I0587258

LUCIENNE DIVER

CRAZY IN THE BLOOD

The Latter-Day Olympians #2

WFP

WordFire Press

ISBN: 978-1-61475-608-8

Cover design by Janet McDonald

Cover artwork images by Kanaxa

Kevin J. Anderson, Art Director

Published by WordFire Press, an imprint of WordFire, LLC PO Box 1840 Monument CO 80132

Kevin J. Anderson & Rebecca Moesta, Publishers

WordFire Press Trade Paperback Edition December 2017
Printed in the USA Join our WordFire Press Readers Group and get free books, sneak previews, updates on new projects, and other giveaways. Sign up for free at wordfirepress.com

 Created with Vellum

DEDICATION

This one has to be for the two loves of my life, my husband Pete and my daughter Abby.

PROLOGUE

"My middle name is Odysseus. Of course, growing up, they just called me Odd."
—Christos Karacis

Christos Karacis
Gypsum Valley, Midnight

Damned silly to be skulking around a campsite at my age like some Boy Scout on a panty raid. Too bad there was nothing nearly so entertaining about my situation. The Back to Earth compound had turned out to be a lot bloodier than a Scout jamboree.

I hadn't slept in two days, ever since I'd seen what I'd seen. Every time I closed my eyes, JD's terror-stricken face, the hot spray of his blood, the sight of his intestines spilling into his hands as they tore him apart played out in my head. Then I'd remember the way clawlike hands had latched on to keep me from lunging to the rescue, the fear that I was next, the suddenly alien faces all around me, and especially the knowledge that even if I could grab up JD's trailing innards and shove them back in, he'd probably die of infection.

He never had that chance.

Suddenly, liberating Mara's daughter from the cult had become a matter of life and death. By the time I'd infiltrated it, she was already inner circle. I couldn't get anywhere near her. I was still too low on the totem pole at the winter solstice even to rate an invitation to their celebration, so it was only at the vernal equinox that I'd seen what the bacchants were capable of. And now that I had ... It was possible that Casey was too far gone to save, but that wasn't for me to say.

I had to avenge JD, if nothing else. Penance for my failure to listen when he'd cracked, started raving about wild women and cannibalism and getting *out*. I'd chalked the rant up to moldy rye, just the way history had for the accusations of the witnesses at the old witch trials. I'd assumed the name bacchant was an affectation chosen by someone who knew them historically as worshippers of the fertility god Dionysus—someone who didn't know about their dark fits, the festival frenzies where they tore men limb from limb and let their blood pour out like libations upon the fields. I couldn't accept that anyone would willfully whip his followers into madness and resurrect human sacrifice. So what in the seven hells had Dion done? Was his name just another affectation or could it be ... No, I'd never believed our family tales that the old gods walked among us—Atlas with a gym franchise, Aphrodite the new Mayflower Madam and the like. Drugs or mass hypnosis ranked far higher on the probability scale than divinely inspired blood lust.

My body shuddered involuntarily at the thought, as if trying to throw it off, and I pressed myself more deeply into the shadows of the building that the solar-charged lights of the compound failed to reach, trying to hide myself from the bacchants sauntering by on their rounds. It was nearly midnight; everyone else was snug in their beds.

When they passed, I forced myself to walk as if I had a purpose. There were, sadly, a few yards of well-lit ground to cover between me and the main building—the only one with a phone so far as I knew. Slinking would certainly get me noticed. If I could pretend to be on a mission, maybe I could brazen it out. No one stopped me on the way, but still a sense of dread clutched at my heart. Between that and the odd heat wave making the air as thick as pea soup, I was gasping like a landed fish by the time I made it to the side door of the office building. I'd never noticed video monitors—they were against the anti-technology stance of Back to Earth—but I wasn't going to stake my life that they didn't exist. The office phone was just barely tolerated as a necessary evil and only for the high muckety-muck, who was presumably beyond corruption. I kept my head down, my face away from where I thought the cameras would be placed, and pulled the promotional postcard I'd swiped—sixty percent recycled paper—from my pocket. I slid it like a key card through the minimal gap between the door and frame. It took three tries. Between the lack of lamination, the tight fit and the sudden weakness in my hands, I mangled two edges before I felt the proper slide.

As quietly as I could, I closed the door behind me and listened. Aside from the hoot of an owl outside, which I tried not to take as an ill omen, all was as silent as the grave. *Eerily* quiet in the way only a place without the constant, accustomed hum of technology can be. The glow from outside barely penetrated the gloom, lighting my way to Dion's inner sanctum. I crossed to his door, staying low to avoid windows, and tried my trick again with the postcard. It was a lot easier this time. I thought I might be getting the hang of breaking and entering.

Dion's office was pitch black, without a single window for illumination. I had to feel my way to the desk and phone. Shaking, I sat in Dion's cushy chair and dialed Detective Beverly Simon's number by touch. I'd thought long and hard about who to call and figured that of all people, she'd listen. Plus, she could take care of herself and had the clout to get things done.

"Simon," she answered with a voice all groggy from sleep. Longing shocked me like a sucker punch to the gut.

No time. "Bev, you've got to listen to me." I kept my voice low.

"Christ—"

"Shh. Just listen. I don't know how much time I have. The Back to Earth movement. Check them out. A kid's been killed. JD something."

God, I hadn't even bothered to learn the kid's full name. The fact that we didn't use them here didn't make me feel any better. For all I knew, JD wasn't even his real name. He might have recreated himself as so many did on joining.

"*What?* You vanish for months with no word and then call me with a *tip?*"

I heard a sound, like someone testing the outer door, maybe preparing to enter.

"Bev, *please.* I've gotta go."

I pressed the button to disconnect, then quickly hit random keys to prevent anyone from punching redial in case I was discovered. I didn't want Bev in their sights. I replaced the receiver as quickly and quietly as I could. Still, the slight sound it made touching home seemed to echo in the resounding silence of the compound.

Over my own pounding heart, I couldn't be sure, but I thought I heard an answering snick of that outer door sealing. Someone was inside with me. The footsteps heading my way confirmed it. There was only one exit from the office and nowhere to run.

CHAPTER ONE

"Beware embossing. It often heralds formal gowns and rubber chicken."
—Tori Karacis, words to live by

Tori Karacis
Los Angeles, CA

The Feds and my cousin Tina's wedding invitation blew in on the same ill wind. Truth be told, one came in bearing the other. It couldn't be harpies or banshees or even, hell, desert scorpions. Oh no, those I could probably have handled. But it didn't seem terribly good form to use my gorgon mojo on guys who could lock me up and lose me in the system without needing much in the way of probable cause.

Not that I was paranoid. I mean, two weeks ago I'd faced down a few gods from the old neighborhood trying to drop LA into the ocean just to announce their second coming. In theory, a couple of mere mortals shouldn't be too much of a problem—

assuming they weren't here to cart me off to some super-secret government lab to explore my more unusual attributes from the inside out.

"Mizz Karacis?" asked the one I was already planning to dub Little Wooden Boy simply because he reminded me of a two-thirds scale model of Al Gore.

"I hope so, I'm wearing her underwear."

"Very original," he answered with no discernable trace of sincerity. "I'm Special Agent Eric Holloway and this is Special Agent Ben Rosen from the FBI." His partner, the one not holding my mail hostage, flashed a badge that I supposed was meant to be good enough for the both of them. "We need to ask you a few questions."

And there it was … the other shoe. I'd been waiting for it to drop ever since Internal Affairs had started harassing Detective Armani … or, as I called him now, Nick. I understood why—an officer dead, Armani's partner disappeared—but that didn't mean I liked it. He couldn't very well tell them the truth—that his partner, Detective Lau, had flown off on the back of a dragon who'd been awakened by a seismic blast caused by Greek gods run amok. Not unless he was willing to earn himself a trip to a padded cell on a psychiatric visa. I still wasn't fully convinced of my own sanity, and I'd seen it all with my own eyes.

But my inquisitors loomed, awaiting an invitation to enter. I said a wistful goodbye to the idea of getting to the beach before all the good spots were taken. It was unseasonably warm for late March, and my air conditioning just wasn't cutting it. If I was going to bake, it might as well be to a nice golden brown. Instead, I sighed. Heavily.

"Sure, come in. Thanks so much for bringing my mail," I replied wryly.

I held out a hand to relieve Holloway of the burden, but he walked right past me without giving it up. His gaze skimmed my sunny yellow bathing suit cover-up and flip-flops, noted the mesh bag containing my paperback and tanning supplies, and moved on to the small condo I was housesitting for Armani's AWOL partner. My own apartment had fallen prey to Zeus's pyrotechnic wrath. I'd packed away Detective Lau's desiccated sea life—dried up starfish, sand dollars, sea urchins and the like —because they creeped me out. Otherwise, the place was pretty much as she'd left it, aside from the dirty dishes in the sink and a centimeter or so of dust. I wasn't much on the housekeeping front.

"Cozy," commented Rosen with that same lack of inflection his partner had mastered. No doubt they'd been at the top of their academy class for dry delivery. Their mothers must be so proud.

Rosen had Charlton Heston's sandy abundance of hair, but that's where the resemblance ended. Beyond that he was unremarkable. Dark suit, crisp white shirt, conservative striped tie, eyes that couldn't decide what color they wanted to be—green or brown. Blending into the woodwork was probably not a bad thing for a federal agent.

I gestured them toward the relatively uncluttered conversational grouping in the living room.

"Can I get you anything?" I asked, just to be polite.

They exchanged a look that might have said *yeah right* before declining in stereo.

I shrugged and took a seat, after which they took theirs, barely sinking into Lau's militantly firm couch. Stiff, just like the missing lady herself.

"Ma'am, we need you to tell us everything you can about the events of March 6th of this year."

Oh, crumb. "March 6th? My schedule is at the office, so you'll have to give me a second." I pretended to think before answering. "I was probably checking the mail for my tax refund. I e-filed early, you know, thinking I'd speed things along, but I guess I'm just a cock-eyed optimist. Speaking of mail, can I have mine?"

Holloway eyed me keenly before handing it over. "There's no

refund check. There *is* a wedding invitation. At least, that's what it looks like. Will you be bringing Detective Armani?"

I forced myself not to react as I flipped through my mail—junk, junk, flier, another bill, embossed card-stock envelope. "I haven't decided yet."

Rosen's hand slammed onto the table, so suddenly and untelegraphed it made me jump. "Let's cut the crap. Last night, several people turned up dead under mysterious circumstances at the lip of a crater caused by an explosion that took place two weeks ago. Exactly two weeks ago, *you* made a 911 call that led to the arrest of three incapacitated men at the Le Brea Tar Pits who are believed to have been involved with the explosion. Your voiceprint is unmistakable. You can start telling us what you know or we can haul your ass in."

It was on the tip of my tongue to ask if the rest of me could come too when I registered what he'd said. "Wait—what? More bodies?" That explosion—that had been the old gods raising a ruckus, but this was new.

The Feds exchanged another expressionless glance. "Show her," Holloway ordered his partner.

Rosen reached into the same jacket pocket from which he'd pulled documentation earlier and snapped a sheaf of papers down in front of me so that they fanned out across the table. I wish I could have said they were grainy or blurred, but ...

"Excuse me." I choked, racing for the sink.

I tossed my cookies, every last one from Yiayia's special snickerdoodle care package. They weren't nearly as good coming up with a chaser of bile. I ran water down the drain and grabbed some in my cupped hands to rinse out my mouth. I wished my mind was as easy to scour, but it would take the world's most impressive roll of mental floss to rid myself of those scream-scene images.

"Gum?" I heard from behind me.

I whirled on them. "Oh yeah, that'll make it all better."

"It's for us," Rosen said, "so we don't have to smell your breath while we talk."

What the hell do you say to that?

"Sit," Holloway ordered. "It'll pass."

I sat, but only because my body told me it was a damned good idea. I was shaking and my knees had gone to Jell-O. "Those people weren't just killed, they were shredded," I said.

"Yup," Rosen agreed. "Holloway lost his lunch, same as you. That's how I knew to bring the gum. You ready to talk to us now?"

Well, hell, they'd already seen the contents of my stomach, what more did I have to hide? I told them what I knew. Oh, not the god part of it. The way I spun it, Zeus, Poseidon and Hephaestus, under their street names, of course, were domestic terrorists whose activities I'd stumbled upon during one of my private investigations. I didn't know what in the world had possessed them to plant explosives at the tar pits, and I claimed no knowledge of what had caused Mount Lee to explode, knocking the *H* from the Hollywood sign. Based on their questioning, I guessed that was where the bodies had been found. In life, the newly deceased had been seismologists and volcanologists monitoring the equipment they'd set up to explain a magma-free eruption of a previously docile peak.

"This investigation that led you to the terrorists, that would be …" Holloway consulted his BlackBerry, "the Circe Holland murder?"

I agreed that it was.

"According to the police report, you described her assailant as *green around the gills, kind of scaly*."

Uh oh. Now it got dicey. "If you know that much, you probably know that a body fitting that description was fished out of the water under the Santa Monica pier. Case closed," I answered, like it was an everyday occurrence.

Rosen tapped on the table until I returned my attention to

him. This back and forth of theirs was going to put a crick in my neck.

"Yes, we've examined the body. Very strange, wouldn't you say? Like something out of legend." His eyes held mine. And held. And held. He wasn't blinking.

I had a moment's concern about how I would play it before my natural smartass stepped in. "Wait, this must be some kind of new reality show, right? Like *X-Files* meets *Main Street Mysteries*?" I pretended to look around. "Where's the camera? Which one of you is Scully?"

He still wasn't blinking or smiling. "So you *don't* think it's strange?" he asked, refusing to be put off track.

"Is this relevant to those bodies on Mount Lee?"

Holloway jumped back into the fray, "We're not at liberty—"

But Rosen cut him off. "The bodies on Mount Lee—or rather the parts found—had been gnawed. Forensics hasn't matched the bite marks yet, but I think there's a good reason for that. They seem too large to belong to any currently living carnivore."

I noticed the look his partner threw him, the first genuine expression from Little Wooden Boy. Okay then, so Rosen was Mulder.

"What are you saying?" I asked.

"I'm saying that it's possible Circe Holland's killer isn't the only abnormality out there." I so wanted to start humming the *X-Files* theme, but I couldn't carry a tune in a bucket with both hands. Rosen was apparently a true believer. And that made him dangerous as hell.

"Speaking of which," Holloway said, leaning in as if to relegate his partner to the background, "did you happen to encounter any evidence of biological terrorism during the Holland investigation?"

I narrowed my eyes at him, wishing I had some kind of *useful* power, like mind reading. Biological terrorism? Dead and dismembered bodies? What could they possibly think I knew?

"Like what?" I asked.

Holloway was warming to me. Really, I could tell from the dead stare. "Vapid doesn't play well on you, Mizz Karacis."

"Possibly because I'm not playing." Wait, that hadn't come out quite right.

They fired a few more questions at me before finally giving up, threatening to be in touch and showing themselves to the door. I followed so that I could throw the deadbolt behind them, then leaned against the door for good measure, still shaking, legs feeling about as supportive as Silly Bandz. But it wasn't all the Feds' fault, and I knew it. I hadn't been the same since—But no, one crisis at a time. I had my hands full with this one right now. I kept hoping that if I ignored the other it would just go away.

My first thought was to call Armani—Nick—but what in the world would I say … And could I trust that Internal Affairs wouldn't be listening in?

I trudged back into the living room and collapsed into a chair—to the extent it allowed anyway—to do some thinking. In a way, it was comforting to know that no human was suspected of what had been done to those bodies. The kind of carnage in those pictures … it would have taken a madman. Not that they were exactly in short supply in my world.

The crime scene photos were gone, but my mail still sat in the center of the coffee table, taunting me as only inanimate objects can. It's hard to win a staring contest with unwanted responsibility. It never blinks. And kickboxing your mail was wholly unsatisfying. My cousin Tina was a whole other matter. Drop-kicking bridezilla would be a hoot and a half—only I didn't suppose I'd ever make it back into the family's good graces that way.

As if I didn't already have enough to chew on, there was the catch that came with the wedding invitation. I had to find Uncle Christos, Tina's godfather and my absentee mentor, so that he could give the bride away. Her own father was six feet under and therefore unavailable. Truth be told, I was starting to get a bit concerned about Christos myself. His sabbatical from the PI business had now taken on Odyssean proportions and no one had heard from him since the beginning. But as the fellow black sheep of the family—one of the few not to go the circus route— I felt compelled to support his decision to go walkabout. He was a big boy. He knew how to take care of himself. It warred with my innate nosiness not to pry, but I'd thus far given him his privacy. If I wanted back into the family fold, that was going to have to change. Yiayia's snickerdoodles had been a bribe for me to give in to the family's request. I wondered if the fact that I hadn't kept them down voided the implied acceptance of having eaten them to begin with. But really … *Yiayia's snickerdoodles* … what other choice had there been?

On some level, I realized I was off on a tangent. That had been happening a lot lately. Focus was a friend I hadn't spoken to in a while. But I tried. The vision of those poor dead scientists gave me something to hang on to. It was hard, in fact, to look away, even in my mind's eye.

No one had hired me to investigate. No doubt Rosen and Holloway would be happier if I didn't, but I needed something to take my mind off my tremors and a new case would be just the thing. Plus, I couldn't *not* help, just as I couldn't unsee what I'd seen.

Research was definitely in order, and that meant the office. My old place might not have had enough furniture for a conversational grouping, but at least it'd had DSL. Lau's place had bupkis, unless you considered dialup, which I didn't. She didn't even have decent Wi-Fi in her area that I could piggyback onto.

My hands shook as I used the arms of the chair to help myself up. Only through sheer force of will had I kept them relatively steady throughout the interview with the terrible twosome, but I would *not* consider that the weakness was getting worse. I was also not thinking about pink elephants, Elvis sightings or that growing feeling of need, pining for something no multivitamin was going to supply. It would pass. Ambrosia addiction had been known to kill mere mortals, but I had it on good authority that I wasn't ... or not entirely. So, I wasn't thinking about withdrawal or the sexy god who'd dosed me with the stuff in the attempt to save my life. *First one's free, little girl.*

Nope, I was Cleopatra, Queen of Denial.

I spared one more wistful thought for the beach before changing into black slacks, sandals and a teal top—business casual on the off chance a client wandered into the office while I was there. I'd take as many distractions as I could get.

On the way, I stopped off for a triple shot latte worth every inflated cent. By the time I reached the office, at least I had a reason for the shakes. My stomach was dancing the jitterbug, threatening revolt.

The Karacis Investigations office was located in old Hollywood—the part that held classic theatres like the Orpheum and Rialto, many of which had since been turned into discount stores or offices. The buildings were antique, the rooms small and the rent relatively cheap. It was the only reason I could afford to stay. Certainly, I wasn't rolling in the dough. Hollywood stereotypes aside, no one had yet come through my door asking for help finding a Maltese falcon or stolen diamonds and offering to share the award. *Yet* being the operative word. I lived in hope.

I rode the creaking elevator up to the third floor rather than take the stairs on shaky legs. At my door with the peeling paint and semi-discreet gold plaque bearing our company name I had to focus to get the key into the lock without further scratching the paint. I'd just made it and was about to turn the knob when something behind the door went *thump*, loud enough to be heard over the gurgle of my insides. I froze, listening intently, waiting for the sound to repeat to be sure I'd heard anything at all and hadn't just entered some auditory hallucination phase of withdrawal. But there it was again—the sound of something rubbing against something else. Friction, like of desk drawers poorly fitted or our closet doors sliding on their tracks.

Someone was in there. Good, well, at least I'd mastered the obvious.

Quietly, I set down the last of my overpriced coffee and removed the key from the door to get to the canister of pepper spray I kept attached to the chain. I thumbed off the safety, then slowly, silently turned the unlocked knob. As soon as it unlatched, I slammed the door open with my shoulder. The door didn't bounce back at me, and no one instantly pounced. That didn't mean the coast was clear.

Holding my pepper spray like a gun, since my actual weapon was helpfully locked in my desk, I moved through the office. Entryway—empty. No tingle of my god-given early warning system as I approached the coat closet. Still, I chose one side and slid the door back as quickly as it would go. Nothing. I could see to the other side of the equally intruder-free closet. There were only three other rooms besides the entry foyer where my assistant Jesus (pronounced *Hey-Zeus*) greeted clients and dealt commentary with every sniff, eye roll and pointed riposte—my office, Uncle Christos's office and the bathroom.

A little ripple of tension shot through me at the thought of Christos's office. So, I had my direction, but also an extra kick of adrenaline because *this was new*. My scant precognition had only kicked in before when something was coming at me. It had never before given me directional signals.

No time to think about that now. I crept toward Christos's office as if I hadn't already broadcast my presence with the slam-ming and sliding doors. I stopped just short of entering. His door was ajar. I planted one foot on the floor and gave a *"ki-yah!"* as I blasted a sidekick at the door, blowing it in to hit anyone who might be hiding behind it in ambush. The door didn't get far before meeting an immovable object and rebounding toward me. I was out of range of a knob to the ribs, but not bullets if they were the next thing coming at me, so I whirled to the side to put a wall between me and the intruder.

I would have been content to wait him out until he was vulnerable coming through the doorway, but there was another way out of that office, through the connecting door into mine. I was torn—guard the exit into the hallway or go in after the intruder and hope he wasn't fast enough to do an end run around me. The first was probably the sane, sensible choice, since it seemed a good bet he hadn't planned an escape route out my third-floor window in broad daylight in downtown LA.

Problem was, I was riding a caffeine and adrenaline high. Every neuron was screaming go, go, GO. I went, aiming another mighty kick at the door. This time it nearly jumped out of my way. A frisson of alarm rippled through me, warning of the blow a second before it landed. I ducked and rolled, catching it on the shoulder, but I only knew because of the force. I was feeling no pain. Unfortunately, neither was I still in possession of the pepper spray.

I came up in a crouch and swept one leg out to knock the guy off his feet, but he jumped it, suddenly past me with a running start toward the outer office door, a blur in basic B&E black. I leapt to my feet and ran after, catching his shoulder just as his hand stretched for the knob. His elbow missed my ribcage by centimeters, but my kidney punch arched his back and caused a grunt of pain. It didn't keep him from turning the knob and hotfooting it toward the staircase.

Something dark—my inner adrenaline junkie maybe—screamed at me to pursue, but I fought it down. There was no guarantee he'd been the only intruder. If I gave chase it left his partner free to ransack the office.

Besides, I didn't trust my compulsion to pursue. The fight had been over way too quickly, and it bothered me that I felt like that was a bad thing. Fighting had always been a means to an end—fitness, primarily—never something I craved.

I forced my mind to turn down more productive pathways

and began by taking stock of the damage. Jesus's desk was no longer obsessively neat. A first smile of the day teased at me when I imagined his upcoming hissy fit. I peered into Christos's office and found the personal mail we'd been saving for him scattered to the four winds, the contents of his desk drawers littering the floor …

Definitely time to give Armani a call.

What I didn't expect was his barked response—"Call property crimes"—and subsequent hang-up. I was still staring in shock at the phone when the one on the desk rang. My heart twisted, knowing it wasn't Nick ringing back to apologize but hoping all the same.

I was too curious to worry about destroying evidence like prints. But I wasn't so far gone that I didn't use my shirt to pick up the receiver, exposing the bottom of my bra to anyone who might have stuck around, and nearly giving myself a Charlie horse as I contorted to make it work.

"Karacis Investigations," I answered.

"Tori, thank God I caught you." It was a woman's voice. Husky, familiar, but I couldn't immediately place it. "It's Beverly Simon—uh, Detective Simon. I've heard from Christos."

Detective Beverly Simon, Christos's poker buddy … and, I suspected, something more. Not that he'd ever said as much.

"Speak of the devil! Do you know where he is? Tell me he's all right."

My heart sank at her hesitation. "I'm not so sure. I'd like to come by and talk to you."

"Well, that's a coincidence. I was about to call you. We've had a break-in here, and it seems the perp was pretty interested in Christos's office."

"I don't believe in coincidence," she said.

"Neither do I."

"Don't touch anything. I'll be right over." A click indicated the line had gone dead.

She probably expected me to step outside the office, close

the door behind me and leave well enough alone until she arrived, but … I was only (mostly) human after all. Snooping was like a siren's song I was powerless to resist. Besides, I needed to be sure the intruder hadn't started a fire somewhere or set a bomb to cover his tracks. The fact that I didn't smell anything burning in the first case and didn't know what I could do in the second didn't stop me. Logic was just a tool—twisty as a garden hose.

Which sent my brain off on one of the tangents it'd been so fond of lately. The hose put me in mind of snakes, maybe the poisonous kind that could be left to lie in wait. Other scenarios played out in my head—deadly spiders, anthrax, Barry Manilow mix tapes. I tried to reel in the paranoia, but the fear had taken on a life of its own. I needed a reality check. I needed—gods help me—Jesus.

I yanked my cell phone from its belt holster and hit speed dial. At my retelling of events, Jesus gasped in horror—probably at the idea of disarray rather than at my brush with danger—and promised to be right over. My dark thoughts seemed to melt away. With Jesus assuming all of the drama, it was hard to maintain it myself. Begin with *Monk*, the obsessive-compulsive detective, pass *Top Model* on the way to diva, take a left turn at Albuquerque, and you might hit Jesus. Maybe. If he wasn't feeling ornery. I was calmer already.

Now there was nothing to do but wait, a four-letter word if ever there was one. Mentally, I ran back over the details of the break-in, so I'd have them straight for Detective Beverly. What I kept coming back to was the contradiction of the intruder himself. I mean, basic black head to toe to break into a place in downtown LA on a beautiful morning when most people were in tank tops and sandals? Not that any kind of affectation was exactly unheard of in La La Land. Everything had happened so quickly that I couldn't remember if the guy had been wearing gloves or not. It seemed likely, though, especially since he'd taken the B&E cliché to a whole new level, which screamed amateur.

On the other hand, he certainly knew how to fight, jump a kick and take a punch, which said he wasn't completely without experience.

If only I'd gotten a decent look at the guy's face, I might not only have a good description for the police, but the man himself, frozen in his tracks by my gorgon glare. As it was, I'd seen only enough to mark him young, twenties at the latest. Medium brown hair, medium height, average build. Helluva description.

The sound of a key rattling in the office door derailed that train of thought, and a millisecond later Jesus breezed through, breathing as if he'd powerwalked the five blocks from his apartment. He air-kissed the space beside my cheek as he brushed past me, headed toward my office. He looked like a man on a mission.

"We're not supposed to touch anything!" I called after him.

He waved me off with a fluttering hand over his shoulder. I followed behind him like a puppy and watched as he used his pinky to pull open a side drawer of my desk. He gingerly removed two sets of the cheap sandwich bag type gloves we kept around for handling evidence we intended to turn over to the police.

"Now why didn't I think of that?" I asked, taking the pair he held out to me.

Jesus straightened and raked his gaze over me. "Because you are shaken up. Literally. *Chica*, how much caffeine did you *have*?"

I smiled, the Jesus effect. "Too much. The intruder was in Christos's office when I caught him. Let's start there."

Jesus went right for the files, so I squatted on the floor to look over the debris scattered there. Paper clips, staples, sticky notes, pens, pencils, lightly-used napkins, binder clips—the usual desk drawer detritus—lay among fliers, credit card offers and the occasional piece of personal mail. I didn't want to touch anything, so I just stared, first taking note of each individual piece and then trying to see some kind of pattern—what was missing, what had been flung farthest afield. I knew there was something ...

"Jesus?"

"Yeah."

"I think our visitor made off with Uncle Christos's bank statements." The sound of flipping folders halted.

"*Qué?*"

"Well, unless you've been filing or forwarding them, they seem to be missing. I haven't been paying attention to what's been coming in, so I can't account for every piece of junk mail he's received, but the accounting statements are pretty noticeable in their absence."

"But that doesn't make any sense. It's easy enough to request new ones."

"Maybe the intruder wasn't trying to keep *us* in the dark so much as access the information for himself."

Jesus sniffed. "Must be why you're the highly paid detective, while I'm a lowly office clerk. You're the one with the theories."

I wasn't touching that with a ten-foot pole.

The intercom chirped. Jesus's gloves disappeared into a pocket, but I kept mine on to buzz up Detective Beverly.

"Been investigating on your own?" she asked, looking pointedly at my hands as she stepped through the doorway.

Jesus leaned casually against his desk, one butt cheek propped on the edge. "Not quite on her own," he answered.

Great, an admission of sorts. I shot him a look, which he ignored.

Beverly's lips thinned, but she wisely saved her breath on the admonishment. "Guess you'll be able to save me a little time then. Tell me what's missing."

"My phone message pad," Jesus said, surprising me. "And bank statements."

"Anything else?"

"Not that we've noticed so far, but when you see Christos's office, you'll know why we can't be sure yet," I answered.

Something flashed behind Beverly's eyes, a mixture of anger and determination, and she went to see for herself.

"Check the computer files yet?" she asked from the entrance to Christos's office.

Jesus and I exchanged a look. We hadn't gotten that far.

"The monitor light is blinking, like someone did an incomplete shut down," she explained in the face of our silence.

Then she took a harder look at me. "You feeling all right?"

I let my lip curl just a bit. I'd always hated that question. By the time anyone asked it, it was usually pretty clear that you weren't. Either that or you were holding it together just fine and resenting the hell out of the implied criticism.

"Fine," I said, hiding my hands out of sight behind my back. "Still a little jittery with adrenaline overload, but I'll live."

She gave me that *cop* look, the one that said she could see right through me, but she let it go. "The crime scene techs should be right behind me. I want to talk to Tori, get her description of the intruder, but there's no reason for you to stick around on a beautiful day like today."

Jesus bristled at the clear dismissal, and I jumped in to head off the collision I could see coming between my drama king of an assistant and the detective who'd dare to muck up his kingdom with her fingerprint powder.

"Jesus will be as good as gold. Won't you?" I asked him pointedly. To Beverly, "He's an aspiring actor. I'm sure he'd just like to get a firsthand look at the way things are done, in case it's ever useful to him."

"I'm sure we could arrange a ride along or something later in the week," she countered. "For now, I need him out."

Jesus huffed in response and shot me a martyred look. "Fine. I am going."

"But," he said, still looking at me, "do not expect *me* to clean up the mess." Heaven forbid.

CHAPTER TWO

"If at first you don't succeed, pry, pry again."
—Christos Karacis, on perseverance,
the #1 tenet of PI work

Detective Armani—Nick—called as I was on my way to
the storage unit where Uncle Christos had socked
away his stuff when he'd decided to go walkabout.
"Where are you?" he asked without preamble.

I told him, biting off the words, stung by his earlier brusqueness. "I'll meet you there," he said.

It was on the tip of my tongue to tell him not to bother, but
he didn't give me the chance.

I sighed. Fine; if there was another intruder at the storage
site, Armani was welcome to him. But based on the fact that the
key had still rested in the top drawer of Christos's desk, under a
probably fossilized pack of gum, I didn't think it was on the
intruder's radar. The computer, however, had been another

matter. Detective Beverly had been right about that blinking monitor. I should have caught it myself. The hard drive had been shut down, but I must have interrupted the intruder before he finished covering his tracks. Whether the computer files or the financials gave it away, it was only a matter of time before the storage unit came to light. If there was anything interesting inside, I wanted to be the one to find it.

My hands shook on the steering wheel of my shiny red Camaro. When the car seemed to be shaking too—or lurching, more like—I realized my foot was bouncing up and down on the gas pedal like it was bopping to a beat I couldn't hear.

Maybe I needed more caffeine—or less. Or maybe even food. *Ambrosia*, a soft voice whispered through my head. I swatted the radio on to drown out the voice and was blasted by Green Day, which was a much better soundtrack than the one playing in my head.

I distracted myself further by guessing at what I might find in the storage locker. I'd lived long enough in the circus with my family of folk and in LA with its *Twilight Zone* feel not to take for granted that I'd discover nothing more than neatly labeled boxes peaceably collecting dust.

All the way from my office to my Camaro I'd felt an itch between my shoulder blades, as if someone had painted a target on my back in … in really itchy ink. It was weird. Not the tingly sensation that warned me of imminent danger, but an ice pick of unease. I looked around the crowded street, especially behind me where I'd felt the stare, but this was downtown LA, a far cry from the glitz and glamour of Hollywood Boulevard. The streets teemed not with tourists, but the people who truly lived and worked and kept LA going. If anyone was out of place or paying me particular attention, aside from those people who stepped around me, annoyed that I'd stopped mid-sidewalk, I certainly couldn't tell.

I did my best to shrug it off and continued on to the parking garage where my car, Cammi—yes, I'd named her—sat waiting for me.

The drive took me to an especially unattractive part of the city, an industrial section, nearly deserted on a Saturday. I slid Cammi into a space across the street from the storage place, really nothing more than a cement bunker inset with inmate-orange garage doors. Nothing and no one suspiciously pulled to a stop behind me. A sedan blocked the entrance to an open unit on the other end of the facility. Beyond that, all was quiet on the western front. So in all likelihood no one was watching me. I hadn't been followed. The target I felt on my back was just more paranoia. From withdrawal? Oh yeah, that was *much* more comforting. I looked around once more, this time for Armani, but I didn't see him, and didn't feel compelled to wait. I'd liberated my handgun from my desk at the office and slipped it and its special holster into my slacks so that it literally had my back. Good enough.

The key to the storage unit was burning a hole in my pocket, and the mystery of what lay behind door number one was calling. I looked both ways before crossing the street, waited for a banana-yellow Hummer to pass, and beat feet toward the bay of doors. The key turned easily in the lock of Christos's unit, but the door was badly weighted. It took an immense tug to get started on its upward path. Dust mites took flight, dancing in the air all around me, catching the light and tickling my nose, which wrinkled in reaction. Superheated air from within hit me like a slap in the face, stealing my breath and beading sweat on my forehead.

For *this* I was giving up a day at the beach. When I found Christos, he was going to owe me big time.

Based on the scorched, stagnant air, I was the first person to open the unit in some time. It was not going to be easy to explore. Furniture and boxes of all sizes vied for space, stacked on top of one another to within centimeters of the dirt line marking the door's usual resting place.

I allowed the slam of a car door to distract me from starting on the Herculean task of sorting through the mish-mosh. Okay, it wasn't exactly the stables of Augeas. I didn't have to contend with the acrid reek of horse dung baking in the Mediterranean sun, but still …

My pulse jumped as it always did at the sight of Detective Nick Armani. He was movie star gorgeous in the roughed-up, Daniel Craig kind of way. Only he was dark where Craig was light—his jet-black hair framing a face that was arresting rather than pretty. His brows were a little too heavy, but they worked somehow to emphasize his amazing blue eyes, almost cobalt with a ring of midnight all around. And an intensity that made me feel sometimes like we were the only two people in the world. Like now …

His gaze snagged mine as he jogged toward me and I was helpless to look away, but I didn't have to be happy about it.

"Hey," he said, stopping just shy of my personal space.

"Hey," I answered as neutrally as possible.

He took in my look, hands planted on my hips—a confrontational stance, I realized. Not body language he'd miss. For his part, he looked grim, but that was hardly uncommon. Police work was rarely puppies and rainbows.

"Look, I'm sorry." He reached out to cup his hand around my neck, stroking the side with his thumb. My pulse jumped another few notches, but I didn't let it show. "I didn't mean to shut you down earlier. We just need to keep everything by the book, at least until IA wraps up their investigation. Something's happened in the last day or so. The Feds have been around. I've been getting sidelong glances at headquarters. All I really know is that it involves more murders."

"The Feds haven't questioned you?"

"Matter of time, I guess. Maybe they're gathering stories to compare mine against."

"Lovely."

"They're just doing their jobs," he said.

"Whatever." I shrugged and started to turn away.

"Tori—" It stopped me. My name on his lips always did. I looked back at him. "I've missed you."

That did it. My whole body turned to mush, and this time I couldn't blame it on the withdrawal. I let him turn me toward him and kiss me, the heat rushing through me like a flash fire, burning away the last of my resentment. Damn the man.

When he finally drew back, he said, low and husky, "You're shaking."

"I'm cold," I lied.

"It's got to be ninety degrees out here."

I shrugged. "Maybe I'm coming down with something." He studied me like a crime scene photo.

"You gonna give me a visual diagnosis?" I asked.

His lips twitched into one of his rare grins and my heart did a somersault. "Well, I'd be glad to play doctor, if you think it would help."

I looked around us. "Where?"

He did the same. "You're right. Maybe we'd better clean out this unit first."

"Whatever the doctor orders."

I waved a hand, indicating that he should precede me into the cluttered unit. Truthfully, I wasn't feeling too well, and I didn't want him to see my moment of weakness, where I closed my eyes and struggled to summon up the strength to go on. When the idea of playing doctor with Armani put me in mind of a cold compress and a nice nap rather than a steamy roll in the hay, I knew I was in trouble—and not the kind I usually chased.

Two hours, many boxes and a sneezing fit later, I came upon a box of old statements. I had enough energy left to pull them down off a stack that consisted of a dining room table, over-turned chairs, a table lamp and an old computer monitor before I collapsed to the ground, taking them with me. Armani quickly tossed the tackle box he'd been examining back onto some industrial shelving and rushed to my side. "Tori!"

It seemed too much effort to tell him I was okay, and anyway, I didn't think he'd believe me. Something poked my thigh. Something else jabbed into my back, but it didn't stop me from wanting to lie down and sleep. Or die, as pain blossomed in my stomach—a small thing at first, just a bud, but then it bloomed into a whole freakin' mushroom cloud. I knew I'd blown my analogy. I didn't care.

I must have made a noise or curled in on myself, because Armani's hands were suddenly everywhere, searing and painfully hot.

"Sweetheart, you all right? When was the last time you ate?"

"Dunno," I mumbled. I think I did anyway. I know I thought it.

Then the world tilted on its axis and my stomach nearly heaved up whatever it had left. It took me a long moment to realize Armani had picked me up and was carrying me away. I closed my eyes to blot out the sensation of movement, but it didn't fool my gut. At least I finally had someplace to lay my head—right on Armani's extremely nice chest. It seemed like only a second before I was getting dumped. The world went suddenly purple-gray and when my vision cleared, I was sitting in the passenger seat of my car. Armani was nowhere to be seen. A second later he reappeared—having gone to close the storage unit? I didn't know, didn't care.

All I wanted was—

—*ambrosia*—

Oblivion.

Another burst of pain rippled through my abdomen. I wasn't going to survive this.

Nick got behind the wheel. "Hospital?" he asked.

"Home," I managed.

He stared at me, assessing. I could tell even with my eyes squinched against the pain.

"Food poisoning," I bit out, knowing he'd need something more than that.

I'd had food poisoning before. Wanted to die then too. It gave me hope for the future. Plus, I knew from experience there was nothing to be done but let it pass. Armani would know that too.

Nick, dammit.

Not important now.

A blink and we were elsewhere. Stopped. Parked. I wished I were up to taking advantage. Nick pulled me out of the car and tight to his body, which felt like a raging inferno. My skin crackled and peeled away. I could feel it. My brains were liquefying. I worried how Armani would explain brain matter all over his clothes. I hoped IA didn't notice.

On some level I knew I was incoherent. On another it all made a sick sense.

Armani had my keys. Somewhere along the line he must have frisked me and I'd been too far gone to notice. He let my legs down to have a hand free for the door, but held the rest of me tightly to him as I would have slithered to the floor. He pushed the door open and picked me up again. It probably would have been romantic if I hadn't wanted to puke down the front of his shirt.

Even my back hitting the bed was almost too much to bear. It was a bed of nails or hot coals or razor blades....

Armani vanished and was back, dumping half the contents of my medicine cabinet, water, a half-finished package of saltines and what I guessed was a barf bowl onto my bedside table.

"I'll sit with you," he said, brushing my hair back from my face. His hand was like sandpaper.

Shaking my head hurt, so I worked my throat to croak, "No. Won't be pretty. Don't want you to see me this way."

He didn't move, but sat studying me. I'd never told him about the ambrosia. I was sure I could kick the addiction and was too embarrassed about my own stupidity in consorting with the gods ... well, *god*. But mostly, I was afraid he'd righteously try to kick Apollo's ass. Afraid he'd fail.

Which made me an addict *and* a liar-by-omission.

My stomach lurched and I reached for the bowl. Armani jumped out of the way.

"I'll check in later then," he said hastily. "Call me if you need anything." And he fled. Coward.

It was a false alarm. I fell back against the pillows, bowl clutched in my arms, and prayed for death.

My eyes closed, and I fell into a hell of shakes, sweats and lost time.

My face and neck split open from the razor-sharp claws that slashed from every direction. So quickly that I only registered the pain as I was falling. Teeth flashed then, so many. Drawn by the blood? Definitely slathering—drool dripping down, burning as it hit my open wounds, then seeming to bubble like acid, eating right through me, melting me away. The better to eat you with, my dear. Those teeth—biting, rending—rivaled even the breath, hot as the fires of hell, that seemed to cook me on contact. It smelled of death, and not just one. An entire abattoir.

Spreading numbness started to chase away the pain, and I knew I was lying somewhere, bleeding out. Literally half the girl I used to be. Chill air hit my exposed ... everything ... temporarily whipping up the pain again, bringing the nerves back online. I knew from the breeze that I was outdoors, even as I knew that didn't make any sense.

I burst awake, flailing, panicked, my heart pounding as if to prove it still could. I wasn't going out like this, dammit. I had things to do, a mystery to solve.

It took two tries before I could get my hand to obey me and

move. The buttons on my phone betrayed me, but I still had voice dial.

"Call—Apollo," I managed.

I faded again until his voice startled me out of it. "Tori?" he answered. "You have a lot of nerve—"

"Help," I cried.

CHAPTER THREE

"What doesn't kill you doesn't necessarily make you stronger.
Wiser, maybe, but don't count on it."
—Christos Karacis

I opened my eyes to the face of an angel—the fallen variety. The kind designed to lead others into temptation and have them thank him for it. Repeatedly. To make matters worse, he was sitting on the edge of the bed, his weight slanting the mattress so that my body seemed inclined to slide toward his.

Apollo's golden hair was wild, like the corona of the sun, like it would look after someone had run their fingers through it, clutching his head to their breast or … elsewhere … urging him not to stop. My mind supplied an image of *me* in that position, Apollo above me, gazing down with those impossible turquoise eyes turbulent with emotion …

I shut it down, closed my eyes and focused on breathing. In and out. No, that was bad. Just … bad.

"Move away," I said through gritted teeth.

Apollo shifted fractionally, but I could feel him staring at me still. My body cried out for contact, but I ruthlessly ignored it, even though every single cell seemed to strain toward Apollo. I felt *alive*. More than alive. Manically, enthusiastically, quite definitely, hyper-alive. Full of light and energy. My eyes snapped open at the realization of just what had to be heightening all my experiences.

As my gaze met Apollo's, I struggled to find a well of anger to tamp down my libido and was surprised not to have to look too hard, though I must have known on some level that this was what would happen if Apollo rode to my rescue. Some part of me must have decided deep down that I could die another day but not while the family was counting on me to track Uncle Christos and not while there were new murders, massacres really, begging to be solved. I didn't have the luxury of the moral high ground. No, as much as I wanted to blast Apollo with both barrels of my wrath, I was the one to blame here. I had to take responsibility.

Still, my "thank you" tasted like ashes on my tongue.

"Stop. Your effusion is just embarrassing," Apollo said, brushing aside a sweat-soaked lock of hair obscuring my vision. The jolt it sent straight to my heart made me cranky.

I touched the back of my hand to my mouth and it came away wet. "Drool, eh? Sexy."

"Very funny."

"I feel funny." I couldn't hold his gaze. It was just too intimate. His eyes were aqua and glowed like the sun reflecting off the Mediterranean. They made me think of skinny-dipping and the power of the surf, surging. I cut that thought to the quick. "Seriously, though, thanks for coming," I said reluctantly. "I wasn't sure you would."

"What, and miss the chance to make you beholden to me?"

"Think again, buddy. In my book, this just makes us even."

Apollo tapped a finger on his lip, pretending to consider, but not putting much effort into making it look sincere. "Really? By my count, that makes twice I've saved your life and you've—oh wait, you have yet to reciprocate."

"Damn you and your scorekeeping. Tell you what, you let me know when you're going to throw yourself in front of a train, and I'll be there to stop you. No, really." Two could play at sincerity.

Apollo's eyes rolled upward as if he could spot the heights of Olympus right through my ceiling. "It doesn't work like that."

I sighed. "Fine." I looked down to be sure I was decently clothed, unlike the last time I'd woken in a bed with Apollo, and started to rise. Apollo looked regretful, but didn't try to keep me there.

I was pleased that all my parts seemed to be in working order. It was the first day in what seemed like forever without the shakes. I didn't have to *pretend* I was fine. I wanted to give a rebel yell, but that would be undignified. And heavens, having built up my skid row junkie image, I didn't want to blow it all in one fell swoop. "I need to wash the stink off, and I need food, not necessarily in that order. The least I can do is offer you something."

I wandered into the kitchen and started opening and closing cupboards, as if elves might have stocked them while I was out. "Um, how about omelets? As long as you don't like anything in them. More like scrambled eggs, really. Or, I make a mean cinnamon toast."

He followed me in and lounged against my cabinets. He looked good standing there, and my brain tried to remind me that bedrooms weren't the only places for fun and games, but those thoughts were by now used to being ignored.

"I'm not hungry, thank you," Apollo announced as he watched me play at domestication. "I left a … supply … for you in your refrigerator. I suppose you'll have to let me know when you need more."

"So, what's the catch here? What do I owe you?" Rather than look at him, I went about getting the fixings for scrambled eggs and toast. Normally I'd opt for cereal or a Power Bar rather than actual home cooking, but I felt the need for something hot and filling. Besides, I was bursting with excess energy I needed to channel.

"Dump your detective."

Armed with a tub of butter and a spatula, I whirled on him. "Just because you saved my life doesn't mean you get to dictate how I live it."

"Are you yet on a first name basis?"

"Yes." *Most of the time.* I dropped everything on the counter and attacked the butter with a vengeance, tossing a glop into my pan and barely waiting for it to heat before adding the eggs. "Anyway, it's none of your business."

"He's not for you. I have seen—"

"What do you know about the dead bodies on top of Mount Lee?" I asked suddenly. I didn't want to know my future ... or Nick's. I'd read enough of the myths to learn that knowing the future often led people to play right into their doom. The whole self-fulfilling prophecy bit. The only thing to do with that power was mark it "return to sender."

"The ones in the news?"

"I sure hope there aren't any others." I chopped the eggs to within an inch of their lives before sliding them onto a plate and carrying my feast to the table. Apollo sat down across from me. It was such a strange homey scene with the morning light streaming through the windows. All we needed were steaming mugs of coffee and newspapers to help us ignore each other.

"They are related to the earlier trouble?" Apollo asked.

I froze, first bite nearly to my lips. "Trouble? No euphemisms before coffee. Anyway, I think they are. There's the location for one. Plus, the remains of all the bodies would barely fill a chum bucket, so I'm doubtful it was your average man off the street who whacked 'em. Oh, and the Feds asked me some pretty oddball questions. Wanted to know about biological warfare."

Apollo's face went all over strange before tightening into a mask.

I swallowed the bite in my mouth. "What? Does that mean something to you?"

"Maybe. Can you tell me any more about the attack?"

"Not … really." Not except for that strange dream with the gnashing teeth and slashing claws, the details of which were already slipping away from me. And anyway, it was *just* a dream. A vivid, terrifying, heart-pounding dream, but still. Unless …

"I'll show you mine if you show me yours," he wheedled.

I eyed him. "I've seen yours."

"Innuendos aside," he said.

"Oh, can we do that? I didn't know it was an option. Anyway, that's all the info I have except for a nightmare where it was me on that mountain with claws and teeth coming at me from everywhere."

Apollo went as white as the china, which, with his tan, was an incredibly impressive feat. "That's what I was afraid of."

"What is?"

"You remember that *gift* I gave you?"

"Oh, you mean besides the deadly addiction?" Apollo waited patiently for me to remember manners. I hoped he wasn't holding his breath. "The precognition … yeah, I remember. Interesting side note, it now comes with GPS."

He didn't look entirely surprised. "Well, you may also find that you have very vivid dreams. You'll want to pay attention to them."

Damned to addiction by day, haunted by horror at night. My life was really some kind of John Carpenter dream come true. I wished I'd slammed the door on Apollo back when I'd first laid eyes on him. I'd known he was dangerous, but couldn't resist him any more than a moth could resist dashing itself against the flame.

"So you're saying these dreams have meaning. Are you guessing or do you know something?"

Apollo shrugged. "There've been portents, sightings ... nothing concrete."

"Buffy was right, then. We really are living on a Hellmouth."

"The underworld isn't Hell—well, except for Tartarus. The Elysian Fields are there too, don't forget."

"I was trying to be clever. Okay, Mr. Literal, what does all this have to do with the bodies?"

"Well, the rumors are that a fissure has opened into Hades's realm. Anything could be coming up through it. Escaped souls, Erinyes, Cerberus himself—" He stopped.

"Now that's a thought. The Erinyes ... the Furies ... they wouldn't attack without provocation, but Cerberus ... In your dream, the attack came from all sides?" I nodded. "A three-headed beast would certainly account for that. Plus, it's said that black venom drips from his jaws. I've never had the privilege of seeing for myself, but if it's true, this might be the biological weapon the federal agents inquired about."

"Oh, bloody hell—" I held up a hand before he could protest. "I know, I know, but bloody Tartarus lacks the same oomph. I don't suppose the whole problem can be solved by asking Hades to bring his dog to heel?"

"It might."

"But you don't think so."

"Well, for one thing, they don't exactly have cell towers down there, so it's not like you can call up and ask him. And since you're still alive, you can't just pop down for a visit. But mainly, Hades keeps Cerberus on a pretty tight leash, and I can't imagine that he's just gotten loose."

"So if Cerberus is running amok, it would mean—what? That Hades has lost control? That he's let Cerberus off the leash?"

"Perhaps. We did put his brothers in jail. Hades could be distracted enough to drop his tether. Or he could be letting Cerberus play in our world as revenge. Or ... it could be more than that. He might have Cerberus hunting something specific."

"Something like—?"

"You."

"Great. Really and truly awesome." I pushed my plate away, unable to eat another bite. "I mean, who doesn't like a good fight to the death?"

"Tori, this is—"

"Nothing to joke about. Yeah, I get that. But sometimes life's too absurd not to laugh."

"So now we're finishing each other's sentences?"

"Only because you're so predictable. Don't read anything into it."

He studied me for a moment, a look that made me understand the eyes as windows to the soul cliché. I felt like he could see straight inside me to things hidden even from myself. It was eerie, more exposing than standing naked on the Santa Monica Pier.

"Stop that," I said.

His serious look changed to an obnoxiously knowing smile. "Are there any other *services* I can provide for you before I go?" he asked, reaching to brush my hair away from my neck. The flesh there sat up and took notice.

My mouth dried up as I tried to form the word *no* all while my body screamed *yes*. This was the dangerous Apollo, the one who could swallow me whole. The one I'd run from ... was still running from. I hadn't talked to him since then or since my relationship had heated up with Armani and Apollo had sent me that strange note—*I know*.

He leaned in and bit down suddenly on the flesh that he'd cleared. Not hard. Just enough to flood my system with longing, to start me fantasizing ... He ended the nip with a kiss and rose without another word, giving me his back.

Always leave them wanting more, I thought. And gods, did I want. But I couldn't have. An ambrosia addiction was one thing. An addiction to Apollo ... that I would never survive.

Then suddenly he was gone, and I was left with nothing

more than a plate of congealing butter, half-eaten eggs and my thoughts, none of them sunny side up. Ten minutes later, I got myself in hand. It was Sunday morning. I could either watch cartoons, follow leads or go to church, which would make my mother *way* too happy, now that she was almost speaking to me again. Besides, recent events had thrown a monkey wrench into the belief system I'd never fully developed. Being me, I chose option *B*, or snooping, as my mother called it.

LA doesn't really get moving until well after noon, so the streets were nearly deserted on my drive to the office. I was able to get a parking space right out front. Given the hour, even the mom and pop deli on the corner wasn't open for business, so I was going to have to fend for myself coffee-wise when I hit the office. No biggie, since aside from cinnamon toast, scrambled eggs and grilled cheese, it was the one other thing to which I could apply heat and expect something palatable to result.

There was no supernatural trill of alarm this time when I opened the office door, just the normal *oh my gods* reaction to the sight of fingerprint powder on every surface. It was a wonder that I'd forgotten for even an instant. The LAPD had taken a lot of prints, including Jesus's for comparison—mine were already on file because of my gun license—but it was too soon to tell whether any were unaccounted for by staff and clientele.

I started coffee, turned on Jesus's computer so that I could pop a CD in to make cleaning tolerable and gathered supplies. The Arctic Monkeys belted out a song as I scrubbed.

The coffee was ready before the cleaning was done—I had a sixth sense about these things—so I gave myself a well-deserved break, doctored a Kong-sized mug for myself and sat down at Uncle Christos's desk. Since it was Sunday, the banks would be closed, but I was almost certain Christos would have things set up so that he could manage his accounts online. He was pretty computer savvy for an old guy. All I had to do was figure out his password. If I was really lucky, he'd set the computer to automatically remember. Given his chosen field, I thought he was probably too smart for that, but I could hope.

Sure enough, once the computer was up and running, I played around on his browser, and found that his bank's website was bookmarked, but no account numbers or codes were programmed into memory. Account numbers I had covered. The password was going to be trickier. Important dates were the most common numeric codes, which banks seemed to favor, but after trying Christos's birthday, my Aunt Helen's birthday (taken from us all too soon in a freak accident), and their anniversary I gave up, afraid the browser would lock me out for too many bad attempts.

I turned to Christos's blotter for clues. It was one of those huge paper calendars that covered nearly the entire surface of the desk. The top sheet was still for November of last year, when Uncle Christos had left with a jolly wave and an order that Jesus and I keep the home fires burning. He was fried, he said, and needed an extended vacation. Didn't know where he'd end up or when he'd be back. All we knew was that he was starting out in the general direction of north—toward the Napa Valley, wine country. This did not exactly come as a shock.

There were two numbers scribbled in the blotter's margins that I thought traced to the San Francisco/Napa area. Christos's own cell phone had stopped working long enough ago that the number had been reassigned, which did wonders for the family fears. I opened up a reverse telephone directory we had bookmarked on the web and went to work. The first number traced to a Residence Inn that, when called, had no record at all of a Christos Karacis, not even as far back as November. Or so they said. The second number I found was registered to an M. Olivieri. I didn't know if M. stood for Mr., Ms., or Marsupial, but I hoped I was about to find out.

The phone was answered on the second ring—a woman's voice, either weary or wary. It was hard to tell based on the simple, "Hello."

"Hello, I'm—"

"Casey?" the woman asked, all trace of reserve gone. "My God, is that you?"

"Um, no, ma'am. My name is Tori Karacis. I'm a coworker of Christos Karacis. I'm trying to get in touch—"

"I'm sorry," she cut in quickly. "I can't help you. I don't know anyone by that name."

"But—"

"I'm sorry, I'm—I'm waiting for a call. I can't stay on the line." And, sure enough, she didn't.

I tried the number again. M. Olivieri certainly didn't pounce on the phone when it rang … and rang … surprising for someone waiting for a call. In fact, I ended up in a perfectly lovely one-sided conversation with her machine, during which I left my cell phone and landline numbers, snail mail and email addresses, and why I was calling. Any time, day or night, I said, she was free to call. I wasn't going to hold my breath.

If I had to drive up to Napa to flash my PI license and Christos's photo … well, I supposed I'd be paying for my own gas. Tina's destination-Delphi wedding had to be costing a small fortune, and I didn't think my expenses were in the budget. At least if I found Christos for her I could plead poverty to get out of going myself. I doubted I'd be missed.

But I wasn't ready for a road trip just yet. Not, at least, until I knew what I was getting into. I had sources … okay, I had the Internet, but it was a start. I Googled M. Olivieri and came up with about a thousand sites, none of which seemed relevant. I tried *Casey Olivieri* hoping that whoever "M" had been so anxious to talk with shared her last name. The first article tagged Casey as the top scorer a couple of years ago on her high school field hockey team. The second was more enlightening: "Mother Cries Cult." It was dated six months ago.

In a cry that echoes the still relevant question, "Where have all the young girls gone?" many California families are lamenting the loss of their children. Less than a year ago, the national Back to

Earth movement swept into town, drawing to it many disenfranchised youth irate over the treatment of our planet and its resources. Many have moved into the Back to Earth cooperative, while others have a more casual connection.

One mother, who asked not to be identified, bemoaned, "We never see Joan anymore. They have no phone—at least, not that they let the kids use. Our letters are returned to discourage 'raping the mother for her flesh,' my daughter's own words! I haven't seen her in five months." Another mother went so far as to call the Back to Earth movement a cult.

According to police spokesman Eric Denny, they've found nothing to support this claim. "The Back to Earth residents are all above the age of consent, and we found no evidence of coercion."

A member of Back to Earth, Casey Olivieri, who asked to be called Narcissa, commented, "We're pretty upset by all the fuss. What nobody gets is that you're all living in a cult of convenience. Disposable everything—fast food, instant gratification. It's all me me me, now now now. Back to Earth is all about renewal, replenishment, respect. Everyone else needs to get a grip and a clue before it's too late."

The group's founder was unavailable for comment, but his California branch officer adds that, "Anyone interested can learn more about us and earth-friendly living on our website. It's our one concession to modern life and a paper-free environment."

Well. I blinked. A cult. But, hey, if they were hooked in to the Internet, I should be able to hack them. Okay, not *me* exactly. That was illegal, and anyway, I was ill-equipped, but a friend of Jesus's about whom the less I knew the better ... For now, at least, I could check out the website, see what Back to Earth professed to be about, maybe get a phone number or address or something that a hands-on, young-in-body/old-in-spirit kind of gal like me could wrap my skills around. My foot was already beginning to tap with impatience at every hourglass icon.

Casey Olivieri had covered the basics in that article. Back to

Earth's home page was pretty tame. Lots of photos of dewy leaves, tree frogs and the like, vivid enough to warm the cockles of any nature geek's heart. The rhetoric was all philosophy—reduce, renew, replenish, thinking long term, living off the land, leaving no trace, yada yada yada. There were links to organic farming sites, articles on mulching and natural fertilizer. There was a number to call for more info, but no street addresses, no officers' names, just vague references to co-ops on which their policies were practiced in various states—Florida, Oregon, Utah and California among them.

Any group so stingy with contact information made me suspicious. But if they were up to no good, they had to be on someone's radar. I picked up the phone to call Detective Beverly.

"'Lo," she answered, sounding like two syllables were just too much.

"Wow, when was the last time you slept?" I asked politicly. Because I was known for that.

"What day is it?"

"Um, Sunday?"

"Already?" She sighed. "What can I do for you?"

"What do you know about the group Back to Earth?"

Dead silence. Not a cricket was chirping.

"Where did you hear that name?" she asked.

"So you do know it?"

"I asked you first."

"Actually, I believe *I* asked you. You just chose not to answer."

Another sigh. I almost wished I could feel the breeze through the phone. The office was like an oven. "Christos … might have mentioned it."

"And you weren't going to say anything to me?"

"Tori, there must have been a reason he called *me*. Whatever is going on, it might be too dangerous for you to go poking around. Too dangerous *for him*," she added, before I could protest. "It might require more finesse than you tend to exhibit."

Come on, my finesse ranked right up there with my politicness.

"You're saying what? I'd go in guns blazing? Half the time I keep mine locked in my desk drawer."

"I'm saying you should let the pros handle it."

"*Hello*, PI here."

"Yeah, and how new is the laminate on your license?"

"Look, I got this far on my own. Either you can tell me what *you've* got on Back to Earth or I can just keep poking the turtle and see what snaps."

"Turtle … really?"

"Snapping turtle. Very threatening. So, what'll it be?"

She sighed again. Probably a personal best for me. "Fine, what do you want to know?"

"Only everything."

Which wasn't much. Back to Earth hadn't tried to file as a church for tax-exempt status, but was incorporated as a single proprietorship. Owner: Dionysus Bach. *Dionysus*. I didn't like it. Not one bit. There were far too many gods in my world already. Whether Dionysus was the real deal or just played him on TV, nothing about the name gave me the warm fuzzies. In fact, those bodies atop Mount Lee, the ones the Feds had questioned me about … those had been torn apart much the same way the big D's obsessive followers were known to shred those unlucky enough to fall prey to them at his festivals. Only, the Feds had mentioned *inhuman* bite marks. No, of course the pieces couldn't fall that easily into place. In a way, I was relieved. The thought of Uncle Christos all tied up with frenzied floozies …

"What's that?" I asked, having lost the thread of the conversation about the time I started imagining Uncle Christos being torn limb from limb.

"I said they've more or less stayed away from LA, for reasons we suspect begin with Scient—and end with—ology. They don't exactly encourage competition."

"And you think Christos is on the run from this Back to Earth cult? Or trapped inside?"

"I don't know. We—our phone call was cut off. But he'd definitely seen something, and it had him scared."

Christos scared. The two didn't even belong in the same sentence. He hadn't left the circus because he was afraid of heights and couldn't bring himself to join the family acrobatic troupe, like me. (Or been asked to leave because he couldn't keep his snooping to a minimum and unearthed dirty little secrets no one wanted brought to light.) He'd left because it was too tame.

"Well, damn," I said, because that about summed it all up.

"My thoughts exactly."

CHAPTER FOUR

"So, which is it? Are you crazy by nature or nurture?"
—soon-to-be-ex boyfriend to Tori Karacis
just before she decked him

A trip to the San Francisco area was definitely in order. But first, I had some snooping to do here. Those bodies atop Mount Lee hadn't shredded themselves. I had to know what I was dealing with. I didn't know what I'd find that the Feds hadn't. It didn't seem likely they'd left any evidence behind. But maybe the Oracular powers Apollo had given me would kick in at the site. They had to be good for something besides lost sleep … right? I hoped so anyway.

Before I could so much as grab my car keys, my cell phone rang and "Yiayia" come up on the display in all her hirsute glory. Yiayia—grandmother—was the Rialto Brothers' bearded lady. And a damned good one at that. All natural. Nothing added. Legend had it that our family line had begun when the god Pan had beer-goggled one of the gorgons. I'd recently learned that it was all the gods' honest truth. At least we'd so far managed to avoid tusks and serpent-hair—cousin Tina's aggressive overbite and my unruly curls aside.

One ignored Yiayia at their peril.

"Kalimera," I said. *Good morning.* I forced cheer into my voice.

"You have been holding out on me. *Again,*" she accused in answer.

Well, crap. I was in for it now. I could almost see my snickerdoodle train leaving the station. Yiayia's hobby (*cough* obsession) was running *Goddities,* a tell-all website/gossip rag about the Greek gods. Think WikiLeaks for Olympians. What I learned, I was expected to pass along instantly. Or else.

"Um, what do you think I know?"

"Egona," she said, disappointment in her voice, "the chats are all abuzz. They say you've opened up a portal to the underworld!"

Geez, did everybody know about it except me? Wait, *Goddities* couldn't be Apollo's source, could it? Surely not.

"Um, well, not *me* exactly. I've actually only just learned of it."

"And?"

"And what?"

"Tell me more," she ordered, like it was obvious.

Hermes's hairy heinie. Well, any search engine would probably turn up the story about the bodies I was soon headed to investigate, so it wasn't like I was giving away state secrets. Only … what if, as I'd feared during the worst of my paranoia, the Feds or the police or *someone* really was listening in on my calls? I thought back on what we'd said so far. Probably enough to get Yiayia committed to a nice mental facility. Maybe we could get adjoining padded cells.

"Well, you've heard about the bodies found on Mount Lee?" I asked.

"No-o-o," she said slowly.

"Check them out."

"Are you with someone?" she asked, clearly wondering why I didn't give her the goods myself.

"Yes," I answered. It seemed easiest.

"Is it your sexy cop?"

I smiled. "No."

There was a pause. "Tell me it is not Apollo. I thought you were through with him. Remember what happened to Cassandra."

Ah yes, the prophetess of Troy, who had the power to see but not be believed.

"I know."

"Or Daphne." Who was turned into a laurel tree to escape Apollo's advances.

"*I've got it.* Listen, it's not him, okay. What else is the rumor mill saying?"

A shiver of alarm shot through me, and I knew that whatever she was about to say I wouldn't like. I hoped Apollo's god-granted gift didn't start me jumping at shadows. I had enough troubles.

"They say that Persephone has used the path you've opened to flee Hades ... for good."

"I didn't think that was possible. I thought Persephone *had* to live a certain amount of time in the Underworld or she'd wither away."

"Maybe it's come to that. Maybe it's a small price to pay after all this time ... or she's found some other way. But, this global warming kick that's all over the news right now? They say that's Demeter ... gloating."

"Well, crap."

"If Hades blames you for his big brothers' jailing, even if they weren't on the best of terms, or for Persephone's betrayal ... you'd better watch your back. I—I'm worried about you, *Egona.*"

I was worried about me too. I had to think pissing off the

god of the underworld was a hundred times worse than crossing Apollo, the god of music and light.

"I'll be fine," I lied. "But … if you hear anything more, you'll tell me?"

"As long as you promise to keep me in the poop in return."

"That's *in the loop*, Yiayia."

"Fine, whatever. What about coming on for a guest chat at *Goddities*?" she asked, shifting gears fast enough to give me whiplash. "You're practically a celebrity. The group would go gaga."

At least she had that right. "Uh, I'll think about it." *When pigs fly.* "I'm a little busy right now."

"Any word on Christos?"

Ah, there it was. It was on the tip of my tongue to ask her about Dionysus and Back to Earth, but if she didn't already know anything about BTE, I didn't want to tell her and risk seeing it all over the web. I didn't need them to know I was coming for them, and I didn't want to put Christos in danger. I put her off with a vague, "I have a lead…. But maybe you can help me," I added. "Do you know any important dates in Christos's life that he might use as a password? I already tried his and Helen's birthdays and their anniversary."

There was the smallest hesitation before she said, "Try February 1, 1980."

"What is February 1, 1980?"

"The day of their great sorrow," she said, a tone in her voice I'd never heard before—something like reverence. "Christos and Alexa so wanted to have children, but the only one conceived was stillborn … on that date. They named him and then they buried him. Christos may still honor his birth."

I felt tears prickling behind my eyes, and my nose got all tingly. It was too horrible. I hadn't even been born yet. No one had ever told me.

"I'm so sorry for them," I said, my voice wanting to break.

But apparently Yiayia, who'd had years to get over it, was ready to move on. "I helped?" she asked.

"Maybe."

"Good. Now, what are you wearing to Tina's wedding?"

"Sack cloth," I told her. She didn't seem to find that amusing.

I let her read me the riot act as I again opened Christos's browser, hit the link for his bank's website and keyed in the birth date of the cousin I'd never known. It did the trick. The printer revved up as Yiayia ran down.

Finally, it seemed safe to cut in. "Yiayia, I have to run. You did help. Now I have a clue to follow up on."

"You be sure to keep me postered."

I rolled my eyes. "*Posted*. Sure thing."

I pulled the bank statements from the printer as soon as they shot out, but I didn't really know what I was looking for. Christos had taken out a big chunk of his savings before his trip, but the only action since had been some automatic monthly payments. Uncle Christos didn't believe in debt or credit cards, I knew, so if he'd used plastic on anything, it would have debited his account. But there was nothing. Wherever he was, whatever he was doing, he was off the grid. If Detective Beverly hadn't heard from him, I'd really be panicking. But at least I knew he wasn't dead … yet. Just in a heck of a lot of hot water.

We had a family talent for trouble.

CHAPTER FIVE

"Tori, we do not say crazy; we say eccentric."
—Yiayia scolding a young Tori talking about her family

S o my uncle was missing and caught up in some cult, the god of dead people had a mad-on for me, volcanologists were getting torn to shreds atop Mount Lee, and the Feds were looking to me for answers. My life was nearly complete.

What would *really* ice the cake would be an arrest for trespassing or tampering with evidence, I thought, even as I ducked under the crime scene tape on Mount Lee right behind the Hollywood sign. I wondered whether ambrosia addiction had some kind of side effect in humans ... like rampant stupidity. But then, that would hardly explain all the *other* bad decisions I'd made in my life.

I picked my way over darkened and matted clumps of grass, forcing my gaze over them when all my mind really wanted was to skitter away and defer analysis. I didn't know what I was searching for, but I sure as hell wouldn't find it if I didn't look. Chunks of ripped-out rock littered the landscape, deciding my course as I steered between the bigger bits and twisting my ankles as the smaller bits rolled beneath my feet. By the time I got to the summit, I was lucky to still be able to walk. The mouth of the crater looked charred, as if the Titan Prometheus had tried cauterizing the wound with fire. It still smelled of brimstone and sulfur and … No, I realized. That wasn't a residual scent. It was something living and breathing, flowing out of the hole in waves, like expelled air. There was no breeze at the summit. Yet the scents washed over me, hot and fetid, with the rhythm of expelled breath and the ooky fertile flavor of bacteria incubating in a Petri dish. Yes, I said ooky. It's a technical term.

I drew back in alarm. There was *something* down there. Living, breathing, watching. I was sure of it. I pulled out my phone, thinking to call someone. For backup? So they'd know where to find my body? I wasn't sure. But anyway, I didn't know who to call. Armani? I was trespassing on a crime scene. Jesus? While he could probably cut anyone to shreds with his razor wit, I didn't want to count on him in a fight. My best friend Christie, much as I loved her, wasn't exactly sidekick material. There were only so many times a body could listen to a high-pitched "ewww" without adding to the carnage.

"Looking for something?" a voice asked, low and sly.

I whirled, my heart pounding in my chest, holding my phone out like a weapon and reaching for the pepper spray on my keychain. Behind me—well, *before* me now—stood a foxlike creature. Tufted ears, red-gold fur glowing like a second sun … and a long, slender lizard's tail flicking lazily. He barked out a laugh.

"There is no need to phone-a-friend. I am right here."

"*Friend.* Yeah, right. More like a pain in the a—"

"Ah ah ah, show some respect." He tsked, and it was so

strange a noise to hear coming from the foxy body. Almost stranger than words. "Not nice to curse in front of the gods."

"You're not *my* god."

He—Hermes, in the guise of one of his other namesakes, Iemisch (he also answered to Mercury, Loki, Coyote, humor columnist Thom Foolery and any number of other things)—cocked his head and stared at me thoughtfully.

"God of tricksters, travelers and thieves—no, perhaps not. I tend more toward your competition."

We'd met before. Hermes had supplied valuable intel, in his own way. Cryptic, sometimes in free verse. Never straightforward. Something like an oracle. I had yet to figure out *why*. Maybe I amused him, but I was almost sure he was playing some game and I was a living chess piece he was nudging toward the proper square. No, I didn't trust him as far as I could throw him … in any of his forms.

"What do you want?" I asked.

"So polite." Hermes took three steps closer and wound around me like a cat, his whipcord tail lingering over my legs and other areas in a way that would have been sexual harassment had they been hands. Or if I had a weapon at the ready more threatening than a phone with which to take proper exception. "I came with a warning. There is a war brewing, and *that*"—he nipped playfully at my phone, but let his teeth close on empty air—"is not going to cover it. I doubt you can speed-dial your enemies to death."

"War?" I asked, already adding it to my mental list of taking down a cult, kicking my addiction, finding a semi-formal dress and a date … "Can you give me a little more to go on here? Are we talking War as in the card game, *Cowboys vs. Aliens* or thermonuclear?"

"What have you got to trade for the information?" he asked. His tail lashed the phone out of my hand, and it landed in something I didn't even want to analyze.

"Oops," he said in response to my glare.

Oh, if looks could kill … "I don't have anything to trade," I told him with a minimum of regret.

"Perhaps not now," he agreed, tail swishing like a cat's, "but you will."

"How do you know?"

"I have my ways."

"I'm sure you do, but I'm not dealing. No way am I going to promise you some undisclosed future thing for information of questionable use. Do you think I was born yesterday?"

"Well, in the grand scheme of things—"

"Forget it. Look, it's been nice talking to you. Really. Glad you could drop by, but I've got work to do."

He eyed me. You'd think it would be hard to take seriously a foxy-face with cute little sticky-up ears. You'd be wrong. There was something about the expression, the stillness, the implied threat of those teeth, all of which seemed to be canines and wickedly sharp … "You know, I think you've made the right call, deciding to fight your addiction. I mean, fast-healing, nigh invulnerability, ultimately becoming immortal. Awful stuff. But the flipside—fever, withdrawal, hallucinations, death. Definitely the way to go."

"So, what? Apollo sent you to talk me into staying hooked?"

"Well, I *am* the messenger of the gods," he answered helpfully.

With that, he turned tail, literally, flicked it once and was gone. Just … gone.

Or maybe I'd missed his exit, because right now all I could see was red. I was going to *kill* Apollo. As in *dead*. Deceased. *Bleeding demised.*

I stomped over to my phone and lifted it out of the muck. I was just about to wipe it off with the hem of my shirt when I heard. "Stop right there!"

I froze.

"Put your hands where I can see them." It was the voice of authority. Agent Holloway, I thought, or maybe Rosen.

Slowly, I raised my hands to shoulder level. "Turn around."

I did as he asked, figuring I could go all gorgon on his ass if he made for the cuffs. It was Rosen, and he had a weapon in hand, aimed straight at me, but he didn't seem inclined to use it. He actually seemed satisfied in some weird way rather than angry, as if my presence confirmed something he'd suspected all along ... like my involvement. At least he hadn't seen Hermes. A fox-lizard might have been challenging to explain.

"Do you people have motion detectors set up or what?" I asked, figuring that zipping my lip would only make me look guiltier. Strategy ... sure thing. Certainly not poor impulse control.

"Or what," he answered helpfully. "You want to step out here, away from my crime scene so that we can have a little talk about tampering with evidence?"

The question was probably rhetorical. Just to keep my mind off what I might or might not be stepping on as I complied, I argued anyway. "There was no tampering involved. You think I want to touch any of this? Besides, I'm sure the CSIs have been here and done that."

"The scene hasn't been released." Rosen lowered his gun, but it didn't disappear into that spiffy shoulder holster that always kept the lines from showing beneath the Feds' suits. Not that he was wearing the jacket right now—not in this heat.

I reached the scene tape and debated which was more ignominious to try in front of the Fed—climbing over or going under. Finally, I opted for under and slid out toward Rosen, who stepped back as if I had the cooties. Hey, *I* wasn't the one with sweat stains under my pits and halfway to my navel.

"We don't have anything to talk about," I told him flatly once I could see the whites of his eyes. "I don't know anything."

"If you weren't connected somehow to these deaths, you wouldn't be here."

I rolled my eyes. "I'm stunned by the brilliance of your

reasoning. Oh no, wait, I'm not. *Hello*, private detective, a.k.a. snoop. It's sort of an occupational hazard."

"*Hired* snoop. If you have a client, you haven't said," he countered. Rosen was no slouch at staring contests. My eyes were going dry from the effort not to blink. There was a very short list of things that could outstare us gorgon girls. Fish. The occasional owl. Tikis.

"*You* brought me into this when you treated me like a suspect—in a slaying I still see in my nightmares. I take that personally. So yeah, I've got a client and she's pretty demanding. If you're not going to arrest me—" not that I should give him ideas, "—I'd like to get back to work."

"Does your boyfriend know a former porn star stayed over at your place last night?"

Holy non sequitur, Batman. So that *had* been him. There'd been rumors that Apollo Demas, star of stage and screen (hey, the gods had to do *something* after they'd lost their worship and a great deal of their power along with it) had begun his career in the adult film industry. I might have to stop by the video store on the way home.

"Nick trusts me," I answered.

"Uh huh. You didn't answer my question."

"I didn't figure it was any of your business. How about you answer one of my questions for a change? If this scene's already been processed, what are *you* doing here?"

He eyed me, much like Hermes had, but in the end, he too decided to talk. I was just one of those people, I guessed. Put me on public transport and I'd hear the life story of the lady next to me, whether I wanted to or not. Usually not. There were, after all, limits to my curiosity. "That fissure runs deep and has partially collapsed back in on itself. It's not possible to see down past a few feet. A team's coming out from UCLA and we're going to send a camera down to take a look. I came out to check on the scene and the structural integrity. Now you. Tit for tat."

I grit my teeth. "No, Armani doesn't know."

"It was Nick a second ago."

"So sue me. Anyway, it's not what you think with Apollo."

"It never is."

I glared and he ignored.

"We're friends, okay?" I said. "It may seem odd, the actor and the PI, but we share … a common ancestry."

He raised both brows at that. "You're related? Like kissing cousins?"

The very thought was so absurd I couldn't even get angry. "*So* no. Not unless it's back countless generations." Was Apollo related to Pan somehow? Maybe. It seemed like all the old ones were related somehow—springing fully formed from each other's heads and that sort of thing.

"He'll tell the same story?" Rosen asked.

Call me slow, but I only just realized that Rosen could only know about Apollo's visit if he'd had me watched.

"How *exactly* is this relevant to your case?"

"Who says it is? Maybe I'm just making conversation."

"Yeah, well, this one is over."

His phone rang as I was about to brush past him, and he reached a hand out lightning-fast to grab me by the arm and hold me there. He lifted the phone from a hip holster with his other hand.

"Rosen." He stopped to listen. "Really?" His voice sharpened, and I knew it wasn't a checking-in sort of call. "Send them over right away. I'll stand by."

"Don't move," he ordered me, as if I had a choice. He was hanging on tight, and even if I gave him the gorgon glare, I'd probably have to break his fingers to escape. When he unfroze, I'd have a heck of an enemy. With a badge and a license to kill.

He punched a button on the phone and held it at arm's length to look at whatever the caller had sent his way. It made him suck his lips into his mouth to the point where they ceased to exist.

"What is it?" I asked, not that I thought he'd tell me.

I was wrong. He turned the phone in my direction, and I wished he hadn't. "Another body's been found—torn apart."

"Here?" I asked. I didn't mean *here* here, of course, but LA in general.

"San Francisco area."

"Uncle Christos." It escaped my lips before I could think. More of a prayer than a statement, really, that the body not be his. It was hard to tell with the face ripped off.

CHAPTER SIX

"Happiness is a smoking gun."
—Christos Karacis

Armani was waiting for me when I got home. I'd seen earlier that I'd missed three calls from him, but ... I could lie to myself and say I hadn't called earlier because I hadn't wanted to implicate him in any way in my violation of the Mount Lee crime scene. Or that I knew he'd be busy at work or ...

But that Queen of Denial thing—it's not just an honorary title. I take my duties *very* seriously.

I opened my—Lau's—apartment door, walked into the living room and *boom*, there was Armani, sitting on Lau's stiff-backed chair, incongruously flipping through a fashion magazine Christie must have left behind, no doubt hoping she'd influence me through osmosis.

He put the magazine down, fixed me with a cop stare and said, "You didn't return my calls."

"I see you let yourself in." *Never* get defensive.

"You gave me a key."

"Actually, *Lau* gave you a key. I let you keep it."

He shrugged. "Same difference. Where've you been?"

"Nick, you're my boyfriend, not my keeper."

His eyes narrowed. "*Really?* Because yesterday you seemed to need a keeper. Besides, if I *were* your boyfriend and I'd called three times to make sure you were okay after you practically collapsed in my arms, I'd think you'd care enough to call and let me know you were fine."

And just like that I felt like an ass.

I moved into the room and perched on Lau's coffee table to go eye to eye with Armani. "I'm sorry." All that sincerity I'd saved up not wasting a drop on Apollo? I used it here. "I guess I was just so embarrassed about my weakness ..."

I left it there. It was probably as far as I could go without lying to him, and I'd avoid that if I could. "Let me make it up to you," I said instead. "Have you had lunch? Let me buy us some pizza."

Maybe on a full stomach the news would go down better that I was leaving town, at least for a few days, to hopefully *not* identify the body Rosen had shown me as that of my uncle, but to find out what really had happened to him. I couldn't do that from here.

"You think I can be bought off with pizza?" he asked incredulously.

"Can you?"

He smiled, and at least part of my world righted itself. Gah, had I really just thought that? Romantic drivel. "It's a start," he said.

"Good. The works?" I had to ask, because while most people were predictable, Nick liked to mix things up.

"Except for pineapple. Fruit doesn't belong on pizza."

"Tomato is a fruit."

"Don't go getting all smart ass. You're supposed to be making things up to me."

"Right. Have I told you how incredible you look today? Almost good enough to eat."

"Oh no you don't, woman. No getting distracted. I was promised pizza."

I stuck my tongue out at him and turned for the kitchen to call up the pizza place. He followed me in to raid the fridge for drinks.

I was mid-dial when Armani said, "Hey, you made dessert."

I dropped the phone. "Don't touch that!" I said, suddenly panicked. Armani straightened and fixed me with a *look*. "Why not?"

Thinking fast, I answered, "It's Christie's. She made it for a party tonight, but her fridge is on the fritz. This stupid heat and the brown outs have taken a toll."

"Christie cooked?" he asked—not like he believed me, but like he was confirming that *that* was the story I was going with.

"Don't be silly. Christie stirred ingredients together. No cooking involved. It's ambrosia"—literally, but he didn't have to know that—"marshmallows, whipped cream, pineapple and, um, whatever."

Damn Apollo's sense of humor, that's really how it looked in its inoffensive little Tupperware container.

Armani continued to stare at me over my refrigerator door, but I picked the phone back up and redialed, pretending not to notice. "I'll order us a dessert pizza while I'm at it," I told him, "so you can stop eyeing Christie's goodies."

It was a leading line, and he was supposed to pick up on it, but he seemed more interested in studying me than exchanging witty banter. I should tell him. I knew it. But until I kicked the habit or was at least well on my way … I was already judging myself. I didn't need the weight of his disapproval as well.

"You can tell me anything, you know," he said quietly.

I met his deep blue gaze and nearly let it all pour out … but then the pizza guy came on the line and the moment passed. I placed our order, hung up the phone and asked, "You gonna grab us a couple of sodas or just let all the cold air out?"

He grabbed the sodas and together we walked back into the living room to sit, this time together on the couch. No sooner did our butts hit the cushions then he turned to me. "Okay, Tori, what's really going on?"

That intensity was almost painful, like looking straight into the sun. I spilled … everything but what he really wanted to know. I told him about the Feds' eight-by-ten color glossies, about the latest photo of the body near San Fran that I feared might be Christos, even about Hermes and his cryptic ramblings about war. After all, Armani had been by my side when Zeus, Hephaestus and Poseidon had made their play for power. It wasn't like the mention of Hermes would be a great blow to his worldview.

"What do you think he meant?" Nick asked. We were back to Nick.

Unburdening my soul (mostly) had that effect.

"I don't know how many meanings there are. I think the questions are: who will be fighting and how do we stop it?"

"Okay then, how *do* we stop it?"

"No flippin' clue."

"Well, as long as you have a plan."

"Any luck finding Lau?" I asked, switching gears. Here I was going on about my crap—blah blah *war*, blah blah *missing uncle* —okay, neither insignificant. But meanwhile he had an Internal Affairs investigation against him—a possible career ender—and an AWOL partner unable to back up his story or explain why his girlfriend had temporarily taken over her lease.

"Her mother's heard from her, at least. When Lau makes contact again, she'll pass a message along. There's apparently no way to reach her. No cell reception where she is. Something about dragon breeding grounds and signal disruption."

"Wait, wait, wait, did you say *breeding grounds*? I thought the dragons had all died off or gone into perpetual hibernation. You're telling me they're up and about and *multiplying*?"

"I think so. Lau's mother doesn't speak much English, so I may have gotten things garbled."

"Wow, that's … wow."

"You consort with old Greek gods and you think that's wow?"

"Hey, I grew up on tales of the Olympians, almost like they were my crazy aunts and uncles, which if you'd met any of *them* you'd understand is not so farfetched. But *dragons*? They're mythic."

"Your sense of wonder is seriously skewed, you know that?"

"Yeah."

"So what's really in that tub in your fridge?"

I gave him Yiayia's stink-eye. "Hash brownies, cleverly disguised as ambrosia. You've got me." I held out my wrists. "You gonna apply the cuffs?"

"Maybe after the pizza."

"Good call," I said sourly.

Later, after he'd gone off to the precinct where desk duty was making him insane, I called Christie.

"If Nick brings up the tub in my refrigerator, it's yours."

"Huh?"

"Don't ask."

"Okay." That was when I heard the quaver in her voice.

"Christie, is everything all right?"

"N-no. Jack …" She got a little incoherent after that, but I let her ramble. I might have missed the details, but I'd gotten the gist from his previous months of dickery. That's right, I said dickery. I'd never really had a BFF before Christie, so I'd had no idea how much tongue biting could be involved. Not that I hadn't expressed myself on the matter of Jack now and then when I couldn't help myself.

She finally ran down, blew her nose noisily and added, "I need to get out of town. Just for a few days. His stupid cologne billboard is everywhere. I swear, I'm afraid I'll fly off the handle and drive straight through one of them."

"If they weren't, like, fifty feet in the air."

A choked laugh-sob escaped her. "Yeah, except for that. So what do you say?"

"About what?" I really should have listened more closely. Bad friend. No cookie.

"Getting out of town with me."

"Um, I would, but I have to head up to San Francisco for a few days to—"

"Perfect!"

"But, Christie, it's work. And it could be dangerous."

"Even better! I could help. It would totally take my mind off things, and you'll need back up. It's a win-win. I can make us the best road trip mix."

My mouth moved, but nothing came out. On the one hand, there was the danger and my total commitment to keeping Christie out of it. On the other, an eight-hour drive on the end of which I might face the shredded remains of my favorite uncle all alone didn't seem even remotely appealing. On the third hand, which was entirely possible given my mutant family, if the trip led to the need for any undercover work at the cult, well, I was no actress, not like Christie. Plus, if *I* were recruiting for a nature cult, I'd go for Christie's farm-fresh looks over my gristle and bone any day of the week. But, still, DANGER.

"Christie, I'm not kidding about the danger. I don't know what I'm in for in San Francisco. At least one person's already been killed." Or more ... I still didn't know what, if any, relation there was between Back to Earth and Mount Lee.

"I'll be careful. I promise. Don't make me beg."

Well, damn. How on earth did people say "no" to Christie?

Not that she heard it much. She seemed to have a constant stream of modeling and commercial work, though she still hadn't gotten her big break.

"I'm leaving *really* early in the morning," I said in a last-ditch effort to dissuade her.

"Tell me the time and I'll have the coffee and bagel bites ready to go."

"Jack's an idiot," I said.

"I know," she answered, quietly.

"You want me to put the hurt on him?"

"No ... Well, a little. But mostly no. Thanks for asking."

"I'll see you at 8:00 AM, sharp."

I hung up, wondering how the hell Christie had just roped me into road-tripping her straight into the danger zone. Oh sure, she seemed sweet and innocent, but it didn't stop her from getting what she wanted. Except for Jack. *Idiot.*

That night I dreamed of blood. Rivers of it ... with the occasional lily-white bone floating to the surface. Empty eye socket here, lost limb there.

My heart pounded, my temples throbbed, and I willed myself to wake up.

Wake up. WAKE UP!

I bolted upright, just as a sword sliced the sheets where I'd been a millisecond before. I looked into the face of Death with only time to think *this is wrong; it's supposed to be a sickle* before the blade was coming for me again. I rolled, but the blankets coiled around me like pythons, lashing me in place. The blade landed centimeters from my ear, taking some of my hair with it as I fought to get free. The shock of it flooded my system with juice, as if someone had pushed the plunger on a whole vial of methamphetamines. Like Wonder Woman on speed, I tore the blankets from my body and dove off the other side of the bed.

I planted my feet on the floor, dropped into my kickboxing ready stance and faced the Grim Reaper. Or just about. Except for the whole sword thing. The Angel of Death, Thanatos, Mors —call him what you would—was enough to cause heart failure even without a single sword stroke. He stood over six feet tall with the traditional black cloak and cowl shadowing his face. He was surrounded by a miasma of undulating darkness that managed to convey uncompromising ... cold. Not evil—evil could be swayed in its own self-interest. Thanatos was far more frightening, because it didn't look like a wrecking ball could move him, let alone little ol' me.

"Um, hey, you sure you've got the right girl?" I asked, just in case. "I'm only house sitting."

He nodded. Once. And advanced on me—straight *through* the bed, floating more than walking. I didn't actually see legs move beneath that cloak, nothing so mundane.

Fear tore through me like a flash flood, instinctive and primal. The myths had no stories I knew about cheating death— not successfully, anyway. Achilles, Orpheus and Eurydice— cautionary tales for incautious children.

Desperate, I yelled *"Freeze!"* and tried to whammy him with the gorgon glare, but I couldn't even see his eyes, let alone meet them, and he kept advancing as inexorably as, well, death.

If he could move through furniture, I doubted my pitiful roundhouse kick was going to do much good against him. I didn't have room for a running start, but I lurched around the corner of the bed, set to make a dash for the door. Only to be blocked by the same figure that had reduced even Ebenezer Scrooge to a quivering apologetic heap.

I was the one who froze. Time warped, and everything happened in slow motion and yet too fast to report. His sword came up. My eyes widened, unable to look away from the glistening blade. It flashed as it arced down at me with a terrible beauty, like silver-struck moonlight. The very movement was grace and beauty and terror, and then ... nothing.

"Ares's hairy arse, what on earth was he thinking? Her time isn't up!"

There was a voice. Faint, but compelling …

"Besides, we were just getting to the good part. Who will win—the divine Apollo or the dreamy detective? It can't end on a cliffhanger," someone else said.

"Lachesis! You're as bad as these mortals, getting caught up in their soap opera lives."

"I can't help it. I mean, it's better than Lost. *If you'd put down your clippers every once in a while, Atropos, you'd see. You need to lighten up."*

Lachesis? Atropos? The Fates? I drifted closer, certain I couldn't be hearing right. Couldn't be hearing anything at all.

"Girls, focus," the first speaker—Clotho?—chimed in again. *"We need a decision. Thanatos has usurped our authority, cutting a cord that had yet to reach its terminus."*

"Not acting alone, I'd wager."

"Be that as it may, do we sever the cord or rethread? If Thanatos is doing Hades's bidding and his plot succeeds, it might behoove us to be in his good graces."

"No!" The voice, crusty and deeper than others—Atropos?—was implacable. *"We don't cede him our authority. Even Hades must bow before us."*

"Good luck with that," Lachesis put in.

"Lachesis!" Crusty scolded.

She hmphed. *"Look, I vote no, okay? Tori's life is way too interesting to cancel mid-season."*

"Addict," Atropos accused.

"Sister, I share Lachesis's view," Clotho said. *"The thread is intriguing. It strengthens the weave."*

"Fine," Atropos grumbled, *"then we're agreed?"*

"Yes. Besides, we've got to get back to work on these costumes. Full dress rehearsal is tonight."

I gasped in a breath that felt like a chainsaw unleashed in my chest. My eyes snapped open. I expected to see a bright light or a dark and desolate hell, depending on whether I'd been judged naughty or nice, but my own room swam in front of me. At least, I thought so. I'd never seen it from this angle before—an unlovely view of the dust bunnies and dried, boxed sea life beneath Lau's bed.

I was *alive*. Like Scrooge, I wanted to throw open my window and shout it out to the world. I had some vague retreating memory of the Fates discussing my life or death as if I was some sitcom they'd be sorry to see canceled. It seemed I'd been picked up for another season. Either that or I was in some bizarre version of Tartarus and the dust bunnies were about to swarm.

I tried to roll to my feet, but my eyes were the only things that moved. That was when the panic hit. What if I was paralyzed? How long would it be before someone came to check on me? Long enough to dehydrate? Starve to death? No, dehydration would come before starvation. And hey, if that wasn't comforting … I took a few deep, jagged breaths and put everything I had into pressing my arms to the floor to raise my upper body. I felt … nothing. At all.

Terror choked me, my vision swam, my breathing went so shallow in my panic that no actual air exchange was going on. No feeling was *bad*, I knew that much. The fact that I could breathe on my own, no machine required, didn't mean much if I was to be locked inside an immobile shell for the rest of my life, able to see and think but not respond. Helpless. My own special hell.

Then suddenly—

"UNG!" An inarticulate cry ripped from my lips as my entire body arched off the floor in pain. It tore through me, shredded my mind, burnt out the nerve endings that had just reknit. Possibly my spinal column had just mended itself. Gods bless—

"Arrrrr." Agony stole my breath again, chased my awareness to a dark little corner and told it to stay put as it took over everything.

Mercifully, I blacked out.

CHAPTER SEVEN

"You keep saying 'twisted' like it's a bad thing."
    —Cousin Tina Galanos, contortionist for the Rialto
Bros. Circus

D istantly, I was aware of the ringing of a phone but it
    didn't seem to mean much to me. My consciousness
    kind of dog paddled to the surface, in no rush to
arrive. Equally distant was the cry of pain from one shoulder and
a numbness in the arm that signaled I'd fallen asleep in a bad
position. For some reason, I was soaked to the bone, hot and
cold at the same time. Clammy. It was the taste of blood that
snapped me awake.

Blood in my mouth was bad. Bad, bad, bad. There were
probably other adjectives, but I couldn't think of them right
then. I tested my body, and it moved—sluggishly, because that
numb arm didn't want to cooperate, but I was able to sit. My
tongue was swollen. Probably I'd bitten it at some point and the
blood was only the result. Panic began to retreat.

I fumbled for the phone on my bedside table and answered, "'Ello." Something like it anyway.

"Oh my God, Tori, are you okay? Did you oversleep? It's almost nine o'clock."

Christie. Right. We had plans.

"'M okay," I said, clearing my throat between words. "I'm just … groggy. Give me a little bit? My alarm didn't go off."

"No problem. Do you want me to meet you at your place?"

My bedroom looked like something out of a slasher film. "No, I'll be there to pick you up as soon as I can. Sorry."

"No prob—"

I hung up maybe a syllable early, but the shakes had set in with a vengeance, and the only thing I could think of was getting to my fridge and getting help. I didn't want to want it, to *need* it. But if I died or went insane, Hades would win, and that so wasn't happening. I pulled myself upright and did the zombie shuffle into the kitchen. The sight of my bloody arms as I lifted them for the handle of the fridge didn't do anything to put me off my feed. I hadn't asked Apollo about dosing, but inside the Tupperware container with the sky blue top was a scoop. I was going to guess one would be enough. If not, I'd try two—

I ate it standing. As the ambrosia touched my lips, my mouth flooded with saliva. The flavor burst over my tongue like … like ambrosia-flavored champagne and Pop Rocks. It seemed to fizz and tingle all the way down as my body came back online, leaving me hyper-aware, hyper-alive.

It made me wish Armani was here. And naked. And standing at attention … Okay, so a cold shower before dashing off to pick up Christie. At the rate I was going, the car was optional. I felt like I could run to San Francisco myself and be back in time for lunch.

Clearly the ambrosia had side effects—delusions of grandeur, mistaking oneself for an Indy 500 car.

The shower was … oh no, I was *not* going to wax poetic about the feel of the crisp, incredible water flowing over me.

Except to say that it did nothing to cool my jets. It was *almost* enough to wash away the horror of my near-death experience, though. Priorities. I left Armani an X-rated text message—very life affirming—dumped all the ice from the freezer into a Styrofoam cooler I found in Lau's pantry, and gently placed the tub of ambrosia on top of it. Side effects or no, I couldn't afford the withdrawal while traveling four hundred miles from home.

I wondered how I'd convince Christie that the tub was off-limits. Maybe I'd make up an incredibly high caloric content. It might even be true.

Twenty minutes later I sat in front of her apartment building, calling for her to come down, since I was double-parked. I had time to download a GPS app onto my phone and program in the address of the Residence Inn before Christie arrived, matching Coach luggage slung over one shoulder and rolling along behind.

I popped the trunk and got out to help her. "Jeez, Christie, how long do you think we'll be gone?"

She flashed me the smile that had gotten her the teeth whitening commercial last year. "I don't know, but I figure it's my Girl Scout training kicking in. I like to be prepared."

"You were a Girl Scout?"

"Well, a Brownie, anyway."

She tossed the big bag into the trunk, not needing my help after all, thanks to her personal trainer. Then she dug around in her shoulder bag and came up with a matching hot pink iPod. "Tuneage," she explained, as if I might not get it.

We plugged in, buckled up, fidgeted with settings and mirrors, and hit the road. Christie produced a thermos out of her clown car of a bag, and two stainless steel cups to go with it.

"Not pink?" I asked.

"Can you believe the pink only came in *plastic*?"

I refused to comment on the grounds that she held exclusive access to my caffeine options.

"I hope you like Kona," she added.

"Love it."

She produced some kind of froufrou liquid sweetener. "Sugar?" she asked. I gave her a look.

"Okay, sugar like substance," she amended. "Kid tested, FDA approved."

"Hit me."

She doctored my cup and handed it back to me. I took an immediate sip. It was no ambrosia, but it wasn't bad either.

"Thanks."

"*De nada.* And Tori, thanks for letting me come with. And for not saying 'I told you so' about Jack."

I bit my lip.

"I Can't Drive 55" by Sammy Hagar blasted out of the stereo.

"Really?" I asked her.

It was good to see her grin. "Like I could leave that off the ultimate road trip mix. Just wait, there's more."

"Come Monday" by Jimmy Buffett.

"Little Red Corvette" by Prince.

"Sleep While I Drive" by Melissa Etheridge.

"Take it Easy" by The Eagles.

"Highway to Hell" by AC/DC

"Please Come to Boston" by Joan Baez.

"California" by Joni Mitchell.

Christie's tastes ran a lot more folksy rock than mine, but she'd put so much effort in, I didn't have the heart to tell her so.

I'll skip over the next eight hours of girly stuff, pit stops, smoothies and half-caf, skinny, grande, ridiculously overpriced foamy goodness. But for almost an entire day, no one tried to kill me, torture me with crime scene photos or entice me over to the dark side with six-pack abs, dreamy azure eyes or snickerdoodles. The sun was shining, the AC was working, and Christie, who was as tone deaf as me, didn't give a damn when I tried to sing along with the CD.

Ah, *this*, I thought, was what it felt like to be a real girl. Nice.

The warm fuzzies lasted until the outskirts of San Fran, when the traffic slowed to a crawl, the clock flipped past 5:00 PM, and I was suddenly concerned that I'd have to go another full day without finding out Uncle Christos's fate.

"Hey, you all right?" Christie asked, seeing my smile dim.

"Yeah, just … tired. Hungry." No need burdening her with my problems when she had her own.

"You're kidding—you can eat again after that mondo burger you had for lunch?"

What could I say? Apparently, ambrosia gave me the munchies.

"In one point two miles turn right on ramp onto Restin Boulevard," the GPS on my phone piped up. The voice had gotten fainter as my battery wore down. Any time now I was going to have to locate my car charger.

"That's our exit!" Christie perked. She'd not only mastered the obvious, she had it eating out of the palm of her hand.

It took us eight minutes to go one point two miles, but once we took the turn off, we could see the Residence Inn from the ramp. Two seconds later, maybe three, we were parked.

The kid behind the counter looked up as we entered, nearly hyperventilated at the sight of Christie, and quickly tucked the magazine he was reading beneath the counter.

"Can I help you?" he asked, voice breaking only once.

Christie gave him the thousand-watt smile that still sold that tooth whitening system to the masses, and I thought he would keel straight over.

"Uh, one room or … uh, two?" He gave me a once-over and turned straight back to Christie. If my ego were dependent on barely post-pubescent desk clerks, I'd be crushed. As it was, I let her handle the room thing while I looked around. In a Plexiglas stand by the register was a menu/advertisement for a pizza chain that would apparently deliver. Farther on down the counter was a second stand for something called the Rustic Potato. I picked up a menu out of curiosity before wandering over to the wooden rack of pocket-sized brochures for everything from whale watching tours to dinner theatre. Oddly, no pamphlet for creepy cult tours. Huh.

I wandered back to the desk around the time the clerk was telling Christie about the breakfast buffet and handing over two keys.

"Oh, wait," I said, stopping Christie as she reached to accept them. "Is that the quiet side of the street?"

"The what?"

"My uncle stayed here a few months ago, and wherever his room was, he said the traffic noise was just terrible. The big trucks rumbling by at all hours ... I think you'd better make sure we're not near there. His name is Christos Karacis."

Christie leaned in with her smile and added, "I do need my beauty rest."

The clerk nearly swallowed his tongue. He clacked away on his computer. "I don't see a record of him. Um, how do you spell it? Maybe I've got it wrong."

I spelled Karacis for him, but he came up blank again. He looked at Christie, really anxious to impress. "Maybe he registered under another name. Sometimes guys do, you know, for ..." he turned rose red, "... uh, privacy."

"Oh!" she said, playing flustered really well. "Tori, what do you think? Did your uncle have any, you know, aliases?"

Hell's bells, I didn't know. He'd gone off on his little Odyssey without so much as a forwarding address. The whole thing was weird all the way around. I felt a *zip* go straight through me and froze, waiting for it to repeat. It wasn't exactly the *zing* of forewarning. What then? Okay, think back—Christos, alias, Odyssey, *zip*. Something about *The Odyssey* then? I wondered if this were some kind of manifestation of my oracular powers.

One zip for yes, zilch for no. Definitely it was trying to tell me *something*. I just wished I had some idea what on earth it could be. Clearly something to do with *The Odyssey*. I thought back over Odysseus's adventures ... what I could remember anyway. Suddenly, I had it! Odysseus had used an alias when he and his men had been trapped on Polyphemus's island. When he asked who was there, Odysseus had told him "No one," which in Greek was—

"Try *Outis*." I said, not quite believing it was going to be that easy.

"Let me check." The clerk clacked away again. "Bingo. He was here—C. Outis. But if he had problems with his room, he never complained. He was in the same one the whole time."

"We'll take that one," I cut in.

"But you said—"

Christie leaned in and whispered something in his ear. The clerk went from rose to beet red and gave me a half-frightened look. "Sure, no problem."

He gave us two new keys and made clear to Christie that she could call if she needed anything ... like a cabana boy for herself or a psych referral for her friend.

"I'm pretty good at this undercover stuff," Christie murmured to me as we turned for the door. "We're like good cop, crazy cop."

I gave her a smile. We *had* already gotten closer to Christos than I had on my own. "Let me guess which one I am."

"Aw, don't take it personally. You've just got it goin' on. You're tough. I'm ... not so much. We use what we've got. So, where do you want to eat?" she asked more loudly.

"How about the Rustic Potato?" I asked.

Because I'd just looked—really looked—at the menu, which advertised *Gourmet confections, featuring organic, farm-fresh produce grown locally.* I had a feeling, subtle but there. And if that wasn't enough, I recognized some of the pics on the cover as the same ones from the Back to Earth website.

"That the new hippy-dippy place way out on Green Hills Road?" the clerk asked, overhearing.

"Is it?"

He shrugged. "I don't go in much for rabbit food, but the boss says it's to die for."

Interesting. And hopefully not apt.

CHAPTER EIGHT

"Food of the Gods? Which—that hippopotamus-headed one across the way? Sure enough this ain't people food."

—Pappous on the trendy restaurant Yiayia had insisted on for their 50th wedding anniversary

The Rustic Potato was, in fact, "that hippy-dippy place" on Green Hills. At least, it was *a* hippy-dippy place. This being California, it wasn't like there was any lack of restaurants fitting that description. I wondered what kind of signage a "Rustic Potato" would have. It turned out to be a vivid blue background with an overly cheerful sun looking down on aggressively green fields. I was almost inspired to burst into a song featuring words like zippity doo da, and twittering about the blue bird on my shoulder.

"Cute!" Christie gushed.

"You don't think it's a little ... much?"

"Sourpuss," she said.

"Hey, you knew this road trip was dangerous when you took it."

Christie stuck her tongue out at me. "Jeez, you'd think *you* were the one who just got dumped."

"Sorry."

"No, no—with you doing all the brooding, there's hardly any room for me in the role. I'm left with perky sidekick girl. That's kind of why I love you."

She said things like that, kind of why I loved her.

Christie had taken twenty minutes back at the hotel to freshen up. Her golden blonde hair was high on her head in a thick pony-tail that managed to look cool *and* classy. Her sundress was hothouse orange. Her fingers and toenails were a fuchsia that should have clashed with it, but instead were tied to the whole outfit by the chunky, beaded tri-strand necklace she wore, full of bright, tropical colors. It would have taken a crack team of stylists to make me look half so good, but I gave it a shot. Black capris, a honey-gold silk tank, and some dangly gold earrings, exposed by catching my unruly hair up into a twist with just a few loopy strands framing my face. No one would mistake me for a starlet, but with my Mediterranean skin tone and amber eyes, I didn't need much but liner, mascara and lip gloss to look as good as I ever got.

Beside the sign was a drive that looked like it was paved in clam shells, which we turned onto with a crunch—a cacophony of crunching, actually. The Potato itself looked like a Tuscan vineyard—all pink stucco and light wooden slats with vines curling up and around light fixtures and lattices. Herb bundles hung from rafters. Waitresses in white peasant blouses, black gypsy skirts and colorful scarfs and waiters in white collarless shirts, black chinos and those same headscarves tied about their waists bustled about. None of them were above the age of twenty-one or -two … tops. All looked to be about bursting with health.

The hostess who met us at the door was styled like the

mistress of the hacienda in a wrap dress the same punch-me yellow as the sun on the sign. Her hair was as black as mine, but glossy and as straight as I'd always wished mine could be, hanging in one long, dark curtain to the small of her back.

"Your first time here?" she asked. Christie nodded enthusiastically.

"Well, welcome!" The wattage from her smile probably could have lit a whole Tuscan town. "Right this way."

She led us through the packed restaurant to a small, two-person table at the back under a stained glass hanging lamp made to look like bundles of grapes and leaves, and left us with menus to study.

"Isn't this place great?" Christie gushed. "I mean, did you *see* her complexion? What a great endorsement. I'd about kill for pores like that."

"Um, yeah. Totally." I'd never noticed another person's pores in my life and wasn't about to start now.

Christie propped the menu up before her so that no one else could see her lips move and stage-whispered, "So, what do we do now?"

"We order," I stage-whispered back.

"Oh, right."

The look of the waiter who came to take our order didn't say Ken-doll so much as beanpole, which was a bit of a relief. I wasn't normally an insecure person—because first I'd have to care—but being surrounded by so many perfect people was starting to give me hives. I ordered a mineral water to fit in. Christie ordered an unsweetened ice tea.

"We have a full bar," he said, seemingly disappointed we weren't inflating the price of our bill and thus the size of his tip with booze.

"Really?" I asked. "That doesn't seem in keeping with the spirit of this place."

He grinned—all teeth. "Grapes are organic. So are barley, hops, potatoes …"

I laughed. "You've got me there."

"Besides, there are a ton of antioxidants and other health benefits to red wine, for example."

"Sold!" I said. "I'll have a glass of Merlot." I needed a drink after that drive.

"Great. And you?" He turned to Christie.

"Ack, no. Stains your teeth. I'm good with my tea."

"Coming right up." He vanished off to the bar.

"What're you having?" Christie asked.

Steak, I thought. Medium rare with enough blood still flowing to sop my bread in. To my surprise, it was actually on the menu.

The waiter returned, a half-full glass of deep garnet wine for me, and a tawny tea for Christie. Between the wine and the red meat, I ought to replace all the blood Thanatos had slashed out of me in pretty short order. I just hoped I'd get to keep it this time.

"Ready to order?" Beanpole ... or Martin, as he informed us ... asked.

"I have a quick question first," I said. "How organic is your food? I've heard stories about salmonella in sprouts and E. coli coming from natural fertilizer. I know organic is supposed to be good for you. My friend here swears by it, but ... I'm not so sure." Christie and I had decided on the way over that I'd be the PITA (aka Pain in the Ass), since it came so naturally to me.

"Ton*i*," Christie said, modifying my name and putting just the right note of exasperation into her voice.

Martin turned a beatific smile on her. "No, it's okay. We get that sometimes. The biotech food people do their best to drum up the hysteria about organics." To me, he said, "All of our distributors are accredited, and we wash our fruits and vegetables carefully. We've never had a problem."

"*See*, I told you it was perfectly safe," Christie jumped in.

"Are you interested in organic?" Martin asked, laser-like in his sudden focus.

"Absolutely," she breathed. "Our body is our temple, right?"

They beamed at each other, and I kept my eyes from rolling in their sockets. "We'll talk later," he said with a wink.

We placed our orders and off he went. "Our body is our temple?" I asked wryly.

"Sure, don't you believe that?" she asked, doing wide-eyed for me. Unless it wasn't an act. With Christie, it was hard to be sure.

"Of course I do. I believe all men should worship at my altar."

"I thought Armani was already taking care of that."

Oh crap, Armani. I'd promised to call him when we got in. "Excuse me," I said, rising to take myself and my phone outside.

"What did I say?"

"Nothing. I have to make a call."

"Gotcha, I'll hold down the fort."

I stepped outside the restaurant in deference to the other customers, turning my face up to the sun to catch the meager rays still remaining. There was some famous Mark Twain quote about the city—something about the coldest winter he ever experienced was the summer he spent in San Francisco. It did have that reputation. If Chicago was "The Windy City" because of all the bombast, San Fran came by it more naturally. But you wouldn't know it by tonight. There *was* a breeze, but it was lovely. Cool, but not cold. Refreshing even. The same hot snap that had hit LA seemed to have touched down here as well.

Demeter gloating, as Yiayia had said? Glowing was more like it. Beaming even. I was in the wrong spot to see the sun go down, but the sky was a gorgeous golden-amber. The traditional clouds mere wisps enflamed by the setting sun so that they looked like some dragon's fiery breath blazing across the sky.

I sighed, just as Armani picked up the call. "That for me?" he asked.

"Yes. The sunset is gorgeous. Wish you were here."

"Stopping to admire the sunset? That doesn't sound like you."

"Worse, I was just thinking poetical thoughts about the blazing sky."

"Do I have to worry about losing you to another city?"

"I don't know … maybe," I teased.

"Just remember, we have smog and riots and record-breaking temperatures. Everything you could want, right here at home."

"Um, you do *want* me back, right?"

We'd sparred like this before we'd dated. Old habits were hard to break, like the whole last name thing.

"Is this a trick question?"

All of the sudden, my stomach gave a flutter-kick of insecurity. We hadn't exactly parted with romantic declarations— puppies and kittens and chocolate covered kisses. We'd parted with me hiding something and him knowing it. Stupid cop instincts. I should tell him. Secrets were relationship poison. But … I didn't have the time or patience for an intervention. I was sure that was all there was to it. Really. It was *not* just an addict's rationalization.

"Straight answer, please," I said. "None of your cop tricks, answering one question with another."

"Of course I want you back." His voice was all low and sexy and gave me a little thrill. Then he ruined it by saying, "Why else would I leave my favorite toothbrush at your place?"

"Wait, you have a *favorite* toothbrush?"

"Don't you?"

"I have *a* toothbrush. One. By default, I suppose it's my favorite."

"Well, then, you see?"

I didn't. "That was another question, you realize that, right?"

"Here's another—I guess you haven't been to the morgue yet?" *That* put a damper on things.

"We got in too late."

"Call me when you do, whatever the outcome."

"I will."

"And if you need me, just say the word. Captain doesn't have me doing anything they can't spare me from. I'm pretty certain I can get the time off."

"I think you're going to need that vacation time for my cousin Tina's wedding."

There was a pause during which I held my breath. "You haven't asked me yet."

"I thought I just did."

"Lord, Tori, a man likes to be asked. Women don't let us get away with that kind of crap."

"I'm not most women. I'm liberated. Hence the fact that I just asked *you* out on a date."

"Oh, was there a question in there?"

I huffed. At what point did we get past the banter and into the deeper stuff? Not that I was particularly good at that or any less at fault than Armani. *Nick.*

But ...

"Will you? Save me from my nutty family and the singles table at the wedding?"

"Well, since you put it so romantically ... I'd be thrilled to escort you. But, fair warning, I don't chicken dance."

The very visual surprised a laugh out of me. "Duly noted."

When we rang off I felt like I'd just been through a kick-boxing match. I wondered who had won. At least I had a date for the wedding. Now all I had to do was find a dress and the stand-in father of the bride.

I turned to go back in and nearly jumped as the phone rang in my hand. I checked the display and saw that it was Jesus. It was well after five, which meant it was either a personal call (unusual) or something big had kept him at the office after hours (even more so).

"*Chica*, what the *hell* is going on?" he asked as soon as I picked up.

Since the potential answer covered a lot of ground, I really needed more specificity. "What?"

"I'm still at the office," he said, answering *that* question. "Do you know why?"

Gods save me from men who asked more questions than they answered. It was like an epidemic. "No, why?"

"Because a Godzilla-sized dog ... I'm talking a Hound of the Baskervilles, huge black beast, dripping drool and menace ... parked outside the door and wouldn't let me leave. I had the phone in my hand to call animal control when his trainer or whatever came calling."

"Trainer?" I said stupidly.

"Tall, dark and deadly. Wild black hair, skin pale as any New Englander, six foot five or so, shoulders out to here." I could only imagine. "Looked like he could melt me with his eyes. And not in the good way."

"Doesn't sound like anyone I know," I said honestly. "What did he want?"

"You. And again, not in the good way. It sounded more like he wanted to murder, not hire you."

"Where is he now?"

"Gone. I wouldn't tell him where you were, but that dog of his—I couldn't stop him from sniffing around. I think he left with one of your gym shoes. I don't think he can track you all the way to San Fran, but ... I had to warn you."

"But you're okay? He didn't hurt you?" It was on the tip of my tongue to ask how many heads the dog had, but I supposed Jesus, drama queen that he was, would have mentioned a little thing like a couple of extra heads.

"My nerves aren't all that are shot. I could use a spa day."

I ignored the hint. For now. Christmas bonuses were still a good many months away, and the deductible on the damage Poseidon had done to our offices weeks before had wiped out any budgetary frills.

"Did he leave a name or number?"

Jesus sighed again when I didn't pick up the hint. "Both. His name is Hadrian Boss, and—"

Hades. Had to be.

Jesus read off the number, but I had to make him repeat it twice to commit it to memory. I wondered if they'd finally installed cell towers in Hell or whether Hades was going to be topside for a time.

"Jesus, I doubt this will ever come up but just in case ... don't go anywhere with this guy and don't eat anything he might offer you."

I could practically hear Jesus rolling his eyes. "Right, no candy from strangers and never get into their car. I learned all that when I was five."

"I'm dead serious."

"So am I," he answered, and for once he sounded it. "You don't grow up on my side of the tracks and not know a thing or two. Don't worry, I had my nine mil pointed at his cojones the whole time. He never even knew it."

"Great," I said faintly. I wondered what kind of bullets worked on the god of the dead and his mutant hellhound. I doubted they came over the counter.

"*Chica*, you're starting to scare me with all this concern for my wellbeing."

"You *should* be scared. Look, maybe it would be best to close up the office for a few days ..."

"No ultra-butch white boy is going to turn *me* out of a job, don't you worry." I'd never been very good at taking orders, but Jesus was even worse. If I pushed the issue, I knew, he'd just dig in. The boy could out-stubborn me, and the last thing I wanted to do was go back to the office to find that my keyboard had been remapped and all my high-octane coffee replaced with decaf.

"Fine, just watch yourself."

"Coming *and* going," he promised. It was probably true. I'd never seen anyone else so in love with his own image.

I hurried back in to Christie after hanging up, hoping I hadn't been away as long as it'd seemed and that our food wouldn't be both there and cold. I could see immediately that I was beyond hope on the first part.

Christie looked up from playing with the condensation on her glass of unsweetened ice tea as I approached. She forced a smile onto her face, but I could tell that leaving her alone with her thoughts, probably of Jackass, had been a *bad* idea. There was a suspicious moisture gathered at the corners of her eyes, which along with her nose, looked just a bit pink.

"Another minute and I'd have started without you," she said. "Doesn't this look great?"

The food *did* look amazing. The colors were all so bright, the smells ... a sudden wave of want and need nearly swept my legs out from under me. I knew I was hungry, but I shouldn't have been anywhere near that desperate. Something was wrong.

"You okay?" Christie asked. I *hated* that question.

"Fine," I said, dropping into my chair a little too hard. "Just famished. You're right. This does look good."

My hand shook slightly as I picked up the fork, headed straight for a potato wedge, since it was already pre-cut for speed and ease of consumption.

Christie watched me worriedly as I put it into my mouth before reaching for her own knife and fork.

The flavor burst over my tongue—butter and salt, and something else. Something wonderful. Rosemary? Strength and health, satisfaction and warmth flooded through me. I could *taste* the earth where the potato had grown. Good, mineral-rich soil. The feeling of well-being grew in me like Jack's beanstalk—huge and overpowering. It was like ambrosia ...

I smacked Christie's fork out of her hand as it would have reached her mouth, and it went pinwheeling, the piece of Portobello mushroom she'd speared flying off the end and landing in her tea. The fork itself clattered to the floor.

Christie gasped and stared at me like I'd just grown a second head. "What the hell?"

"Don't eat that," I hissed.

Her eyes widened, and she leaned in close to whisper. "Why, do you think it's poisoned?"

Martin came bustling up with a fresh glass of iced tea and a replacement fork in hand. I certainly couldn't fault the service, even if I was horrified by their special ingredients. No wonder The Rustic Potato was such a hot spot. They weren't just drawing loyal customers, they were creating addicts.

"Is everything okay?" Martin asked, blocking onlookers' views of our table.

Because, oh yes, we had apparently drawn an audience.

Christie and her improvisational skills came to the rescue. She crooked a finger, encouraging Martin to lean in for a secret. "My friend has a sort of impulse control problem. Usually the meds take care of it," she breathed in his ear, "but sometimes … Maybe we'd just better get all of this to go. And—" she shot a worried glance at me "—quickly?"

"Why don't I meet you at your car?" he asked, clearly anxious to get rid of us before we could put anyone off their feed.

"That would be wonderful." She reached into her wallet and came out with a few bills she tucked discreetly into his hand.

He straightened and smiled down at her. "Right away."

Martin ran off to get takeaway boxes, and I couldn't decide whether to give Christie a glare or a standing ovation for her performance. I'd probably go with the latter. It wasn't like I had any shame.

"I can't take you anywhere," she said to me.

"I brought *you*."

"Whatever. Let's get out of here."

She came around to my side of the table and pretended to help me out of there like I was some kind of invalid.

At the Camaro I shook her off and started for the driver's

side, but Christie stopped me with a look. Cursing under my breath, I dropped the keys into her outstretched hand. Probably people with "impulse control problems" shouldn't operate heavy machinery. I hoped I was doing the right thing. Christie, having learned late how to drive, was hell on wheels. Things like lanes and speed limits were mere suggestions; shoulders were for driving on, and corners were to be cut.

She was checking her makeup in the rearview mirror while making adjustments when Martin appeared with a large paper sack bearing The Rustic Potato sun logo on the side. I guessed a lump of starchy tuber just wouldn't have done it. She stepped out of the car to take the bag from him rather than roll down her window for him to pass it through. Given the size of the bag, it might have been tricky.

"I brought the food," he said with a smile. "And your change."

"Keep it," she said. Then, with her tinkling laugh, added, "The tip, I mean, not the food. I'm looking forward to that."

His smile got even bigger. "Thank you! I've included our takeout menu and," he blushed, "my number, in case you want to talk more about the holistic lifestyle. We have a seminar tomorrow afternoon you might be interested in."

With free munchies, I'd bet, *the better to brainwash you with, my dear.*

"Oh," she said brightly. "That sounds great. I'm only here for a few days, but I might just give you a call."

She'd made his night. That was clear enough. I gave them a moment, looking away toward the hacienda-style building illuminated on the outside by small white lights that twinkled like stars and—and froze at what I saw. Coming around the building and getting into a white van half-blocking the exit out of the parking lot was my office attacker. Or someone who looked an awful lot like him.

"Christie," I called, flinging out a hand to hit my window and making them both jump. "We've gotta go."

The van started to roll out.

Christie said a quick goodbye and closed the door between them, hefting the bag into the back seat. Martin continued to stare after her, ignoring his other customers inside.

"Where to?" she asked.

"Follow that van," I said.

"What van?"

Darn it, the vehicle had already disappeared down the hilly drive. "Straight ahead. Just drive!"

I was ready to reach my foot over the central console and step on the gas for her, but Christie didn't even pop the parking brake before she was backing out. Still the van had vanished by the time we hit the street.

"Which way?" she asked.

But the trouble was headed away from rather than toward me, and my oracular powers were no help at all.

I sighed deeply. "I have no idea. Might as well head back to the hotel."

"Yay!" she said. "So we have the rest of the night to ourselves? Chick flick and ice cream?" Her eyes glowed, but not in the supernatural sense.

"Like you eat ice cream."

"I eat ice cream like you watch chick flicks. We'll compromise."

"Chick flick with action?" I asked.

"Fat-free frozen yogurt?"

I stuck my tongue out. "What's the point?"

"Sorry about losing the van," she said.

"Don't worry about it. At least I got the partial plate."

"So what's wrong with the food?" she asked. "And what are you going to do with it? Take it to a lab? Go all CSI?"

Questions I didn't have answers for. How I knew … that one I could sidestep. But what *was* I going to do with the samples? I didn't suppose the police generally tested for ambrosia or even knew it existed.

"It's … something I've encountered before. As soon as I tasted it, I knew. The Rustic Potato is putting an additive into their food that makes it highly addictive."

"Can they do that?" she gasped.

"Not legally. But this is so new, I don't think the FDA's even aware of it yet."

"But you are?"

"I came across it during another investigation. It's bad news."

"So if it's not illegal, how do we stop them?"

"You know the Feds I was telling you about?" She nodded. "Maybe they can help."

But did I want to go there? That was the question. If the Feds already knew about the ambrosia, it was no harm, no foul. Maybe linking it to Back to Earth would give them an excuse to raid the whole setup and free the cult members.

On the other hand, raids on cults had been known to mean Very Bad Things for the members. I thought of Waco, particularly, but other cults, like Heaven's Gate and Jonestown weren't far behind.

I'd have to get assurances … But even then, what if their investigation led the Feds to Apollo and my supply line? That'd be one way to quit, but as ambivalent as I was about Apollo, I just couldn't throw him under the bus. Not when he'd given me that first dose of ambrosia to save my life, by his way of thinking. Apollo had a habit of doing the wrong things for the right reasons and totally mucking them up for the mortals involved, but that didn't make him a bad person … god … whatever.

I was afraid I was starting to think like an addict, making excuses to perpetuate my use. I couldn't be sure my motives were pure, and that scared the hell out of me. Was I reasoning or rationalizing? There wasn't anyone to ask.

"Tori?" Christie prodded.

I wondered how long I'd been pondering and whether she'd said anything in the meantime when she saved me by repeating herself. "I asked if you were going to call them."

"Who?"

"The Feds."

She shifted suddenly across two lanes to take a left hand turn she'd nearly missed. I braced for an impact that never came. I sometimes wondered if she had her very own guardian angel. Why not? I had a god on speed dial.

"I'm too busy praying for my life," I answered under my breath.

"What's that?"

"Car!" I shouted.

For a second, I thought we and the SUV next to us were going to try to occupy the same space. I didn't think it would go well for us. Christie yanked the steering wheel back to center, and I swallowed my heart, which had jumped into my throat.

"Sorry!" Christie said, shooting me a glance.

"Eyes on the road!"

"Okay, jeez. What was *in* that food?" Clearly not Valium.

Christie and I ended up back at the hotel with some froufrou wraps. Hers included alfalfa sprouts and other greenery that only a rabbit could love. Mine ... didn't. We also ended up with not one, but *two* pints of ice cream—one for each of us, since Christie stuck to her guns on the no fat/no fun version, and I insisted on quadruple fudge decadence. I figured the heart attack she'd nearly given me on the drive over had probably goosed my metabolism to the point where I could take it. And anyway, ambrosia gave me the munchies.

"I don't know how you can eat that crap and stay so skinny," Christie said, eyeing my spicy Italian wrap—salami, pepperoni, ham and provolone with salt, pepper and a dash of vinaigrette dressing.

I looked down at myself, as if to double-check her perceptions. "Um, thanks."

"You're welcome."

"So, which should we watch first?" she asked. "*Romancing the Stone* or *True Lies*?"

"Which has the higher body count?"

She rolled her eyes at me, and we settled down for a girls' night in.

CHAPTER NINE

"*The difference between a mare and a nightmare is one you ride, the other rides you.*"
  —Gus Karacis, head of the Karacrobats

The nightmares closed in on me like a pack of rabid dogs with the decaying flesh of the last person they'd torn apart still trapped in their teeth. Poisonous breath laced with the stench of death.

I was in a field, the same one I'd tasted in that single bite from The Rustic Potato. In the way of dreams, I knew it was the same, even though there was no way I could have. Also in the way of dreams, seasons didn't matter. I stood in that field chest high with golden wheat—golden something, anyway—even though it was spring, and there was no way it would be more than a gleam in the sun's eye.

I spun around in the field, my face turned toward the sun, my arms flung out, the breeze blowing my pitch-black hair into my face like a lash. It stung, and I brushed it back only to find that the sky had darkened. Clouds replaced the strands of hair blotting out the sun. They were thin dark wisps, like fingers, skeletal and reaching. It sent a chill over my heart, and I looked around for shelter, as though the darkness was a danger and my life would be snuffed out along with the light.

The sun was no longer warm on my face. The wind no longer blew. It blasted, picking up debris as it whipped through the field, throwing it into my eyes and mouth. I tried to breathe through my nose, but the stench of death came to me on the breeze, choking me. It poisoned my every breath, as if I took in shards of fiberglass, ripping their way through my sinuses, tearing through my lungs. I started to panic.

My frantic search for safety turned up nothing but a solitary figure far off in the distance. He waved to me, calling me over, and I started to race toward him. The wheat stung me like switches, but I didn't stop. My face and arms turned slick with blood or sweat; my lungs labored.

Behind me the thing with the charnel house breath pursued. Teeth snapped, tearing at my clothes, nearly taking me down. I jerked with each snap, tearing myself free again.

The figure I was racing toward was just coming into focus. Familiar. So familiar. And yet, I didn't dare hope. I knew that. The gasp of breath I took in at the sight of him hurt like hell—no longer shards, but throwing knives of cutting pain. Uncle Christos. Alive. Calling for me.

The sight gave me wings. I put on an extra burst of speed, only to rear back like a startled horse when another, darker figure rose up out of the ground between us. He was cloaked and cowled.

And this time he'd brought his sickle. He swept at the wheat between us, cutting it down like he'd cut me down in another step.

My recoil brought me into range of the dagger-teeth pursuing me, and the agony as they clamped down put all the rest to shame. The teeth tore into my shoulder, and I could feel the flesh shriveling away from them on contact, dying, their poison shutting me down cell by cell. The sickle flashed in the last shards of sunlight, streaking straight for me.

"No!" I cried. "Christos!"

"A life for a life," a voice cracked like lightning across the sky. Not thunder, which was a rumble, but truly lightning, electric and deadly.

"No!" This time the cry was cut short by the biting blade.

My whole body spasmed as I screamed and thrashed, as if I could stop death with a badly aimed blow. The darkness was complete, the chill my world.

I made impact with something, though, and it shrieked.

"Tori, Tori, WAKE UP!" Christie said. "Tori, you're having a nightmare. And you *hit* me."

My heart stopped. *Christie? What was she doing here? It was too dangerous.*

"Christie, run!" I said. The shards of air had scored my throat. The words were barely intelligible.

Then the blow landed across my cheek. "I said *wake up*, dammit!"

My eyes popped open, but couldn't make sense of what they saw. "Christie?" I asked, even though the answer was obvious.

"In the flesh," she said.

What happened next was the most startling thing of all—I burst into tears. Huge, great, gasping sobs. Each breath still hurt, but the fact that I could take them ...

Christie dropped down on the bed next to me and folded me up in her arms like I was her child. "Shh, Tori, it's all right. Whatever it is."

"I almost died," I choked out, sure it was true, even if it didn't make a bit of sense. "Christos ... he's waiting for me to ride to the rescue, and I was never going to get there."

She pretended I wasn't a babbling idiot whose very sanity she was questioning and rocked me like a three-year-old with the night terrors. I was so shaken that I let her. I hadn't cried in ...

possibly ever. But this time there'd been no Fates intervening on my behalf. If I hadn't woken up …

I wondered how long Christie had been calling to me, and if she'd just saved my life.

I got myself under control, wiped my nose on the back of my hand like the classy broad I was, and tried to turn it into a joke.

"Sorry, Chris. I guess I'm the worst roommate ever."

"At least you don't snore," she said, looking terribly serious about it. Our eyes met, and we both broke into stupid hysterical giggles.

CHAPTER TEN

"When you're sane, they call it prudence, not paranoia."
—Christos Karacis

The digital clock said 3:16 AM. It taunted me with its cheerful glow.

After a while, Christie went back to her own bed, pretending to believe my repeated assurances that it was nothing but "an undigested bit of beef." Yes, I quoted Scrooge. I had enough to worry about without wondering what that said about my character.

In contrast to Christie, I laid awake staring at the ceiling or the wall or the clock or *anything* but the back of my eyelids. I spent all that time cursing Apollo. Before his "gift" of prophecy I could sleep in peace, knowing that a dream was just a dream. I didn't have to wonder what it meant that death would strike me down in a field of gold. That dog breath would be my downfall. That Hades was coming for me. Anyway, that much I already knew. I guess if ... when ... I met him, I could compare his true voice against the one in my dream. Of course, by the time I could do that and know whether the dream held deeper meaning I'd probably only have seconds of life left to give a damn.

"But it wasn't me!" I said aloud. "I didn't open any damned portal to hell."

Christie mumbled something and turned over in her sleep, and I instantly regretted my outburst. I'd already woken her up once. At least one of us should be getting our beauty rest. She had the best chance between us that it would take. The air conditioner in the wall seemed to cough and rattle and shut off. I looked over to be sure that it was just resting and not dead, since that seemed to be the theme of the evening, and saw something glowing behind the curtains. Had the hounds of Hades found me already?

Paranoid, I told myself.

Duh, myself whispered back.

I had to know. Bracing myself to come face to face with the stuff of nightmares, I got out of bed and crept to the curtains. I took a deep breath, counted to three, and twitched them aside.

It was a car. *Just* a car. Or an SUV, actually. Someone had forgotten to turn off the headlights, and they were aimed straight for our room. Huffing at the lack of consideration, I pulled my shoes on—they coordinated *so* well with my ducky and bunny sleeping pants—and opened the door as quietly as I could. I realized as the air conditioner noisily kicked back on at the flood of hot air I'd let in that the way I'd chosen to deal with things was not necessarily quieter than picking up the phone and calling the front desk from the room. But I was committed now, and Christie was still asleep, so no harm, no foul. I grabbed my keycard off the desk by the door, eased myself out and the door shut behind me.

I knew almost immediately that something was wrong. I couldn't have said exactly how. Just that the night seemed ... dead. There was *no* movement. Not even the breeze from my dream. The early warning system in my mind went on alert, flashing lights at me if not setting sirens wailing.

This time when my brain taunted me about paranoia, I was able to tell myself to *shut it* in no uncertain terms.

Stupid, stupid, stupid, I thought, to be caught without a weapon. No gun, pepper spray or so much as a pocketknife. I was armed only with my keycard and my wits. I wasn't exactly oozing with faith in either. I debated ducking back into the room. Probably it was the safest survival strategy, but if whatever was out there didn't care for locked doors and Do Not Disturb signs, then I'd be inviting trouble in to meet Christie.

If I continued on to the front office, would I be leading danger away or leaving her defenseless?

I decided not to find out. Do the unexpected.

I stepped out into the parking lot, right in front of the head-lights glaring straight at our window, making it impossible to see beyond them.

"You want a piece of me?" I asked the night. "Well, here I am, all defenseless." I hoped my very bravado would make whoever was there think I protested too much and second-guess the wisdom of attack.

It came out of nowhere. One second I was standing, daring danger. The next a ten-ton truck flying-tackled me to the ground, and I was kissing pavement. Tiny little stones ground into my cheek and diced the hands that I'd flung out to catch myself. The ten-ton tackle landed hard on my back, making my skin and those rocks seem to occupy the same space. The weight on my back was too much for me to fill my lungs. I couldn't breathe. Couldn't move. The parking lot lights seemed to blur and recede away from me. I realized that it was my conscious-ness fading, and I fought it, desperate to turn my gorgon gaze on my attacker ... only I could no more move than breathe.

A whistle split the air, and the weight on my back shifted, at first painfully. I could hear ribs groaning in protest. A sharp agony ripped through me as one didn't creak so much as crack.

Another jumped on the bandwagon. I gasped as the weight disappeared from my back to settle less completely and painfully on my legs … like a dog coming to heel.

I tried to twist, to get an eye on my attacker, but piercing pain shot across my chest, reminding me of the broken ribs. I was terrified I'd puncture a lung if I pushed it. I settled for moving as little as possible, just my head and shoulders off the ground looking instead for the source of the whistle. Not that I thought for a second the person on the other end of it was a friend. Someone had halted the attack, but I was willing to bet they'd started it as well.

The lights from the SUV shut off, but it didn't stop the sight of the figure walking toward me. The parking lot lighting was enough.

Sauntering toward me was a man well over six feet, with wild Jonas-brothers' hair, a back broad enough that he looked like he could take over for Atlas carrying the world on his shoulders. I wouldn't have minded terribly getting a look at the rest of his body, but the shape was obscured by a pastel-blue jacket over a pale yellow shirt with a bright yellow cartoon sun ordering "Have a sun-shiny day!" I'd have laughed if I didn't know how much it would hurt.

Plus, one did not laugh at the god of the dead. He was not reputed to have a sense of humor. Based on the T-shirt, his sense of irony might be another matter.

"Good dog," he said as he neared. He lobbed something the size of a softball over my head, and I heard teeth snap together as something snatched it out of the air. My legs were starting to go numb, but I was fresh out of Hound of the Baskervilles-sized biscuits to lead the monster astray.

"Mizz Karacis," Hades began, fire in his eyes taking the place of those dowsed headlights. Literal fire, flaming on like CGI effects around the irises, which were as dark as an underworld night. "I understand we have much to discuss."

I had to spit to clear my throat. It hurt like, well, *Hell*, and I knew this was no mere nightmare, because those were supposed to be in black and white and what I'd hacked up was definitely red. As in *blood*. I knew that for a bad, bad sign. On reflection, the golden color of the field in my dream should have been a warning sign as well.

"Can't ... talk," I managed. There was a wet gurgle to it that I didn't like at all. My head was swimming, and Hades was starting to become a Dali-esque figure with a melty head that was no longer quite on straight.

He looked peeved, as if I'd been wounded just to thwart him.

In two strides he was by my side, squatting beside me, his whitewashed jeans just inches from my face. If I'd ever thought about it at all, I'd have guessed Hades would look like a badass biker or a metal-head—a cross between Ozzy Osborne, Dave Navarro and Alice Cooper. I'd never have guessed Don Johnson from *Miami Vice* with boy-band hair. It was too weird.

He took one of my hands in his, and a chill numbness started to seep outward from the contact to spread throughout my body. In two blinks of an eye, the pain was gone, but so was all other feeling. I couldn't feel my heart. I couldn't tell if it was still beating. I started to panic, yanking my hand back from his, but he had it in a death grip ... *literally*.

"Calm down," he snapped. "I'm not going to kill you ... yet. I said we have to talk, and I meant it. Life is too short to play word games. I should know. Eternity, though ... in eternity we have nothing but time. You have stolen from me the one person who made it palatable."

He let my hand drop, and I tried to roll to sitting, futilely hoping to dislodge his furry friend.

"I wouldn't," Hades said. "I haven't healed you. My powers don't run that way. But I have put your system in a kind of stasis until you can heal yourself. You won't bleed to death internally while we speak."

"But I didn't—" It took an immense amount of strength to force the words out.

He put a hand to my lips to stop me, and it burned like dry ice. I guessed I could still feel *something*. "It doesn't matter whether you contributed materially or not. You are what passes for the law here. You failed to stop the desecration of my kingdom and the kidnapping of my queen. You will return her to me or your world will suffer the consequences."

I couldn't feel enough to know if my eyes went wide at that. "I'm not ... law—"

He stood abruptly, causing me vertigo as my bruised brain tried to follow the movement. "You ARE." His voice cracked like lightning, just like in my dream. "You may not be *their* law enforcement," he said, burning eyes boring into mine, "but you're *ours*. Olympus buzzes with word of your exploits. You captured my brothers, but failed to stop their damage, which means *I* am now your supreme god."

I begged to differ. Silently.

He continued. "You will do as I say. You will find Persephone for me. Or I will do it myself. Churches, hospitals, homes —they are all like pebbles before me, and I will leave no stone unturned to find her."

Cerberus—or whoever was cutting off all the blood circulation to my legs—growled and the earth quaked. A couple walking out to their car took one look, turned tail and ran.

Hades flicked a negligent hand in the hound's direction, and I screamed as his weight lifted and blood returned to my dying cells. The hound ran after the retreating couple. He was easily the size of Hades's SUV, and probably twice as fast.

"No!" I coughed up the word from the depths of my soul, glaring at Hades, at the smile of anticipation on his face.

I tried to rise, but could hardly move.

Out of sight the woman screamed. The man howled—his cry cut off by the crunch of bone. It was a terrible, horrible sound. My imagination supplied what I couldn't see. Rage started to burn away the cold numbness Hades had sent through my system. I tried again to rise, to fight or run or help, but he was able to pin me to the ground with one hand.

"You're a monster," I said. Even less wisely, "No wonder she ran away."

He started to crush me with that hand on my chest, grinding my broken ribs into fragile organs. The world faded to the blazing coals of his eyes. "I had a point to make. Cerberus guards my gates. My power keeps the souls contained. What do you think will happen if he and I are away too long looking for my love and the inmates realize that no one is running the asylum?"

Oh Hell. On. Earth. All those souls lose in the world, some probably fractured or tormented, angry or confused … For once my imagination failed me.

The havoc they could wreak….

"I see that you understand." He smiled, and I thought of his shirt. *Have a sun-shiny day!* Yeah, right. "You have my card."

He snapped, and it appeared in my hand.

Hadrian Boss, it said in fiery red letters. *Acquisitions*. It gave two numbers; the same two Jesus had given me.

"I'll be waiting for your call."

He snapped again, and suddenly his spot was vacant, just like his soul.

A car pulled into the Inn parking lot, headlights slashing across my broken body—and probably those the hellhound had mauled. *Just like the bodies on Mount Lee*, my brain supplied. I tried to call out, not so much to save myself from being run over as to warn the car off in case Cerberus hadn't vanished along with Hades.

I didn't manage enough sound to be heard over the car's engine. At least, I didn't think so, but it stopped short anyway and a woman jumped out, half-hysterical.

"Ohmagod, ohmagod, ohmagod. What happened? Are you hurt?"

It seemed like an odd question, since perfectly healthy people didn't generally have a lie-down in the middle of hotel parking lots, but I kept my snark to myself.

"Couple," I said, spitting blood in order to get the words out. "Around the corner. Check on them?"

The woman looked where I looked and ran off in high-heeled boots to see what I was talking about. Her scream told me she'd found it.

"Ohmagod, ohmagod, ohmagod," she said again. Then, into her cell phone, "Hello. Ohmagod, you have to help. There's been ... I don't know ... a blood bath. The Residence Inn—"

By which I figured that help would be on the way and it was finally okay for me to pass out.

I opened my eyes to another nightmare ... only this one I was awake for.

Rosen and Holloway stood over me as I lay prone in a hospital bed. It was the second time tonight I'd been stuck lying down while powerful men looked over me. I didn't like it one bit.

"Wanna tell us what happened?" Holloway asked as soon as I blinked him into focus.

"Why, I'm feeling fine. Thank you so much for the concern," I responded wryly. "And you two? How are the wife and kids?"

"No wife," Holloway answered.

"No kids," Rosen chimed in.

I rolled my eyes. Even that hurt. "Why do I waste my sarcasm?"

"For that matter, why waste time with rhetorical questions," Rosen asked, "when the standard variety is already on the table?"

I tried to sit up—to look for a nurse or a few shots of espresso. Not necessarily in that order. Dealing with these two on a full bladder and empty stomach was more than I could handle.

I quickly gave it up. My ribs were no longer screaming at me, either due to really good pain meds or the miraculous effect of the ambrosia, but someone had bound them so tightly I felt like a mummy. I could move, but it took a buttload of effort, and my reserves were nil.

"Will you call a nurse for me?" I asked, ignoring them for now.

"Will you answer our questions?" Rosen asked.

"I promise, if you let me pee and come back to me with caffeine and something I can hold down, I'm all yours."

Holloway looked like I'd just waved a dissecting frog under his nose. Must have been the reference to pee. Rosen just looked amused. "Fine, we'll be back in five minutes. You'll get a sip of coffee for every question you answer."

I looked at him with new respect. "Damn, you play hardball."

"Believe it."

He herded Holloway out ahead of him, and moments later a plump nurse with red hair and freckles came bustling in. She gave me the option of the bedpan or hobbling with help to the facilities, and I chose option B.

I was pretty sure it took the allotted five minutes just to get there, let alone back. Rosen and Holloway were waiting when we returned. They got an eyeful of thigh and probably a little more as I got up onto the bed and adjusted the covers. Why on earth did they have to make hospital beds so huge and gowns so short?

The nurse left, closing the door behind herself and shutting me in with the agents. I was now entirely focused on the cup in Rosen's hand. The contents of the pastry bag could wait.

"Coffee," I said.

"You haven't answered a question yet."

"Coffee," I growled.

I sounded suitably zombielike, and I think he thought I might return from the dead if he let me have my way … or that I'd reinjure a rib lunging for the cup if he didn't. Rosen stepped toward the bed and held the cup along with me as I tipped it to my mouth. I resented the lack of control, but forgave him the second the too-hot beverage hit my tongue. He let me take two scalding gulps, then pulled it away.

"I thought our constitution outlawed cruel and unusual punishment," I accused. "Caffeine deprivation is crueler than water boarding."

"Wanna try it and see?" he asked.

Okay, so I'd pushed him as far as he was going to go. The last time I'd had to give an official statement (that one to the LAPD), I'd had to describe the perp as green and scaly, looking something like the Creature from the Black Lagoon. This time, at least my story sounded a lot more credible. Maybe someone else had seen Hades. Per his threat, maybe he was staying topside for a while and a hotel canvas would turn him up. Even as I thought that, though, I considered what it would mean for all those restless souls he guarded. When I got to Cerberus I stuttered to a halt, lost in the memory of the screams of the couple he'd killed and the sound of his teeth crunching bone …

I reached clawlike hands for the coffee, needing the heat to counteract the chill stealing over me. Rosen surrendered the cup this time, and I held tightly to it to keep my hands from shaking.

"That couple … are they …" I was too afraid of the answer to finish the question.

Rosen and Holloway exchanged a look. "Dead," Holloway supplied. "I'm sorry. Did you witness it?"

I shook my head. "I saw what did it, but not the actual … mauling."

"Describe what you did see."

For once my mouth had no urge to run away with me. I'd never actually *seen* the extra heads, so I left those out of the equation, but when I described Cerberus as being the size of a horse but twice as wide, they exchanged a look that said maybe my head should have been examined along with my ribs.

"Wait, what time is it?" I asked.

"8:00 AM. Why?"

"I have to get to the morgue."

I started to rise, already feeling better than I had on my trip to the facilities. I was surprised when neither one tried to stop me.

"That's where we're headed next," Holloway said. "We can give you a ride."

"Only you haven't been released yet," Rosen added.

As if he'd summoned her, the nurse appeared in the doorway. "Agents, if you're finished here, Mizz Karacis's friend is going to stage a revolt if we don't let her in here soon, and regulations limit visitors to—"

Christie appeared behind her. "Tori!" she called over the much shorter nurse. "They wouldn't let me in to see you. I've been so worried!"

"No need to concern yourself with regs," Rosen told the nurse. "Mizz Karacis was just about to check herself out."

Holloway and I both gave him a surprised look. "Well, weren't you?" he asked.

The nurse's freckled face tried to do disapproving, but wasn't really made for it. Now, if Jesus had been here, we'd have had a world class stare down.

"I'll get the doctor," she said.

"Don't bother. Just the forms. Now, where are my clothes?" I muttered.

That was apparently Christie's cue. "All right, everybody out. My girl's got to change, and she doesn't need an audience."

The nurse sidestepped past her, and Christie took advantage of the unrestricted room access to come in and shoo the agents out.

"I may need some help," I said quietly when she was close enough I could believe no one would overhear.

"No problem." She pulled the privacy curtain shut behind her, but neither of us could find my clothes. A voice hailed us from the other side of the curtain. When Christie pulled it aside, we found the nurse standing there with blue-gray scrubs in hand. "Her clothes had to be taken for evidence. I can offer her these."

"Uh, thanks," Christie said, taking them.

"No shoes," she continued. "I don't think she'll get far in paper slippers, but I'm sure we have something better in the gift shop downstairs."

I narrowed my eyes at her. At least that much of me didn't hurt. "Why are you suddenly helping me out the door?"

She turned red enough to hide her freckles and dropped her gaze to her toes. "I just realized where I'd seen you before."

"Me?" But Christie was the famous one.

She looked back up at me. "Aren't you the girl Apollo Demas rescued from the ocean a few weeks ago? I mean … I must have watched that clip online, like, half a dozen times. So romantic. I don't know how it took me so long to recognize you."

It was my turn to … well, not blush, because I didn't do that sort of thing, but … Yeah, no surprise she hadn't recognized me out of context, grimacing in pain, probably being cut out of my stylish ducky and bunny sleeping pants.

Christie grinned at me and back to the nurse. "Yup, that's her." She leaned in toward the nurse confidentially and said, "They have a *thing*."

If I'd had anything to throw at her at that moment, I would have. "We do *not* have 'a thing.'"

Christie winked at the nurse, who beamed like the sun on Hades's shirt. At least *someone* was having a sunshiny day.

She turned back at the door. "Don't worry, I won't tell anyone else. I don't want you to get mobbed."

"Thank you," I said, well and truly embarrassed now by the whole thing. "I really appreciate it."

"No problem. I'll be back in a flash with your paperwork. I checked in with the doc, and he says it's amazing you didn't reinjure your ribs. You're healing fine, and he thinks you're good to go. Otherwise, I might have had to be a hardcase."

That I would have liked to see.

Then she was off, and Christie was glaring me down, holding the scrubs hostage. "*Re*injured your ribs? When did you hurt them in the first place? Tell me you didn't insist on a full day of driving up here with busted ribs. What were you thinking?"

Crap. If I hadn't been all tied up with the Feds it might have occurred to me how my speedy healing would look to the outside world. Not that I could have done anything about it, unconscious as I was.

"Don't worry about it," I said, unable to meet her gaze. "You heard the nurse—the doctor says I'm fine."

"I'll be the judge of that."

"How?"

"Oh, just shut it. *I'm* doing the driving from here on out. I don't want to hear another word about it."

"You think *that* will be safer?"

She threw the scrubs at me, forgetting that I was supposed to be a fragile little flower.

"You're my best friend, and if anything happens to you ... Well, I'm just going to have to go all Rambo on somebody's ass, and I'm not all butch like you are. Remember that."

It was all I could do not to laugh. Steam was already coming out of her ears, and I knew it was her concern making her lash out.

"All butch, huh?" I asked, fighting even a smile, afraid it might be my gateway drug to hysterics.

She broke first, a sort of sniffle-laugh escaping. "Well, comparatively."

I looked at her sparkling white tracksuit with the silver bedazzled detailing.

On me it wouldn't have stayed white for the time it took to put on. "Okay then, Sundance. Guard the door. I've got this."

Christie turned away and surreptitiously wiped a tear from the corner of her eye while I got into my stylish scrubs. Together we looked like the odd couple.

When I was done, I signed all my papers and told Rosen and Holloway we'd meet them at the morgue, now that I had my very own driver.

The nurse insisted on wheeling me out in a chair, so I never even had to get my paper slippers dirty. Even though I was sure the scrubs and paper booties were perfectly appropriate morgue attire, Christie had an absolutely unreasoning terror that I'd step in something "ooky"—her word—like liquefied body parts they might leave just lying around. Nothing I said would sway her to take me to the morgue directly, though I did manage to convince her that the twenty-four-hour pharmacy would be less out of the way than our hotel. It was clear to me she had no idea until then that pharmacies actually *sold* clothes, and even less idea why anyone on earth would want them. That made two, because even in his absence, I could *feel* the glare of Jesus's disapproval at the drawstring pants, two-to-a-pack tank top and plastic flip-flops I chose based on wholly economic considerations. Lime green on the tank and thongs. Goosy-gray on the pants. Christie pursed her lips and didn't say a word except to convince the clerk that it wouldn't threaten their insurance premiums to let a customer into their employee-only restrooms to change.

I thought it was pity rather than persuasion that won the day. I hoped the clerk didn't come to regret her agreement when she discovered I'd nearly decimated their paper towel supply in the effort to clean myself up a bit before putting on the clean clothes ... as if I had to make myself presentable for the dead. The very thought hurried me out, putting all the filth I'd picked up in that parking lot into perspective. I was alive. The ambrosia would probably take care of any stubborn little microbes that wanted to change all that. Everything else was just vanity.

Christie tossed her purse into my lap as we got back into the car. "There's a brush in there," she said. "Use it … and anything else you might want."

"Sir, yes, sir," I said, giving her a mock salute.

She stuck her tongue out at me. "You're famous now, haven't you heard? You have a certain image to maintain. In case you get mobbed by the paparazzi."

"Screw standards," I said.

She took her eyes off the road to widen them at me. "Bite your tongue!"

I turned her head back toward the street and took advantage of her brush. I left everything else alone. I somehow didn't think Kissable Peach or Approachable Apricot were my colors.

Try as I might, I couldn't find a single scrunchie to tame my crazy curls, which meant I looked something like Medusa—my possible progenitor—only with hair more fright than bite.

The personal primping took my mind off things, more or less, until we reached the morgue lot, at which point any care for my appearance went right out the window. I got snapped back into my seat as I tried to exit the car without unhooking my belt. I had to force myself to take a second to just breathe.

"You okay?" Christie asked.

"No," I answered, tired of pretending otherwise. "Let's go."

Rosen and Holloway were waiting for us just inside, and we all approached the desk together. They flashed ID. Christie and I signed in and had our IDs scanned as well, and then a man dressed a lot like I'd been earlier—in the slate-gray scrubs but with booties bagging his shoes instead of paper slippers—came to escort us back. I noticed that Christie watched his feet as he walked to be sure he wasn't leaving any kind of trail.

He asked us to wait outside for a minute while he went in to check that everything was ready, and though I tried to get a look inside as he swung the morgue doors open and shut, I was totally unsuccessful.

He came out two seconds later, offering booties to the rest of us. We bypassed three autopsy tables currently occupied with sheets pulled up over the bodies to protect the privacy of the dead. I shuddered thinking two of them might be the couple from the Inn.

Two men and a woman already stood against the steel-drawered far wall. The woman was not one of those glamorous television detectives in a wardrobe way above her means. She had on navy pants, a matching cardigan and a man's or non-tailored woman's light blue, button-up shirt beneath it. She could have as easily been a postal worker as a detective if not for the badge hung around her neck. Her non-bottle-brown hair was pulled back into a low, tight ponytail, and if she wore anything on her face it was ChapStick. Still, she looked like a model's "before" shot. She was slim, fit, and had nice enough features. Anything more and she'd probably have more admirers than respect among her peers. Being a woman sometimes sucked that way. Her partner looked weathered—hair buzzed to hide the bald, face ruddy and eyes slightly squinty.

The third man was probably the ME. The scrubs gave it away, as did the white hair peeking out from under a paper cap that matched his booties. He wore thick, square-rimmed glasses that were either retro or relics.

The detectives shook hands with the Feds, who introduced everyone around, but after that one quick glance at the gathering, I had eyes only for the morgue drawer we were standing around, and so I missed who was who—though Penny Raab probably wasn't either of the men.

"You ready?" someone asked.

I nodded without looking away.

I felt a hand on my shoulder, guessed it was Christie's, and let it stay.

The ME stepped into view, twisted the handle and yanked

on the drawer. It came sliding out, as expected, and I nearly crumpled to the floor.

With relief.

It wasn't Christos. There wasn't much of a face left for identification, and the hair was the right color, but it didn't cover his body like a gorilla's. Not that there was much of *that* left either … the body. The ME had done his best to replace the lengths of skin that had been shredded away, but so much of it was simply missing. One of the man's arms had been placed next to his body, the other was AWOL. His stomach looked like a meat puzzle that was only half finished.

"Excuse—" Christie started. She gagged and ran from the room. Involuntarily, I took a step closer to see if I'd seen what I thought I had … "Are those bite marks?" I asked, tamping down my own gag reflex.

"Is it him?" the ME asked. I shook my head.

"Verbal confirmation," he prodded.

"No," I answered. "Not him."

He replaced the sheet.

"You didn't answer my question," I said.

The ME shared a look with the detectives, who passed it on to Rosen and Holloway.

Rosen gave him the nod. "Miss Karacis is a PI whose partner has been pursuing his own investigation. As long as she continues to be cooperative, I see no reason not to share this information."

"We're keeping this from the press," the female detective—Penny—said, giving me the hairy eyeball, "so if it turns up anywhere …"

"They won't have gotten it from me. I'm camera shy."

"That's not what I hear."

Great. Just great. My five seconds of fake fame were going to ruin my life. The ME cleared his throat. "Right. Well, you agree then?" he asked me.

When I nodded, he continued. "Yes, human bite marks. Multiple assailants. Female, based on the DNA."

You could have knocked me over with a feather. "So then, not canine?"

"Well, I suppose you could call them bitches, but it would be scientifically inaccurate."

We all gave him a look. "Sorry, a little medical humor."

Good thing he'd opted to work with stiffs rather than a live studio audience. But I was respectful. "Thank you all for your time. I'm glad it wasn't him, but I'm sorry for … whoever this was. And his family. If there's anything I can do to help …"

"Is your partner still pursuing his investigation?" Detective Penny asked.

"He's dropped out of touch. Hence my concern."

"Have you filed a missing person's report?"

"I'm not sure that's what he'd want. I suspect he's gone undercover, and I don't want to draw any official attention or waste resources if he's just in deep."

The ME replaced the drawer and the others started to move toward the exit. I went with the flow.

"Undercover where?" Detective Penny asked, sticking by my side.

"I suspect the Back to Earth movement."

"Suspect?"

"He's off the clock on this one, pursuing an investigation of his own. He's not reporting in."

"So you've come looking for him?"

"Yes."

"And what have you found?"

So far, a whole lot of nothing … and a fridge full of guilt and temptation. I justified withholding the evidence from The Rustic Potato because of the whole chain of custody issue. Who could say for sure that I hadn't doctored the food myself? No, better they should discover it on their own.

"We just got in last night, so not much. But we're investigating the theory that Back to Earth is a cult and that Christos —my uncle and the founder of Karacis Investigations—has disappeared inside. Your DB—" *dead body,* "—you might want to check missing persons for anyone with connections to the Back to Earth co-op or The Rustic Potato."

"The what?" the male detective asked.

"That organic place I've been urging you to try," his partner answered for me.

"You've eaten there?" I asked, maybe too sharply.

They all looked at me. "Christie and I went last night." I said, thinking quickly. "There was … something funny about the food. I don't usually get all euphoric over steak, no matter how good."

Penny raised a brow in her partner's direction, and he nodded to her in unspoken communication, then answered for them. "We'll check it out. You suspect … what? That it's drugged?"

"Wouldn't be the first time. Remember original Coke?"

There, I'd done my due diligence, hopefully in a way that would leave Apollo out of it.

Speaking of whom … Apollo had said something to me way back when about ambrosia—that it was dangerous to mere mortals (a category from which I was apparently exempt on the mediocre strength of long ago gorgon/god blood). Beyond addiction, it supercharged the body in a way that overloaded the human system, like a jolt of electricity might jumpstart the heart or stop it. Was Back to Earth another killer cult, like Jonestown, or had they found a way to modify ambrosia for humans? I had to know.

"Was there … anything else wrong with your DB?" I asked. "I mean, beyond the obvious?"

"I'm not certain that privacy laws—" Detective Penny began.

"Cancer," Rosen interrupted her. "Tumor the size of a walnut pressing on the brain. Why?"

So whoever John Doe was, he hadn't been drinking the Back

to Earth Kool-Aid, because then the San Francisco PD would have a remarkably healthy body on their hands. Overly healthy ... cells literally bursting with life. Or maybe he *had* and the tumor was one of the side effects to the human body.

"I don't know yet," I answered him, "but it seemed important to ask." Nobody commented. You didn't get far in our fields without hunches ... parts of the puzzle you instinctively knew fit or didn't. It was how you prioritized your time and decided which leads to chase.

We'd hit the outer door beside the desk where we'd signed in. I could see through the window that Christie was waiting for us on the other side, still looking a little green.

"Are we finished here?" I asked.

"We're going to want to get your official statement on the attack last night. Was that related to your investigation?"

"The agents can give you the statement I gave them. I'm available for any follow-up questions, but for now, I think I'd better get my friend out of here while she's still speaking to me."

"You brought a *friend* along on an investigation?" the male cop asked, making me not-so-sorry I'd missed his name. I thought *ass* would work just fine.

"I brought a friend along for support when I thought I might have to ID my uncle's remains. I had no idea San Francisco had such mean streets and that I'd be jumped in a hotel parking lot. Now, if you don't mind—"

I didn't wait to hear whether he did or not, but pushed my way through the door and got Christie out of the morgue.

I had to buckle her seatbelt for her when she just sat in the passenger's seat like a lump, staring at nothing at all.

"You okay?" I asked her, not because turnabout was fair play, but because ... okay, I *got* it, sometimes you just had to ask.

"That was horrible," she said.

I expected her to talk about the blood or the gore, but I should have known better by now.

"That poor boy. What can I do?"

"Do? No way. I'm sorry I dragged you into this. It's way too dangerous. I'm putting you on a plane home. Today."

I started to pull away so that I could shut Christie's door, but she grabbed my arm in a death grip, holding me in place. She turned those baby blue eyes on me, but the irises had nearly eaten all the color.

"Don't treat me like a kid. I'm tougher than I look. It just … takes me a minute sometimes. I'm not like you. I haven't had the chance to get used to any of this. But that in there—" she waved her hand vaguely back the way we'd just come, "—*that's* real. It puts all my problems in perspective. Jack's an idiot, but I'll get over him. That guy in there, *he* had problems. He'll never get a chance to get over them. I want to do something about that. I want to make a difference."

"You don't think legions of people have whiter smiles because of you?"

She turned away from me. " *Thanks* so much for taking me seriously. Never mind. Just take me to the airport."

I slammed her door shut and cursed myself all the way to my side of the car. What was the right thing to do here? Take her to the airport—tough love and all that? Put her on a plane and watch her fly away to safety, probably hating me forever for being such a jerk? If I sent her home now, would the damage to her psyche outweigh the potential physical danger should she stay? Or did I let her risk herself? She was a grown woman, and she was right, I wasn't treating her like one. If anyone had tried to tell me what to do, I'd have told them where to go and how to get there. But Christie was too ladylike … or too hurt.

I yanked open my door, snapping, "Okay."

Christie looked at me, her eyes bright with tears. "Okay?"

"You can help. But if anything happens to you … well, I'll beat myself up and then I'm going to start in on Jack for setting this whole thing off."

"He has nothing to do with it."

"Still."

She cracked a smile. "Deal."

I was going to regret it. I *already* regretted it. But I thought I was doing the right thing. Only time would tell, and there would be no take backs if I got it wrong.

"So where do we start?" she asked.

"You call Martin and make a date."

She crinkled her nose. "Can we call it something else?"

"Call it whatever you like."

"Are you going to tag along?"

"I have something else to do."

"What's that?"

"Recon on the Back to Earth co-op."

"Alone?"

"You've got your job, I've got mine."

"But I saw what they did to that guy … that body at the morgue. You need backup."

She didn't know about my gorgon glare or the super-healing side effect of the ambrosia. All she knew was that just this morning I'd been in the hospital, and it wasn't a huge leap from a gurney to a slab. The concern was sweet but inconvenient.

"How about this—I'll call or text you every hour. If I miss, you call the cops."

"If you miss, it might be too late."

"That's my best offer," I said. "One way or another, I'm going in."

She sighed hugely. "Anyone ever tell you before that you're a massive pain in the butt?"

"First I'm butch and now I'm massive? Some friend you are."

It made her crack a tiny smile. "Whatever. You make sure you hit that timeline or there's going to be hell to pay."

I pretended to tremble in fear. Now *Hades*, he knew how to lay down a threat. And with him, Hell was a very real possibility. But, hey, all I had to do to keep him happy was find his estranged wife and send her back into servitude … that or let him unleash Hell on Earth. No pressure.

I was still working on an option C. If Persephone had left Hades of her own volition, I couldn't be party to her renewed imprisonment. Unless, maybe, she turned out to be a psycho hose beast the world would be better off without. No, not even then. There had to be another way.

"Will do," was all I told Christie. She didn't need to bear the rest of the burden along with me.

We stopped off on the way back to the hotel to buy and activate a few prepaid phones. That way if either got ours confiscated, we'd hopefully have backups that wouldn't be found. We preprogrammed in the agents' numbers, the detectives, etc., and yet I still felt wrong leaving Christie behind to make contact with the cult. That it was her choice would not make me feel any better if something happened to her.

Hating myself as I did it, I waited until Christie left the room to freshen up before taking a three-fingered scoop of the ambrosia Apollo had given me to speed the healing of my cracked ribs and protect me from whatever was to come. Then I grabbed an expensive bottle of water off the television console and made my way out.

Jesus had texted me the address he'd found for the compound. I forwarded it to Christie so she knew where to send backup if I didn't report in. Then I programmed it into the GPS on my phone and let it guide me. And guide me. I was well out of the city, and had bypassed signs for quite a few vineyards by the time the GPS finally informed me in its cultured computerized voice that I should turn in five hundred feet. The only problem was that when the turn came up, the sign for it said "Private Drive" in all caps with an additional sign tacked below that said "No Soliciting." An orchard obscured all view of what lay at the end of the drive. While none of that especially intimidated me, it didn't give me the warm fuzzies either.

I decided not to take the turn, but drove past until those twisted trees gave way to a piled stone fence that I hoped marked the next property line about a half mile down the road. I pulled off to the shoulder and opened my glove compartment. "Gone for Gas," I wrote in the notebook I kept there for recording mileage, which I always meant to do but rarely actually did unless I was on a paying case and needed it for the expense report. I also grabbed the fanny pack I kept there with a camera, first aid kit and power bars for stakeouts and other emergencies. I added the bottle of water from the hotel, and I was good to go. I tucked the note under my windshield wipers in plain sight of anyone curious about the abandoned vehicle to hopefully keep anyone from calling the cops.

Then I locked the car and crept into the trees. They weren't humongous, but they were taller than me, which made skulking convenient. If I'd been a country girl, I could have told what type they were from the buds and little white flowers, but there was no fruit yet—it was way too early in the year—which meant no harvesters or whatever to dodge. Still, I kept my ears perked and crept toward the private drive, figuring that if I travelled parallel to it, I'd be sure to hit the complex. I caught sight of the road through the trees and was ready to pull back to make sure nobody who might be on it would catch sight of *me* when I heard a car crunching over the pits and loose stones of the dirt drive.

My heart seemed to kick into overdrive like it knew something I didn't, and consequently my blood went rushing around like a kid who'd downed the mother lode of Pixy Stix. I took a few steps closer to the path; the better to see what was kicking up my alert system, though it was giving me more of a heads-up than a *duck*!

I was just in time to see a big black Town Car with livery plates slide slowly into view, the better to save its suspension. And in the back, through the lightly tinted windows, was an unmistakable figure. Golden hair, wavy and glorious, falling like a lion's mane or the rays of the sun, broad shoulders, commanding presence, and while I couldn't see them at the moment, eyes the color of tropical waters. Apollo. Sun god and snake.

I pulled back into the orchard, put my back to a tree, and whipped out my cell phone. I had it out and speed dialed before I knew what I was going to say.

"Where are you?" I asked when he answered.

There was a pause on the other end, then Apollo said, "I'm in the Napa Valley. Where are you?"

"Why?" I asked.

"Why do I want to know or why am I in Napa?"

"The last part."

"When did you become my keeper?"

"When you stumbled into my investigation."

I could hear him breathing on the other end of the line and remembered that same breath in my ear. It sent a pulse of crackling electricity shooting through my system that had nothing to do with my prophetic powers.

"You're *here?*" he asked sharply.

"In the flesh."

"Where?"

"Did they send a car for you or did you hire your own?"

"I picked up a ride at the airport. Why?"

"Look out the back."

I navigated around the gnarly trees to poke my head out toward the road and wave one arm.

"Stop!" Apollo shouted, and the car leapt forward as if the driver had been startled and then froze in place, the purr of the engine and the buzzing of bees the only sounds to be heard.

"Get in," Apollo demanded.

I'd faded back into the trees and now stared at the phone in disbelief. "You're not the boss of me."

"You've got the place staked out," he said. It was more statement than question, so I didn't answer. "You want to get inside?"

I wished I could see straight through the phone to his intentions. *That* question definitely demanded an answer, but what? I had no idea how much I'd be able to see of the compound from the outside. Going in through the front gates would definitely give me a better lay of the land and the chance to size up the players so that I knew what I was up against, but it would let them see me as well, limiting my stealth or undercover options. Not that I was a long con kind of girl in any case, but … Well, if what Hades had said about me was true, that "all of Olympus" was buzzing, that ship had probably already sailed.

"What's in it for you?" I asked. Because strings were *always* attached.

"In gratitude, you'll have dinner with me tonight."

"I'm traveling with a friend—"

"Alone," he said, in a way that let me know there was no room for negotiation.

"Fine," I grated out. "In a nice restaurant. No room service."

He laughed. "Afraid I won't be able to control myself in private?"

Put that way it sounded silly. I was hardly irresistible. "Yes," I answered anyway.

He sighed. "You're probably right. Coming?"

Not yet, I thought. Then I spent my brisk walk to the car beating myself up for it. *Not at all*, I told myself. Bad Tori. No cookie.

The door to the Town Car popped open at my approach, and Apollo slid over to make room for me, though not as much as I would have liked. As luxurious as it was, there wasn't enough room for comfort. Apollo's presence was huge, overwhelming, like he was a junkyard magnet and I was an old clunker car. I wanted to slide over beside him, feel his heat and his … *heat*. I wanted to—

"Dial. It. Back," I said from between clenched teeth.

"Sorry, I didn't mean—"

"Whatever," I snapped.

In addition to being the god of the sun, music and prophecy, Apollo imbued the muses with their powers—poetry, literature, all the arts. He himself could inspire a host of wet dreams. I was doing my best to stay dry.

"What are you doing here?" I asked, suspicion giving me a tiny little wedge to drive between us.

"Dionysus and I go way back. I don't know if you know, but we shared a sanctuary together at Delphi."

"So, you're old drinking buddies getting together to talk about old times?"

"No, business."

My *oh-shit*-o-meter was going completely off the rails. Suddenly my head felt like a bell with the Hunchback of Notre Dame pulling on the rope. I know, wrong cultural reference. So sue me.

Didn't Apollo hear the warning bells? He *was* the god of prophecy. Or maybe getting into bed (figuratively) with Dionysus meant something different to him. It was a good reminder that however well he played it on TV, he was *not* human and didn't necessarily share my agenda for protecting them … us. On the other hand, he had stood with me against Poseidon and the other Olympians when they'd threatened LA. Possibly he'd earned the benefit of the doubt. If I didn't have this powerful urge to throw myself on top of him, I'd be much better able to trust that impulse.

"What business?"

He eyed me, clearly debating what, if anything, to say. "On the QT?" he asked.

"Who am I gonna tell?"

"Your grandmother for one."

"I promise, my lips are sealed." I mimed locking them up and throwing away the key, which only riveted his gaze on my lips. Probably not a good thing.

"They're rolling out a new product line," he said, still not meeting my eyes. "We're going to discuss getting some of my talent involved in the promotion."

"A product line?"

I managed to sound only mildly curious, when inside I was screaming. If they rolled out with something mass-produced, it could affect thousands ... *millions*. Nationally and even internationally.

We were at the gates now, and I had to divide my attention between looking around and pinning Apollo with a piercing gaze. What if promotion wasn't all they had to talk about? What if Apollo was actually Dionysus's ambrosia supplier? Or vice versa? Apollo might not even see anything wrong with what Back to Earth was doing. After all, he'd been quick enough to addict me when ... okay, when I'd needed it, at least in his opinion.

I kept all those thoughts on the inside as Apollo flashed his ID and we were waved through the compound gates.

As the windows closed again, he answered me. "They're planning an all-organic version of a grocery delivery service. Today they're talking about regional distribution of their homegrown products, but they've got expansion plans in the works—full gourmet meal delivery via their restaurants, three squares a day with snacks to compete with those diet plans, and once they have more facilities and distributors—" He stopped. "I probably shouldn't be telling you all this, but at least it's not a publicly traded company, so you can't go out and buy stock or anything."

Oh yeah, because I *so* had the money for insider trading.

I couldn't ask any of the questions I wanted to. If he was in league with Dionysus, then talking to him would be just like tipping my hand to the enemy. He'd know I knew. And if he was threatened by that knowledge ... well, I'd already had Thanatos try to kill me. I figured my odds of actually dying went up with each and every god I crossed. Not that it would stop me from investigating, but it might force me to learn the subtlety that had eluded me all my life.

I made a noncommittal noise, like he could talk or not, it made no difference to me, and focused out the window. As far as I could see, the place was immense. Everywhere there were wooden plank buildings, like log cabins if the logs had been sawed flat rather than left to their natural curvaceous selves. There were a few men and women in natural weak-coffee-colored fabric, rather than the blinding white I half expected of a cult. Although, I supposed that would involve bleach, which was probably a no-no for children of the earth. Some had baskets on their hips, heads or shoulders, and some had children by the hand. But there weren't as many as I expected. Maybe everybody else was out working in the fields I could see rising in tiers above the compound. Those nearest turned their heads to watch us as we went by, and one of the children pointed excitedly while jumping up and down, but for the most part our arrival went ignored, which demonstrated to me a surprising lack of curiosity.

"Which building?" the driver asked, talking for the first time that I was aware of.

"Anywhere's fine," Apollo answered.

The driver stopped short as if *here* suited him perfectly. Apollo paid him, and the driver handed over a business card with the receipt. "That's my cell number on there," he said. "You want outta here, you just call. I'll pick you up or send somebody out for you."

"Thank you, but I don't think that'll be—"

"My sister got sick from somethin' she ate from these people —one of their stands. Couldn't prove nothin', but it was the only thing she ate different. Gave me the heebie-jeebies when you told me we were coming out here. If I was allowed to refuse a fare—"

Apollo looked troubled, and I asked, "Do you have a second card, in case I want to go and he's not ready to leave?"

The driver met my gaze in the rearview mirror. "Sure, doll. I don't know what you've got goin' on, coming out of the bushes like that, but you be careful, *capisce?*"

Oh, I *capisced.* I wanted to hear more about his sister, but that would have to wait. I pocketed the card, thanked him, and followed Apollo out of the car.

Three figures had come out of one of the central buildings—two beautiful women with flowing hair, one a bronzy copper and the other so dark brown it was nearly black. Between them stood a man who looked like the love child of W.C. Fields and Zack Galifianakis. In other words, tall but round, at least in the belly area. Attractive-ish, but with a red nose that let you know exactly how that gut had come about. Perfectly appropriate for the god of the grape. Yet his dark eyes glittered with mischief and knowledge, calling you to look no further. He had, in a word, presence. In two, charisma. He didn't look like any kind of health guru, which might explain the need for a spokesperson. On the other hand, he looked exactly like the kind of figure that would lead you into temptation … or a crazy cult.

Apollo stepped forward to greet Dionysus, not with a hand-shake, but with arms outstretched. They hugged and kissed on both cheeks, then Dionysus held Apollo out at arm's length to get a good look at him.

"LA agrees with you, my friend. You don't look a day over … thirty-five."

"I'm supposed to be creeping up on fifty," Apollo answered.

"Ah, but fifty *is* the new thirty-five."

"In the city of angels, it's halfway to dead."

"It is a good thing we spring eternal, no?"

Dionysus put Apollo aside and turned those glittering eyes on me. "And who is this beautiful young lady you bring with you? One of your rising stars?"

It was all I could do not to roll my eyes or step back when he approached, arms outstretched as they had been for Apollo. I knew what came next—the hug, the kiss … both cheeks. I stood for it all, not finding it as difficult as I should have to smile back. His grin was infectious, and the mischievous glint in his eyes invited me to share a joke to which I hadn't even heard the punch line.

Apollo returned to my side and hugged me to him, a possessive move. "This is Tori Karacis," he said. "She's a … good friend."

If the name meant anything to Dionysus, it was covered up by his "Ah ha!" of understanding at Apollo's none-too-subtle implication that "good friend" was a euphemism for "bed bunny."

I seethed, even though it was in my best interests to be dismissed.

"Well," Dionysus took my hand and kissed it, even though he'd already gotten both of my cheeks, "it is a pleasure to meet you, Mizz Karacis. Come, both of you, there is a beautiful spot where we can talk business and you can see the fruits of my labors." *Oh yeah*, his *labors*. "So much better than standing around in the heat."

He tucked my hand into his arm without asking permission and escorted us inside. We barely had time to appreciate the rustic lodge feel of the place—plank floors with colorful area rugs covering them, what looked like handmade wooden furniture arranged group-therapy-session style around a huge fireplace above which was a tapestry of winemaking. Then we were out again onto a lovely terra-cotta patio overlooking the terraced vineyards. An overhang prevented direct sunlight, cutting down on the heat to which Dionysus had referred.

"Wow," Apollo said, eyeing the land. "You've done well for yourself."

"As have you, my friend," he said, giving my hand a squeeze. *Smarmy* didn't begin to cover Dionysus. Neither did the shirt straining across his midsection.

"Sit," he ordered, leading us to a table and chairs that were absolutely gorgeous, made of rough cut, gnarled wood that had been sanded and polished until it was smooth and glowing but still retained its unique shape and character. There were no cushions, but when I slid into my seat, it seemed to fit just fine. The table looked to have been carved out of a single monstrous tree. I mourned that it had been turned into even such a lovely set.

"A lightning-struck oak," Dionysus said, as if reading my mind. "This set works in harmony because it was carved from a single tree that lightning destroyed last year. So devastating. The tree had to have been over two hundred years old. But nothing is ever lost, eh?" he asked, finally surrendering my hand to take his own seat. "That's our entire philosophy here—reduce, reuse, renew, recycle. We compost everything. The takeout containers in our restaurants are biodegradable. We plant even as we reap."

Oh, he had the patter down.

"It's impressive," Apollo said so that I didn't have to. He gave me an amused look, in fact, as if Dionysus wasn't the only one reading minds. I forced myself to relax my face and even let myself ease back into my seat as if the peace of the place was working its magic. "But you didn't bring me here just to impress me. I believe we have business to discuss?"

Dionysus looked at the two women who'd accompanied us. "Gracelyn, will you bring us the marketing plan? Pansy, would you send Narcissa to serve us? Then you can get on with what we've discussed."

That made me sit up and take notice. I hoped it didn't show. Narcissa ... I'd heard that before. I also noted that though Dionysus called his acolytes by name, he'd never introduced them. Clearly, we were to address ourselves to him and him alone. What was odd was that the women didn't seem to mind. If I weren't here strictly on a fact-finding mission (for the moment, anyway), I'd have been organizing a revolt. Smiling back at the women as they smiled at us to take their leave nearly did me in.

I focused on not reacting when "Narcissa" came out with a huge tray laden with a bottle of wine, three glasses, grapes, crackers and assorted cheeses. *Casey Olivieri*, in the flesh. The very person I wanted to find. She looked good. Sun-kissed. Her tanned skin a nice contrast with her lighter-colored threads.

What she didn't look was approachable. Casey's smile was just for Dionysus, though to be polite she swept her gaze over us to imply inclusion.

I hoped at some point I could find a way to isolate her and get her to talk. But not here and now, as Dionysus watched me watch her set down the tray and pour the wine.

He knows, I thought. He'd chosen Casey to serve us specifically to see my reaction. I was certain of it. I kept my poker face in place.

Gracelyn reappeared with the portfolio Dionysus had requested and gracefully, like her name, took the fourth and final chair around the table. A dragonfly flitted casually over the table before zipping off toward the fields, and Dionysus ruined the idyll by sending Casey back for another glass. Only three because I'd been unexpected? If so, he could have had "Pansy" tell "Narcissa" to set another before she came out with the tray rather than send her back. Was it some kind of petty power play?

"Excuse me," I said as Casey disappeared inside. "I need to use the facilities." I didn't wait to actually be excused before rising.

"Certainly," Dionysus said magnanimously, his teeth stained eerily red from his first deep sip of the wine. "Gracelyn will show you."

Gracelyn … who'd only just sat down.

"If you'll point the way," I said, delegating the task back to him, "I'm sure I can find it on my own."

"Oh, but there are instructions that come with the facilities. As I've said, we recycle everything here."

I didn't even want to *think* about that.

"Oh, okay." I looked to Gracelyn. "Sorry about that."

She smiled beatifically, as if she couldn't think of anything she'd rather do than escort me to the crapper. "I'm happy to help. This way."

I followed the glint of her coppery mane of hair, a little jealous at how glossy and smooth it lay while mine was a rat's nest of curls seldom tamed and then only with care and lots and lots of product that was likely frowned upon here.

She didn't lead me into any of the buildings, as I'd expected and hoped. Oh no, that might have given me the chance to snoop. I feared I knew exactly where we were going as we approached a very small shack that looked like an old-fashioned outhouse. I could hardly hear her lecture about fertilizer and decomp over my mental cry of "Oh *hell* no." I could smell it already, and my ambrosia-heightened senses were in full rebellion. I wondered how any of Dionysus's acolytes tolerated the stench, which begged the question—does a god shit in the woods? Or did Dionysus have his own private potty stashed somewhere?

"Um, seriously?" I asked, trying not to sound all citified and stuck up. "There's no other option?"

"Oh, you get used to it." She gave me the special instructions. "I'll be right outside if you need me."

For what? I wondered but didn't ask.

The smell inside was everything I feared it would be and more. The unseasonable heat didn't help. If I'd actually been planning to *use* the facilities ... Well, let's just way it was a good thing I wasn't. Instead, I was going to be hunting hot spots of the non-meteorological kind.

Outside of probably half the teens and amateur ghost hunters in the world, not many people realized that Android phones could be used as portable EMP meters. Oh yeah, there was an app for that. Maybe it even came in handy if you were searching for the ghost of your dear old Aunt Gertrude on a deserted island, but for the most part, those apps were only useful for impressing the impressionable, who'd get positive readings all over the place from technology here, there and everywhere. The readings were enough to convince some that they were looking at future careers with Mystery, Inc.

I'd found the app useful only a time or two myself, but I was ready to make it three. If Back to Earth was as dedicated as they said to a simple way of life and a small carbon footprint, any tech at all should stand out like a virtual sore thumb.

I already had my phone set to silent, but the red and green lights of my app told me everything I needed to know about the hot spot. Not the building we'd been led through, but somewhere off to my right. I couldn't tell how far, just that it was nearly due south of my current location. It gave me a place to start if I was able to sneak back. It was impossible to run a modern business without a communications network, and that meant files, records, a trace. It seemed likely they'd keep all their secrets in one place, rather than scattered about. There had to be some sign of Uncle Christos. Maybe even the man himself. I had a sudden image of a conservationist's version of Tartarus, with Christos facing something like Sisyphus, only instead of constantly pushing a boulder uphill, he was trapped in a giant hamster wheel generating the power to run all of Back to Earth's electronics.

Maybe the outhouse fumes were getting to me.

Before I left, I dashed Christie a quick text so she wouldn't call out the cavalry for me. There was one already waiting from her.

Made contact. Off to a rally or seminar or something. Yippee? More soon.

I didn't feel the least bit bad for her. She'd had the chance to be on a plane back to La La Land. She'd given it up for the glitz and glamour of undercover work. As evidenced by my current surroundings. I used the hand sanitizer attached to the wall before letting myself out. I hadn't actually touched anything but the door, but it was enough to make me feel unclean. Or maybe that had been Dionysus's touch.

Gracelyn was waiting for me when I got out, smile still in place. "All set?" she asked.

"Yes, thanks. Do you suppose we'll be getting a tour later? I'd love to see the grounds. It's so peaceful here."

"Isn't it?" She took a deep breath of air and managed not to gag. It had the effect of inflating some rather prodigious … lungs. I wondered if Apollo had noticed, then reminded myself I didn't care.

The two men were bent over the table as we approached, going over promotional plans, I guessed.

"We'd really like your guy Randy Vargas to direct," Dionysus was saying as we reseated ourselves.

"I thought we were here to discuss onscreen talent."

"Well, for that we have one of our own in mind. We want someone truly committed to the Back to Earth lifestyle, a spokesperson with no skeletons in her closet—no drugs, affairs, cosmetic surgery, clothing lines sewn in sweatshops …"

"Vargas is very particular about who he works with, and he doesn't like amateurs," Apollo said apologetically. "He likes to deal with a certain stable of his own. Plus, he doesn't do commercial."

"We have a budget in mind," Dionysus said, flipping a page of the portfolio.

Apollo's eyes nearly telescoped right out of his head like an old Tex Avery cartoon wolf at the sight of a foxy lady. I wondered what it took to so impress a god. I wondered if he'd tell me. "He might consider it," Apollo said, face back under control. "And the talent?"

"Come, I'll introduce you." Dionysus grabbed the bottle of wine from the table and waited pointedly while the rest of us picked up our glasses. "We can't let such a wonderful vintage go to waste," he said as a prompt. His eyes fell to my untouched glass. "You don't drink?" There was unfeigned horror in the question.

"Acid reflux," I lied.

"Ah, you want *white*." He snapped his fingers, and Gracelyn flitted from his side, presumably to find me another varietal. Dionysus waved away my protest as though it were a polite fiction. I wondered if he viewed the word "no" the same way.

I took Apollo's arm before Dionysus could claim me again.

In contrast, Apollo's arms were rock hard and invited caress ... not that I took them up on their invitation. I thought about Armani and *his* nicely muscled arms. And blue eyes that went dark and depthless when his interest ... intensified.

"What are you thinking about?" Apollo bent to whisper in my ear, no doubt believing it was him.

"Nick," I answered.

"Liar."

I let it stand. It was much safer that way. Historically, women who thwarted Apollo's will didn't fare so well. Like Cassandra, the prophetess of Troy, who'd been given the power to see the future but not to change it. It always came back to Cassandra. It was better than a cold shower, at least my hair didn't frizz. As long as Apollo felt he still had a shot with me, I was probably safe from his wrath.

And doesn't he have a chance? my inner minx asked, dying to rub up against him.

I told her to go play in the street. I was not going to be one of those battered women, attracted to danger, thinking it would never turn on me.

People change, my minxy-me purred.

Gods don't, my sane-brain responded.

As evidenced by Dionysus, back in the minions and massacres game after all these years. He was going on about fields and yields, fertilizer and other loads of crap, but I only paid a cursory amount of attention. After all, I was only along as Apollo's "good friend.." I wasn't expected to buy what he was selling. Anyway, I had way more important things to do, like mentally mapping the complex, trying to identify the various buildings based on what I saw going in or out and trying to get a sense of the number of residents.

The mapping was easy. As I looked back over my shoulder, the buildings appeared to be arranged in a rough semicircle like the talk-therapy grouping around the fireplace at the first building we'd visited, only here the centerpiece of the complex was the circular drive we'd driven up. Patterns. People had preferences—circular, square, oblong, symmetrical or asymmetrical. Often people weren't even aware of their predispositions.

The purpose of each of the buildings was a lot murkier. From where I was I couldn't see a lot of the movement between the structures. Hard to determine functions.

I turned back around, surveying the fields, pretending to be awed and interested. The rows were not nearly as high or as dense as the orchard, so it was easier to see the people here. And there. And ... everywhere. If they were all cult members and not hired labor, we were in some serious trouble. Crossing a god was bad enough. Crossing one with his own fanatic army was nothing short of suicidal.

Ambrosia didn't make me invincible *or* insane. Not completely anyway. But I was between a smarmy rock and a hellish hard place. Besides, there was Uncle Christos to consider, and that guy back at the morgue. I didn't know if he was the first, but I didn't think he'd be the last.

My heart rate must have sped up, because Apollo patted my hand and squeezed it against his chest. I smiled up at him and realized our footsteps were slowing. We were in a row like any other, and Dionysus had been going on about what wine they made with which grapes and the kind of year it had been, but he stopped now. I heard Apollo's breath catch and looked to see what we were stopping for.

Not a what. A who. And she was stoopid gorgeous—like glossy, airbrushed cover model perfection. Like Selma Hayek, Catherine Zeta-Jones and pure, unadulterated sex all merged into one. *My* heart almost skipped a beat, and I didn't roll that way.

Seriously. Instead of the wheat-colored clothing the others sported that covered pretty much wrists to ankles, she wore a white sports bra bandeau-style across her breasts, which if not melons were at least well-rounded apples. Her waist was tiny, but flared into real hips reminiscent of an old-time starlet. In short, she looked like every conception ever of Eve straight out of the Garden of Eden, except that, thankfully, she wore a pair of khaki shorts instead of a fig leaf, though those shorts were small enough to reveal indecent amounts of sleek shapely leg.

It took me that long to even work up to her face with all the other flesh revealed, and I had a split second of sympathy for men, who we expected to meet our eyes at all times … not that it was generally a problem in my case. Her face was arresting enough on its own—beautiful almond eyes framed with dark, absurdly long lashes. Her hair was held down by a bandana matching the color of her shorts, but I could see that beneath it her black hair was not unlike mine on a very good day—thick, wavy, untamed.

Apollo let my hand drop as he stepped forward to greet the girl—woman?—Dionysus was introducing as "Sinestra, the spokesperson I told you about."

"Sinestra" raised those stunning almond eyes to Apollo, blushed and quickly dropped them again. *She's shy*, I thought, shocked. Somehow, I'd expected such beauty to come with a certain amount of arrogance, but all I saw in that brief glimpse was knowledge, and maybe avoidance. Then I realized just why that face was so unlined and why, perhaps, she was dressed so differently from the others. All that flesh on display was nearly as pale as her bandeau, cartoonishly pale, like a cinematic Snow White. I'd bet my life that here was our missing goddess—Persephone, born Kore, daughter of Demeter and runaway wife of Hades. I could hardly blame her for wanting to feel the sun on her skin after the chill of the underworld.

I realized then that Dionysus was introducing me and watching my reaction very closely. Luckily, I'd already put on my game face.

I stepped forward to take "Sinestra's" hand, which she offered with the flutter of eyelashes, her gaze there and then gone. "Karacis," she said, rolling it around on her tongue. "A good Greek name. Where are you from?"

"My brother and I were born here, but my family comes from Kalambaka."

"Oh, the outskirts of Meteora, the holy city," she said.

"One of them," I answered, watching her. Meteora was a place of extremes—rocks shot straight up out of the earth, mountain-high but with sheer cliffs all around, atop of which now sat monasteries and churches dedicated to a religion a lot less ancient, but no less influential, than that which sprung from Mount Olympus to the north. How the monasteries had originally been built was anybody's guess. Word was that hermits retreating from the ever-expanding world finally climbed the cliffs, finding nowhere else to go to escape but the inhospitable pillars of rock at Meteora. I guess with enough determination and religious fervor, one could free climb almost anything, but erecting *structures* … without roads or ramps or the means to build them, it was nothing short of miraculous.

"*Sinestra,*" I said, throwing the focus back where I thought it belonged. "It means *left*, doesn't it?" It was a cultural bias that sinister/left got associated with evil.

"You know your Latin," she said, sounding surprised.

I let her think so. Truly, I had no idea where I'd picked up the tidbit, but if it made me seem smarter than I was, so be it.

Since Sinestra was looking away, studying the fields and no doubt the work still to be done, I did the same. Yiayia had said that Demeter, Persephone's mama, the earth-mother goddess of the ancient Greeks, had joined the movement, but, if she was present, I couldn't spot her.

"Having met you," Apollo said, stepping into the conversation now that I'd left it, "I can certainly see why Dionysus feels you'd be perfect for his marketing campaign."

Sinestra blushed even more deeply, the red of her cheeks the only color beyond her ridiculously dark lashes and mane of hair. "Thank you. My mother and I are so dedicated to the Back to Earth ideals. I'm happy to help, though I'm uncertain …"

She never said exactly what she was uncertain about, but I

think we could all guess it was the idea of all the attention focused her way.

Apollo turned to Dionysus. "I'll present your proposal to Vargas. If he should want to meet your spokesmodel?"

"We can arrange that, of course," Dionysus said, slapping him on the back. "Now, let us drink to our new potential partnership!"

He steered us away from Sinestra, away from the fields and his followers, and back to that shaded verandah to finish off the bottles of wine and one more before we were allowed to leave. Perhaps *allowed* was a little strong, but his patter was so constant that we'd have had to churlishly interject in order to leave. Since I was at Apollo's mercy and had no urge to explain that I had my own wheels waiting at the bottom of the hill, I took my cues from him. I excused myself once in the meantime to use the facilities in order to text Christie that I was still alive and kicking.

Shopping, she responded in return, by which I knew that all was right in her world and that no one had managed to brainwash her as yet into thinking that consumerism was bad and that wheat-colored clothes were the new "in" thing.

That froze me. In my dream, I'd been standing in a wheat field waiting to be torn apart. It seemed telling.

I kept all that on the inside as we took our leave. I tolerated Dionysus kissing me again on both cheeks and even sliding his hand down my back until he could nearly cup my *other* set of cheeks. He stopped just at the *on-no-he-didn't* point, which meant that I had no excuse to put the hurt on him and demand the whereabouts of my uncle. Considering that I was surrounded by followers who'd bought into his "charm," that was probably a good thing. But I'd be back. Tonight, under the cover of darkness.

"I feel like I need a shower," I said as I got into the car with Apollo. Our driver, Alonzo Rayez, according to his card, hadn't

gone far, it turned out. He was at a coffee shop about ten minutes away.

"Need someone to wash your back?" Apollo asked suggestively. Fresh from Dionysus's clutches, it kind of just gave me the creeps.

"Gah, the two of you … no wonder you're BFFs," I said, exasperated.

"We are *not* BFFs," he said, sliding away from me on the seat, clearly offended. "When I said we shared a sanctuary, I meant that he was there when I was not. It was best that way."

"Come again?"

"He has a dark side," Apollo responded.

"No one else at the compound seems to notice."

"They've all fallen under his spell."

"Didn't work on me."

"No," he said bitterly. "If it were that easy, you'd already be *mine*."

That caused a stupid little flutter somewhere in the vicinity of my heart, but he looked away before I felt I had to respond. In fact, he gazed out the window and didn't say another word to me as the Town Car cruised down the hill and I instructed Alonzo to pull over and drop me at my car. Was Apollo lost in his own deep thoughts or had I inadvertently hurt him?

"Are we … still on for dinner tonight?" I asked as I popped open my door to the continued sound of silence.

Uncomfortable with his admission, I hoped he'd say "no" and let me off the hook. I was surprised at my relief when instead he answered, "I kept my part of the bargain."

"Oh, uh, all right then. Where should I meet you?"

"I'll pick you up at six."

I didn't like the idea of being without my own getaway vehicle, but it seemed petty to protest, and it appeared I'd already offended him once, so I told him where I was staying and that I was looking forward to seeing him. It should have been a lie. Sadly, if the flutter in my stomach was any indication, it wasn't.

I had to look away from him then, afraid he'd see it in my eyes.

"Hey, kid," the driver said, breaking the spell. "You need me, you call. For any reason." He gave me another card, and I took it, even though I still had the first.

"Thanks, Alonzo," I answered. "You be safe."

"Back atcha."

They drove off, and I got into my car, sitting there for just a second too long before it occurred to me to turn the key and start the AC so I didn't swelter to death. I jumped when my phone vibrated and nearly fumbled it in my haste to answer.

"Christie?" I asked, recognizing the number of her burner phone.

"Oh. My. God." It came out just like that, staccato. "I am shopped out. You won't believe the stuff I got. So cute! Meet me for dinner?"

Ah, retail therapy. I wondered if Jack knew he could be so completely erased by the purchase of designer duds. I mentally kicked myself for that. There was way more to Christie and way less to Jack. Good for her if the only thing hurting was her credit card balance.

"Um ... I have ... *plans?*"

She was as quiet as Apollo in his snit. "Huh? I thought you were going out there for recon. You didn't make contact, did you?" She drew in a sharp breath. "You haven't been sucked in?"

"Worse," I said solemnly. "I bumped into Apollo."

"*Apollo Demas?* Here? Wait, you said *I* have plans. Not we. Do you think that's smart, going out with him alone?"

"It's ... complicated."

She mulled that over. She only knew Apollo as an aging actor and new-ish talent agent, the heir to the Circe Holland— aka Circe the enchantress who'd turned Odysseus's men into swine—empire that had been built on the backs of dreamy young stars and starlets who hadn't read their contractual fine print. Luckily, Apollo, being an immortal rather than a witch who had to steal her eternal life, offered much better terms. But I don't think any of that was going through her head at that moment. It was more the way he'd looked at me the one time she'd met him ... like he was the Big Bad Wolf and I was Little Red Riding Hood. That brought me straight to thoughts of the one and only mind-blowing, sense-stealing, earth-shattering kiss we'd shared that night.

"Well then, I guess I'm *not* through shopping for the day then."

"What—*why?*"

"Because wherever Apollo plans to take you, I'm fairly sure you don't have anything appropriate."

"You think he'll want to go someplace fancy?"

"Oh, honey." She said it with such pity. "Hollywood types do *not* eat at Taco Bell."

CHAPTER ELEVEN

"Infiltration is like invasion ... you want to go in clean and under the radar."
—Christos Karacis

At 5:57 PM I sat on the toilet seat in the bathroom at our little Residence Inn letting Christie work her magic on me. It was the only way she'd agreed to let me forgo the shopping and borrow one of her new couture pieces instead. I had to do it justice ... or else.

I wasn't short by any means, but the same race car red wrap dress that hit Christie at mid-thigh and made her look like a Nordic Helen of Troy caught me just above the knee and made me look ... okay, smokin' stoopid hot. Or maybe it was what she'd done to my hair that was transformative. Somehow, she'd enticed it to lie in gorgeous waves rather than crazy interlocking curls. Or maybe it was the smoky eyes she'd given me. Or the "Kiss Me Quick" red lips. No kidding, that was actually the name of the color.

"Okay, now stand," she ordered.

Christie'd been all apologetic that she didn't have shoes to match the dress, but the silver stilettos she'd offered instead were both stunning and deadly. I was likely to kill myself in them before anyone could "Kiss Me Quick."

I wobbled to my feet, walked two steps, twisted my ankle and said, "This is ridiculous," just as a knock sounded at the door.

"I'll get it!" Christie said cheerfully, now totally on board with the dinner after her portrayal of Glam fairy godmother.

"No, Christie, don't leave me—"

I stood in the center of the room, afraid to take another step without her support, lest I fall on my face.

"This is stupid." I tried to kick the shoes off, but was foiled by the ankle straps. I dropped onto the nearest bed, making the dress ride halfway up my thighs so that I wondered how Christie ever hoped to sit in it without exposing her hoo-ha. That was, of course, when Apollo walked in.

He whistled at the sight. "All this for me?" he asked.

I glared. "No, all this for Christie. It was the only way she'd let me out tonight."

Apollo looked at my friend, who beamed at her handiwork. "Impressive," he said.

"I know, right?"

They shared a moment, and I wanted to throw a heel at him, but the buckles were defeating me.

"Don't you dare," Christie said when she saw what I was up to.

"I'll kill myself trying to walk in these."

"That's why you have an escort."

She drew Apollo forward, and then almost forgot to let him go, looking slightly stunned at the contact. I knew the feeling.

"M'lady?" Apollo said, offering an arm.

"What if something happens?" I said weakly. "What if I have to chase a mugger or something?"

Apollo and Christie exchanged a look.

"Stop that!" I said, cranky.

"Oh, fine." Exasperated, Christie rooted around in one of her many bags and offered me a little black purse.

"How's this going to help?"

She rolled her eyes. "Look inside."

I unzipped the zipper, and inside were sparkly black ballet flats, folded in half.

"Brilliant," I said.

"Aren't I?" she answered. "Now, you two have fun. But not too much," she said, fixing Apollo with the evil eye.

He smiled, but not in a way that was reassuring, and Christie momentarily forgot to breathe.

"She means that," I said for her.

"I know," he answered. "Shall we?"

I refused to agree or disagree until I heard the rest of that sentence, but I did precede him out of the room. I looked back and caught Christie checking out Apollo's butt as he followed me. I shot her a grin, but I didn't think she even noticed.

Sometime between when Apollo and I had parted and now he'd picked up a rental car several tiers up from my sliding-toward-antique Camaro. The car that beeped at us when he pressed the key fob was sleek and silver with lines like the bunched haunches of some jungle cat ready to spring.

"Nice," I said.

His lips quirked up in a smile. "I figured you here meant trouble, and for that I might want to have some autonomy … like my own set of wheels."

"I hope you got the extra insurance."

"Oh, I did."

He held my door open for me and checked out my legs as I slid into the passenger seat.

"Nice," he echoed me.

I stuck my tongue out at him. Because maturity was so my copilot.

By the time he popped his door open, I'd given up on the buckle of the first strappy shoe and had instead risked stretching out the strap by pulling it down over my heel to release myself from my fashion bondage.

"You're undressing already?" he asked. "Not that I don't approve, but usually I have to buy a woman dinner first."

"I bet you don't," I muttered.

"Well, okay ..."

"Anyway, don't get your hopes up. I'm just working on my own autonomy. There's no way I'm going to be slave to these shoes."

"That's too bad. I was having visions of all sorts of things I could do to you in those shoes."

My mouth was suddenly *way* too dry as I caught some of those same images—me still in the shoes with the little red dress pushed up over my hips and Apollo pushing into me from behind, my hair tangled in his fist, being used to bow my neck so that he could graze it with his teeth.

I gasped as my body struggled for the air I'd been denying it, unconsciously holding my breath.

"Stop," I said when I could.

"Tori?" he asked. His confusion seemed genuine. "What's wrong?"

He leaned in toward me, hand outstretched as if to touch me, and I cried, "Don't!"

He froze, uncertain, which was a new look for him. "What's going on?"

"Don't know," I grated out.

The car was *way* too hot and enclosed, the dress too tight. I wanted to shed it like I had the shoes ... one of them anyway.

"Did you have ambrosia today?" he asked. "Are you going through withdrawal?"

If anything, this felt like an overdose. Everything was far too intense. "Had ... ambrosia," I gasped out, then swallowed, trying to get my heart rate and sudden hot flash under control.

"Must have been something I ate." *Or drank.* Maybe there'd been something in Dionysus's wine … something other than the ambrosia I should have been used to. "Just drive," I ordered. "Give me a minute. I'll be fine."

Was this how Dionysus whipped his followers into a frenzy? It seemed a long way from wanting to tear my clothes off to wanting to tear into another human being, but then the thing stimulating me was an oversexed god. There was no telling what Dionysus's presence would inspire.

The very thought of him was like a bucket of cold water thrown in my face. My breathing slowed, and after a moment I felt like I could relax the too-tight hold I had on myself. I uncurled my hands from the fists I hadn't realized I'd formed, nails biting into my palms to give me pain instead of pleasure to focus on. It hadn't even registered.

"You're bleeding," Apollo observed. "Just a bit."

I wouldn't meet his gaze, but instead focused on releasing the second strappy sandal without ruining it. Apollo watched me a second longer, then turned the car on. It purred like the jungle cat it resembled and leapt forward out of the parking space, which, luckily, he'd backed into earlier.

I felt better when my feet were tucked into Christie's ballet flats. "Are we going to talk about what just happened?" Apollo asked.

"Nope."

"Why not?"

Because to expose myself like that I'd have to trust him. Trust led to intimacy, and intimacy would bring us full circle right back to the problem at hand. I had two very good reasons for avoiding that.

Nick Armani.

And my sanity.

"Hades attacked me last night," I said, tossing out the first conversational monkey wrench I could think of.

Apollo looked at me, blowing straight through a red light he should have been paying attention to instead. "*The* Hades?"

His eyes were about as wide as Charon's coins and dark in the dim interior of the car.

"As if there's more than one."

"And you survived?" he asked, stunned.

Since that was self-evident, I didn't feel the need to answer.

"Why?" he asked.

"To make a point."

"Tori, what's going on?" His voice was soft rather than demanding, and I couldn't help but confide ... part of it anyway.

"Persephone has left him. He blames me."

I told him about the explosion—or, more accurately, the dragon's awakening—opening a path to Hell.

"And you're investigating Dionysus because ...? Wait a minute, his new spokesmodel?"

"You didn't recognize her?" I asked. I'd wondered. I figured all Olympians knew each other.

"I met her once, *maybe* twice, like a few millennia ago. She was a mere girl."

"Well, she's all grown up now," I said. *As if you didn't notice.*

"I'd have to be dead not to."

I snapped my gaze to his face. I *knew* I hadn't said that out loud. "Did you just read my mind?" I asked.

Apollo took on an *oh shit* expression and focused on the turn he was taking like his life depended on it. Half a second later, he took another turn into a drive where white-jacketed valets waited to take the car off his hands. He put up one finger to hold them off and turned toward me.

"You have to believe it wasn't intentional."

"Reading my mind?"

"Creating a link." As hot as I'd been earlier, suddenly I was ice cold.

"I think you'd better explain."

"When I gave you the gift of foreseeing, it opened up dormant pathways in your brain. For the rare person who is already predisposed to certain things, sometimes it has unforeseen effects."

"Very poetic. Except that you're *the god* of foreseeing. What 'unforeseen' effects are we talking about?"

"I swear, I didn't know. It's only happened once before."

"*What* has?" I asked, teeth grinding.

"Forging a link."

"Between us," I asked, just to be clear.

He didn't look away. "Yes. It's faint. I only feel it in times of extreme emotion, like—"

"Take me home."

"I could have lied," he answered, the look in his eyes begging me to understand.

But I was putting things together now, understanding far too well. "That's how you knew ..." I couldn't even complete the sentence. When Nick and I had first ... gotten together ... I'd received an ominous, two-word note from Apollo.

I know.

Now that I knew *how* he knew, I felt violated. Apparently, the intimacy I'd feared had already been forced upon me.

Flames engulfed me again, but this time there was nothing sexual about them. In fact, if I could shoot lasers out of my eyes or fire out of my fingers, Apollo would be a crispy critter.

"That's your defense?" I asked. "*I could have lied.* Oh yes, so virtuous. You freakin' *changed me* against my will. Or, at least, without my permission. There's a word for that, and it's not pretty. And that connection let you spy on something that was intensely private." I felt sick.

"Do you think that was fun for me? I didn't know what was happening at first. Then when I felt ... what I felt and knew what was going on ... Trust me, if I could have shut you out, I would have. I. Didn't. Know. I gave you that precognition for your own good, because your job is dangerous and you needed protection."

"I'm not yours to save or protect."

"Yes," he said, "you are."

I was so upset I nearly swung for the valet when he startled me by opening my door, apparently deciding that our time was up. He must have seen something in my eyes, because he hesitated before leaning in to take my hand and help me from the car. It looked like a strain to keep that smile stretching from one of his retro sideburns to the other, but he managed.

Apollo handed his keys to a second valet on his side and came around the car to escort me into the restaurant. I backed away, fumbling open the clutch Christie'd leant me to find my cell phone.

"I'm calling a cab," I told him.

The look in Apollo's eyes was infinitely sad. I almost—*almost* —felt sorry for him. If he really hadn't intended the connection, then I couldn't really blame him. He would have been punished enough, I thought, knowing what Nick and I were doing—what *he* wanted to be doing. But the invasion … My anger needed an outlet. Someone to blame. And who else was there?

Had he been there every time Nick and I had …? No, I couldn't even think it. And that thing between us, Apollo and I, in the car—that overwhelming tsunami of feeling—was that some kind of feedback loop with our link? If so, he was more dangerous to me than ever. If it ever came up just after the rush of ambrosia or another life and death situation where I was vulnerable and on adrenaline overload … there was no telling what would happen.

"Tori," he said, reaching out to me. "If you really want to leave, I'll drive you."

"Go!" I said sharply. "I'll … be there in a bit."

I still needed to pump him for information. I battled down the image that rose to mind of a different sort of pumping entirely. I had to fight this.

But first, I needed a minute or twenty.

Apollo put on his public face. I watched it transform right in front of me. If he was still hurting, there was no longer any sign.

I waited for him to disappear inside and voice-dialed Nick, who picked up on the first ring. "Tori," he answered, in that voice that could melt me—deep, grumbly, a little rough around the edges. Only tonight it just made me ache.

"Tell me, is murder still illegal?" I asked.

He laughed, but cut off abruptly when I didn't join in. "Wait, you're not serious, right?"

Then I remembered Internal Affairs and potential phone taps and how that was probably the dumbest thing I could have said. "Of course not," I lied. "It's just … Apollo's here."

There was complete and utter silence on the other end of the line. Then, "In San Francisco. With you?"

"If you mean with me in the sense of being seconds away from having his head handed to him, then yes."

"Tori, don't joke like that."

"Who's joking? Anyway, yes, he's in talks with the very group I'm investigating."

"That's it, Tori, I'm coming up."

"Can you?" I asked.

"No," he sighed. "Probably not."

"Of course not. I couldn't get that lucky."

"Tell you what—you come home and you can get lucky any time you want." Home and Armani—Nick—in the same sentence. It was a lovely thought.

Marred only by the knowledge that we wouldn't be truly alone. "I'll be back soon."

"How soon?"

"Not soon enough."

We both contemplated that.

"They discovered the identity of the body you drove up there to see," Nick said after a moment.

"Oh?" That snapped my mind straight away from getting

lucky. I wondered nastily if Apollo was getting whiplash at my changing emotions.

"Jeremy Clarkson, a string reporter from the Associated Press. He was undercover investigating … You'll never guess."

"Back to Earth," we both said together.

"Bingo," Nick finished.

"Thanks, Nick."

We sat on the phone a second longer with nothing more to say, but wishing it was different.

"I'd better go," I said finally. "Apollo's waiting."

"Tell him I said hi," Nick told me, knowing how *that* would go over.

"I'll give him your love."

"Nope, that's all for you." My body ran hot and cold all at once. It was the closest Armani had ever come to a declaration, and I didn't know what to do with it.

"Okay then," I answered, going for breezy. "I'll save it for myself. Good night, Nick."

"Good night," he answered, and I wished I could read his mind like Apollo could mine. Had Nick really meant that love part the way it sounded? How did I feel about that? No time to think about it. Apollo waited for me inside, and the anger he inspired was nice and pure and uncomplicated. I held on to it as I made my way inside.

Apollo waited beside the hostess stand of the lovely, elegant restaurant that I had no taste for. The amber-soaked lighting gave the place a warm, intimate glow. Just right for an assignation … or an assassination. *His*, I thought hopefully.

The hostess, who'd been flirting with Apollo, sized me up as I approached and apparently found me wanting. I blamed the ballet flats, but I didn't regret my choice. If she wanted the god, she could have him. Now would be good.

Apollo studied me intensely as I walked up, and I glared back but didn't look away.

"Everything all right?" he asked when I arrived.

"What do you think?"

"That you're still here."

"We had a deal. You help me, I have dinner with you. I thought about it. I don't want to end our relationship owing."

"End?"

"Show us to our table," I told the hostess. I'd had enough of audiences already.

She smiled professionally at me, more than professionally at Apollo, as if to tell him that if I was stupid enough to pass him up, she'd be glad to pick up my slack, and led the way.

While the front of her little black dress had been demure, the back dipped indecently low, revealing what on a man I'd have called plumber's butt. I wondered how one wore a bra with a backless dress. Christie would undoubtedly know.

Apollo's gaze didn't follow the hostess as she retreated … as if I'd care.

Instead, he was disconcertingly still focused on me. "End?" he repeated.

I looked him in the eyes. I didn't want him to think that I was in any way unsure about this. "After this case, I don't want to see you again." It was dangerous, cutting a god off cold turkey, but I didn't see what choice I had. "There's nothing I can do about the fact that we've been thrown together again, and I can't tell you what to do about Dionysus, but once this is over and I have my uncle back, I don't want anything more to do with gods or goddesses."

"What's this about your uncle?" he asked, ignoring the rest of that rather important sentence.

"He's missing," I answered shortly, determined to get back on track. "He's in trouble and his last known whereabouts involved the Back to Earth movement. *Cult*," I added. "Dionysus either has him or knows where he is."

"Why did you not tell me?"

I seriously considered giving up the glare, for all the good it was doing me. If I spent much more time around Apollo, my face might freeze that way. "Did you miss the part where me and mine are *none of your business?*"

His eyes narrowed. "It seems to me you're my business when it's convenient. When you need ambrosia or a way into the Back to Earth complex you have no problem calling me up. When my usefulness is over, you dismiss me like a servant. And you call *me* insufferable."

"If I'm so insufferable, don't suffer me," I countered rather than admit he'd made a very palpable hit. My voice must have risen, because several diners looked over at us disapprovingly.

Our waiter appeared and offered to take our drink orders, probably hoping that would mellow us out. I was sticking with water.

The way Apollo had put things, I was a spoiled rotten brat taking advantage of his feelings for me. But he ... *what? Did what he thought was right only to have it blow up in his face and have you blame him on top of it?* I didn't know what was right anymore. That was the thing with gods. They'd had eons of practice running circles around us mere mortals.

Still, I hated myself just a little bit.

"Dinner's on me," I offered instead of an apology.

"Why?" he asked suspiciously.

"Because you're right," I mumbled into my water glass.

"Come again?"

I put the glass down. "You're right. I'm wrong. But we're still done. I don't think we're good for each other."

"I think you're wrong," Apollo answered. "Therein lies the problem."

I ignored him then to study the menu, afraid that if I looked his way again, he or my conscience would get the better of me, and I'd take it back, find some way to make amends that would really be a veiled excuse to remain in his presence. Because no matter how angry he made me, no matter how much I wanted to ignore him, it wasn't really possible. And now I knew there was no hiding those feelings.

"Are you reading me right now?" I asked, tense.

"No," he answered. "It doesn't happen all the time. When it does, it's a single, clear, strong feeling striking me like a bolt to the heart. Right now all I feel is churning."

"So it's really my emotions you read, not my mind?"

"I don't read, I receive."

"Whatever."

"Yes."

It made surprisingly little difference to my feelings on the matter. *Churning* was a good description of my emotions and my gut. If there was anything rising to the top it was wanting not to want him. As clear as mud and pure as the LA air.

It was a relief to get back to the room and prepare to head into danger. It was clear-cut with no messy ambiguity. I wondered whether Apollo was feeling *that* and what he'd make of it. It pissed me off that I bothered to wonder, but I put the anger to good use. It kept the fear at bay. Because as tough as I liked to pretend I was, the thought of sneaking into a cult compound by the dark of night after seeing what had been done to that reporter was enough to shiver me timbers.

But first, I had to face down Christie.

"Oh no, you don't," she said. "I'm putting my foot down." I looked at her foot. I was unimpressed.

"Christie, this is what I *do*. If you weren't here, you wouldn't even know I was in danger."

"But I am here."

"Same deal then, I'll check in by text or phone every hour, or you can call in the cavalry."

"You mean the cavalry almost an entire state away?" she protested. "Unless … maybe Apollo can go with you." I knew she was seriously worried if she suggested throwing the two of us together again.

"No," I said sharply. Then, at the hurt on her face, "Sorry, it's just … *no*. Things are complicated with us."

"Then take me."

"You don't think that two of us sneaking in are *more* likely to get caught than one?"

"I can drive getaway."

"I thought you had to get up early tomorrow for some sort of greet-the-dawn, cleansing ritual with Martin."

"I do."

"Well then, you stay. I promise, I'll be all right."

"I'm going to hold you to it."

"Deal. I'll be back in plenty of time to take you out for a huge breakfast of bacon and eggs after your cleansing."

"Make it egg whites and turkey bacon, and I'm your girl."

"Turkey bacon—really? Isn't that an oxymoron?"

"Don't knock it until you try it."

I scrunched up my face. "Pass."

"Child."

I finished checking the gear in my fanny pack and adding in a few things, like camo face paint and lock-picking tools. If I was caught there'd be no way to claim innocence, but I figured that was the least of my worries.

Part of me wanted to get an hour or two of sleep in before setting out, but I knew I was too hopped up on adrenaline for that. Anyway, I didn't want to risk waking up groggy. I was going to need all my wits about me.

Christie hugged me like she was saying goodbye. I shook off the thought, sure it was just that and not premonition.

"I'll check in," I said again in reassurance.

She nodded and pushed me toward the door. I took a glance back and caught her still looking after me, concern written all over her face.

I called my new friend Alonzo on the way and asked him to meet me at an Internet café I'd spotted on an earlier drive. I needed copious amounts of caffeine, since I might be up all night; I needed to research the dead journalist, and I wanted to hear more about Alonzo's sister. I could kill three birds with one stone. Typically, it was two birds, but I was an overachiever.

He was available but on duty, so I told him I'd pay him as if he'd taken me for a ride, and he wouldn't even have to use up the gas. Plus, I'd tip generously. He had no problem at all with my terms.

I spotted a white SUV following me. Either OJ was taking another leisurely run from responsibility or Hades was on my ass. I didn't like either thought.

But I was almost at the café. I pulled off the road and watched the SUV roll right past me. Maybe I was paranoid.

I'd just retrieved my triple espresso from the counter and slid my credit card through a slot at one of the computer terminals, holding my breath about whether or not I'd hit my spending limit, when Alonzo walked in. He gave me a nod and took the insulated cup he'd brought with him for a fill at the counter before joining me.

I used the time to look up Jeremy Clarkson. He'd been the one to write the article I'd previously found calling Back to Earth a cult. More recently, he'd done a piece on a recent string of disappearances in the San Fran/Napa area. He hadn't drawn any conclusions, but speculated that there might be something sinister at work.

Living in LA, a city that seemed to have more than its share of serial killers, most recently Michael Hughes, Louis Craine, Chester DeWayner Turner and others, my mind might have gone that way, but together with his cult interest, I thought Jeremy's suspicions lay elsewhere. His last article had been four months ago. Before he'd decided to go deep?

Alonzo joined me a second later, taking the lid off his mug to let some of the heat escape. Steam rose from the brew like the warning signs of an active volcano ... or maybe the pits of Hell.

"How's your sister?" I asked.

"Not good." He took a sip of his coffee, hissing as it hit his tongue. Then, "She has no energy, no focus, stomach aches and pains, the shakes so badly she can't drink a half full glass of water without half of it ending all over her. She's right now in the hospital for dehydration and malnutrition."

It all sounded familiar from when I'd gone cold turkey off the ambrosia. It had felt like an amped up case of food poisoning. Not good.

"Malnutrition?"

"She hasn't been eating."

"You said you traced the beginning of her illness to Back to Earth?"

"She works at a nearby winery. She started on this raw foods and probiotic kick, getting her lunches and everything from the Back to Earth stand—fruits, nuts, the whole bit. Within a week she was jaundiced, sick. Her kidneys were shutting down. There was nothing she'd eaten that should have done that. Their stand was the only thing different in her world. So either those culty people were lying about being all organic and were using some serious chemicals on their crops that made her sick, or ... something else. I don't know, I'm no scientist, but growth hormone or something. I've been doing some reading."

He looked miserable. His eyes were bloodshot, and the bags under them were certainly not designer.

I put a hand on top of one of his where it cupped his mug. The heat radiated up through his hand to mine.

"What do the doctors say?"

"They're baffled. I'm working nearly around the clock to pay for her care. She's got shit insurance. I can't pay for no kind of private lab to analyze their food and see what's what."

"Maybe you don't have to." I pressed on his hand and then took mine back. "Would you be willing to talk to a few friends of mine? They're federal agents." *Friends* might be pushing it, but they'd at least accept my calls, mostly, I was sure, because they still considered me to be a person of interest.

"FDA?" he asked.

"Homeland Security."

He didn't look like he thought too much of that, but he said, "I'll do anything. She's my baby sister." The tears were there in his voice, but he never let them flow.

I dialed Rosen. "I have someone here you might want to talk to," I said when he picked up. I put him on speaker and sat the phone down on the counter.

"Oh?"

"His name is Alonzo Rayez. His sister is sick. He blames Back to Earth."

"Evidence?" Rosen asked.

"Maybe in her medical records. Look, do you want to talk to him or not?"

"What about *her*?"

I looked to Alonzo, who said, "I can meet him at the hospital. She's a little tough to understand right now. They had to intubate her for a while until they could get enough nutrition into her."

"I'll manage," Rosen said.

I let them work out the details and checked my watch. It was already almost half past eleven. Good little cultists ought to be snug in their beds, particularly if they kept farmer's hours. It was time.

I dug through my purse to find money for Alonzo, but he tried to push it back at me. "I should never have agreed to that. You're helping us. I can't take your money for that."

"Relax, I have a client," I said. It wasn't completely untrue. Hades *had* asked ... ordered ... me to look into the disappearance of his wife. He agreed to an exchange of services—he'd do his job if I did mine. He never said anything about expenses, but I'd deal with that bridge if I lived long enough to cross it.

Alonzo looked relieved. He needed that money, even though he'd been prepared to relinquish it. "I meant what I said in the cab ... if you ever need anything ..."

"You've already done a lot, trust me. If the agents can talk to your sister and find other people with her symptoms, maybe they can start building a case. We can take Back to Earth down."

Now there was a tear, but I didn't comment. Alonzo insisted on walking me to my car. I'd swear I could feel eyes on me the whole time. There was something about the way my spine itched. I stopped just before we hit my Camaro and took a good look around.

Nobody and nothin'. But Hades, I remembered, was rumored to have a helmet of invisibility the way Zeus had his lightning bolt and Poseidon his trident, so the lack of a visual proved nothing.

I gave the night a one-fingered salute, just in case. Alonzo looked at me funny, to which I responded, "Don't ask."

He didn't.

Just like earlier that day, I parked my car on the outskirts of the Back to Earth property. Only this time I risked my suspension by driving it off road and parking it on the far side of that stacked stone wall to keep anyone from becoming too interested. In case anyone was paying attention, I thought it might be a wee bit suspicious to run out of gas twice in one day in the same spot.

I crept again through the orchard, the gnarled arms of the trees making it look like the Forbidden Forest or something equally imposing. I paralleled but never stepped onto the road. Once free of the trees, I was faced with a high, wire mesh fence. The whole no carbon footprint thing led me to suspect it wouldn't be electrified, but I tested my theory by tossing a twig at it. Both fence and twig were summarily unimpressed with the exercise. So I laced my fingers through the mesh and gave the fence a good tug to make sure it was tough enough to climb. The cacophonous sound of jangling bells met the motion. I froze. *Really?* I thought. It was the equivalent of putting pots and pans underneath windows as a low-tech alarm. Like something out of *Home Alone*.

But if the voices heading my way were any indication, it was pretty effective. "—see the way he fawned all over her? I'm telling you—" a female voice was saying.

"I know, you've *been* telling me," another answered. "But what's one bacchae more or less? It doesn't diminish you."

"I'm telling you, this one's different."

"Can we focus here? The alarm bells sounded."

"Probably those cheeky raccoons again."

I faded back into the trees and watched as two women holding LED flashlights stepped up to examine the fence. One I recognized right away—Casey Olivieri. The other was a mystery. Luckily, their lights didn't penetrate the tree line, although they shined them my way.

"Nothing," announced the one who wasn't Casey. "Better organize a perimeter check, just to be sure."

"That's another thing," not-Casey was saying, "these patrols. I don't get it. What do we have to steal?"

By the corona of their lights, I saw Casey roll her eyes. "Only our freedom. Remember when Moss's mother sent that cult reconditioner or whatever to kidnap her?"

"Or when your mother sent that PI?"

So they *knew* about Uncle Christos? I'd expected as much when he'd contacted Detective Beverly and then dropped off the face of the earth, but the confirmation after what I'd seen in the morgue was chilling. I willed them to say more, but Casey was silent for a moment. Guilt over whatever had become of him? My heart clenched.

"Yeah, or him. Not everyone understands. When you withdraw from the world there's always going to be someone who wants to drag you back into it. Acknowledging that our way of life is valid means admitting theirs might be flawed. We threaten them and their comfortable consumerism."

"You sound just like him," the other girl commented.

"You say that like it's a bad thing," Casey said, something ominous in her tone.

I hoped the other girl realized it before something happened to *her*. "No," she answered quickly. "It's just … thank you for clarifying, sister."

Casey studied her in the darkness. "We have enough enemies from without. We can't afford them from within."

"Of course not. I'll get the others."

"Have them bring the dogs."

The other girl nodded and ran off.

Dogs! I hadn't seen any dogs when I was about earlier. I did carry emergency doggie treats in my go bag, but trained canines wouldn't be swayed by them.

But Uncle Christos's life could be at stake, assuming I wasn't already too late to save him. I couldn't call things off.

It was now or never. One lone bacchae. No dogs … yet. I dug deep, trying to access whatever strength the ambrosia and my gorgon ancestress might have left me and leapt for the fence. Casey called out as she saw me, but I was noisily up and over the fence and diving down at her before anyone had the chance to come to her aid. Her hands formed into claws—not in a shape-shiftery way, but more like a veteran cat-fighter—and she lashed out at my face with one set of spiky nails while the other pierced my scalp as she raked my hair to hold me in place. I stared down into her crazed eyes and said with force, "Freeze!"

Power flashed through me, and the gorgon glare held her still. Petrified. It wouldn't last but long enough for me to get away. From the not-so-distant depths of the compound dogs began baying in a way that suggested they couldn't wait to get at me. I pushed myself off the fallen girl and raced for the nearest building. I was on the wrong side of the compound from the area I'd pinpointed earlier as the likely center of operations.

There were shouts now too as I was spotted, not just by dogs but by their handlers. A cacophony split the night, loud enough to wake the dead. I reached a door on the closest building and ripped it right off one hinge. It slumped toward me, and I shoved it out of the way. I found myself in the midst of a dorm of sleeping people, some half-awakened by the noise. I ran. The place was built like a longhouse. If there wasn't another exit at the other end, I'd have to make my own.

The dogs burst through the door I'd left off-kilter. I made the mistake of looking back to gauge how much lead I had, only to see the handlers release them. It cost me a second, long enough that roused sleepers were able to grab at me. One had me by the sleeve and was yanking me in for a better grip, but I tore myself out of her grasp, hearing the shirtsleeve rip. I aimed myself at the second door and kicked it with a great crack of wood and answering pain, which reverberated up my shin to my knee. The door popped open, and I was through. There were more cultists waiting for me on the other side— one man and two women, but they were surprised by the flying splinters and just a second too slow to stop me, though not to pursue.

Something ... some*one* hit me from behind, sliding down my body until he—she?—was hugging my butt, bringing me down to the ground in a flying tackle. I kicked out, caught something that gave, and the grip loosened but didn't let up. Two more bodies fell on top of us, and all the air blew out of my lungs. I was suffocating.

Panicked, I thrashed and fought like a woman possessed, knowing that if I couldn't fight off these three, it would soon be a whole army and all hope would be lost. I fumbled for the pack at my waist, taking the blows aimed at me as I dug for ... ah ha, pepper spray! My Taser would have done just as well, but I was happy to take what I could get. I thumbed off the safety button and heaved to shift the weight on top of me enough to free that hand. I found my opening and sprayed indiscriminately around me.

Howls and hisses greeted me, drowning out the baying dogs, now close enough to split my head open with their triumphant sound. Bodies rolled away from me, and I got my own under me, bursting up from the ground for another dead run.

The dogs lunged for me. One caught something at my waistband and nearly pulled me over before it gave. I half whirled and let loose again with the pepper spray, feeling really badly about it. They were only doing their job. I *liked* dogs. But it was them or me.

I ran a mad dash, ignoring the closest building, heading for the hot spot. I'd lost the element of surprise. I was not going to lose out on possibly my one chance to find Uncle Christos. If they captured me, so be it. Maybe they'd throw us in the same pit and at least I'd have my answers. We could figure a way out together. Better still if we could fight our way free tonight. I wondered how many I could tase, spray, or gorgon glare before they could take me down. Enough?

I couldn't hear pursuit over the blood rushing in my own ears. Hopefully, I'd screwed up the dogs' sense of smell with the pepper spray, but the cultists … I hadn't gotten them all, not by a long shot.

I dodged behind a building, listening for pursuit before using it as cover to bolt for the next. Behind me, someone was calling for a building-to-building search.

If I ripped the door I wanted off the hinges, they'd know just where I was. I reached for my pack, for the lock picks I kept inside, only to find the pack gone. Suddenly, I knew what had given way beneath the guard dog's razor-sharp teeth.

Zeus's zits. I hit the door and thought fast, but I had no gods-given gifts that would help me out of here.

A zing of forewarning had me leaping back from the door a bare instant before it opened, covering me.

Two women came out arguing.

"But, *Mother*, people are getting sick, even *dying*."

I recognized the voice—Sinestra-slash-Persephone. I was torn between my need to grab the door and my need to listen. With no time to decide, I did both, getting my fingers smashed by the door and leaving myself totally exposed should they look back.

"Only the weak," her mother answered. Demeter. It had to be. "When planting, you toss aside the bad seeds; when reaping, you sort the wheat from the chaff."

"These are *people*."

"I believe *people* call it Darwinism. They post videos and give out awards in homage. Some will fall, but the rest ... we will be the Latter-Day Olympians. A new breed, dedicated to the earth and free of the petty squabbles of the old guard. Already, Zeus and Poseidon have been taken out. By a *mortal* girl. All that's left is for Hades to fall."

"Yes," Persephone said faintly.

Pounding feet and raised voices let me know the building-to-building search was close. I couldn't waste any more time.

I ducked inside the building they'd just left and eased the door closed behind me, which left me in pitch darkness. I didn't dare risk turning on a light, but I had to chance *some* kind of illumination or go in blind. The trouble was, I'd lost my pack and my flashlight with it. I felt along the wooden walls, giving myself a splinter in the process. I hissed in pain, but continued on until I hit a desk. Elated, I began opening drawers and rooting through them for a light. The detritus of an office nipped at my fingers—loose staples, paperclips, pens, pencils and paper. But finally, something rolled away from my questing fingers, then back again. I closed my hand on something cylindrical and found the on switch, aiming it down at the floor. Success meant a faint light. Perfect.

I shone the light around the room. It didn't go far, but I could see an old-fashioned projector sitting on the beat up wooden desk I'd been exploring and a pull-down white screen against the opposite wall with rows of chairs facing it.

That was all there was to the room except for a hallway leading off of it. Too dark to make out any details. I'd have to check it out. Someone rattled the handle of the door through which I'd come, and this room offered nowhere to hide. I'd be found in an instant if I just ducked down behind the desk.

Instead I crept into the hallway, quickly but as quietly as possible and tried the first door I came to—locked. The second —locked.

The outer door opened, and I raced to the third—unlocked! I ducked in just as voices filled the room. I found myself in a closet. A teeny, tiny little cubbyhole filled with a mop, a broom, rags, eco-friendly cleaning supplies and *no lock on the door*. None.

I started to panic and then to contemplate fighting my way out, but the voices hadn't yet come any closer.

"Demi and Sinestra were just here," someone was saying. "They said no one had come this way."

"We've checked everywhere else," someone answered.

"Every inch of field?" the first woman asked.

"Any sane person would be long gone."

"Check anyway, just to be sure. Leave no door unopened," said that first voice again. I heard two respond. I was dealing with at least three then. I didn't like the odds.

"Meanwhile, I'm going to go through this pack and see if there's anything to tell us who we're dealing with."

Crap.

I heard one of the hallway doors unlock and the door swing open as the other two resumed their search. My heart was pounding. I didn't need my precognition to tell me I was in trouble.

"Cell phone," the first woman announced. I heard the second door go. I readied my pepper spray and prepared for a fight. "Let's find out about the last number dialed." I couldn't hear her doing it, but I tried to remember who I'd last called— Armani, Jesus, Christie?

The knob on the closet door started to turn when a voice rang out—strong, annoyed and the kind of loud that comes from a phone on speaker mode. "Agent Rosen. This had better be good, Karacis."

The knob stopped moving, as the search party froze at the voice.

"Shit," someone cursed. "Whoever this Karacis is, she's certainly well-connected."

"We'd better let Dionysus know right away," said the first voice I'd heard, who seemed to be the boss. "Star, Kestrel, you go. I'm going to finish going through this stuff."

I let out the breath I'd been holding. Star and Kestrel had to be the women conducting the search, because I heard their steps suddenly retreat. I breathed a silent sigh of relief that I was free from discovery … for the moment anyway. There was no telling how soon the search might resume or the guard dogs might regain their senses of smell and alert to me.

Now was my chance. There was just one woman left, as far as I could tell. I could freeze her, grab my gear and make my escape. I'd no sooner started to turn the knob than the building flooded with more people checking in. I was trapped. There was no way I could pepper spray or freeze enough people to get out.

But I'd missed a check-in while I was playing at escape. Now it was up to Christie to rally the troops. And I'd thought she was being silly.

CHAPTER TWELVE

"When investigating, if someone gets aggressive, you've struck a nerve. Just make sure it's not their last *nerve."*
—Christos Karacis

I woke with a start and fell forward, conking my head on something that resounded with a wooden *thunk*. Totally in the dark, closed in on all sides. I had a panicked moment thinking I'd been buried alive and come to in a coffin. Then I realized that I'd somehow fallen asleep standing in that closet praying for my life. And what a weird one it was when waking in a coffin seemed a perfectly plausible explanation of my condition.

The *thunk* would have given me away, except that there was a much bigger commotion going on outside. Huge. A distraction worthy of a true drama queen, which, unless I missed my guess, was exactly what we were dealing with.

Christie had sure enough called in reinforcements, and Jesus had arrived with both guns blazing.

165

"Where is my sister?" he shouted at the top of his lungs. He then let out a string of rapid-fire Spanish of which his real sister, I was pretty certain, would never approve. "I know you have her!" he concluded.

It was impossible to ignore Jesus in a hissy fit. Gods knew I'd tried.

I smiled to myself and risked a peek out of the closet. As far as I could tell, the guardhouse or whatever I was in was deserted. I slipped out, listening as I went. I was a little shaky after all the action yesterday, the pummeling I'd taken and then being on my feet all night. I needed breakfast or ambrosia—or a breakfast *of* ambrosia. Stat. Oh, and caffeine, a shower, and a couple or three aspirin. But all that, obviously, had to wait. First and foremost, I needed to get out of here and let Jesus know he could do the same.

Quickly, I crossed to the desk and rifled through it for my cell phone and belongings.

"She was coming *here*," Jesus insisted loudly to whoever was trying to calm him down. "She left behind her two-year-old baby, and my brother-in-law. He is not to be consoled. If you don't bring her to me, *I* will bring the police!"

No cell phone. I found and pocketed my Taser, but everything else seemed to be AWOL, and I was running out of the time Jesus had bought me. Someone else could be back at any second. I had no more time to search.

I opened the outer door a crack. Everyone was focused on the action in the middle of the courtyard where Jesus ranted and raved in front of a red rental car, just the sort you'd drive if you were looking to draw attention. I didn't sneak. Sneaking only makes a person more obtrusive, not less. I simply walked out. No sudden or furtive moves. I slipped around the side of the building. As I did, I saw Jesus turn his head my way and quickly back, setting up a wail of "*Dios Mio*. What will *madre* say? She will have to be told. And her heart—"

He fell back against the car, clutching his own chest in demonstration, and I started to run. Now that I was out of sight of the gathered crowd, I bolted for the orchard and escape, not worried about the alarm bells. I could get up and over the fence easily enough, and then I'd be home free. I heard Jesus's holler that he'd be back with the authorities, and then his car started up. It was perfect timing to coincide with my leap for the fence. I was up and over, dropping to the other side in what was probably a land-speed record.

Well, that was easy, I thought. I silently blessed Jesus and his hissy fits, even though I suspected I'd be paying for this one for some time. He'd saved me; he'd never let me forget it.

I tore through the trees, angling in the direction I thought led to my car and freedom. My footsteps slowed as I got close. There were red and blue strobing lights penetrating into the tree line from about where my Camaro should be. I approached the edge of the orchard slowly, that sixth sense of mine flashing louder than the lights. That meant this was something more than an abandoned vehicle check. When I looked out and saw the ambulance, my heart sank to my toes.

Too fearful for caution, I burst out of the woods, running for my car as I saw the gurney beside it, a white-sheeted figure on top. I couldn't imagine who it could be—Christie? Uncle Christos? I thought my heart would explode with the pounding. I *had* to see who was hurt.

An officer came out of nowhere to stop me, catching my upper arms in an iron grip.

"I'm sorry, miss, you'll have to stay back. This is a crime scene."

"But that's my—" I swallowed hard. "Who is it? Who do you have there?"

The cop's grip on me tightened painfully. "Your car?" he asked. "Is that what you were going to say? Are you Tori Karacis?"

Sure, my name would have been on the papers in the glove

compartment. I nodded, unable to take my eyes off the sheeted figure.

"Mizz Karacis, you're under arrest for the kidnapping and assault of Christos Karacis. You have the right to remain silent—"

My legs went out from under me, but the grip on my arms held me in place. "Assault, not murder?" I asked with relief, hardly able to believe I'd found him ... well, *they*'d found him. But still, he'd been found.

"Yes, he's still alive. He'll be able to testify against you."

And that was when the rest of it sank in. *I was under arrest.* They thought I—"But I've been looking for him," I protested as the officer whipped my arms around my back and slapped on the cuffs. He frisked me, finding the Taser in my pocket and waving another officer over to bag it for evidence.

"Looks like you found him," the cop said grimly.

"Could I just see him? I need to know he's okay," I said desperately.

"I think you've done enough," he answered.

The paramedics had finished securing the straps and started to wheel Uncle Christos away.

"No," I cried, "just let me see him!"

But the cops held me fast and wouldn't let me go anywhere but the back of their cruiser, where they tucked me none too gently, letting my forehead hit the doorframe on the way down.

I wondered if Jesus had seen any of it or if he'd already been gone before the police jumped me. I'd been on foot and he in a car. He would have turned in the other direction—away—to head back to San Fran. Even if he'd seen the flashing lights in his rearview mirror, he had no way of knowing they applied to me.

"Why won't anybody tell me what's going on?" I asked my interrogators, frustrated. "At least tell me that he's okay. The officer mentioned Uncle Christos had been assaulted, but that could mean anything. Is he conscious? He'll tell you I didn't hurt him. *Just ask him.*"

I was at my wits' end. I didn't know what kind of impression I was making, but I didn't so much care. I knew I should, but it didn't seem nearly as important as Christos being all right.

Neither the balding, blond gentleman playing good cop nor his hard-eyed partner with the shaved head would tell me a damned thing.

Finally, they exchanged a glance and good cop said, "When he regains consciousness, I promise you, that's the first thing we'll do. For now, your uncle was found in the trunk of *your* car. I don't think it's unreasonable that we have questions that need to be answered, do you?"

"Does he have a concussion?" I asked. "Will he be all right? What do the doctors say?"

He looked at me steadily. "You tell us what we need to know, and we'll see if we can get any of your questions answered."

I tried to calm myself. I knew it was the best I was going to get. They'd already let me cool my heels alone in an interview room for an hour, softening me up for the interrogation. I supposed the world wouldn't end if I had to wait another hour or more to find out about Uncle Christos. Knowing wouldn't change the diagnosis. But the urgency to know didn't go away just because logic suggested it should.

"Now, you say you'd been staking out the Back to Earth compound?" his partner asked. He was standing. Looming, really. Not coming down to my level. It was a power tactic.

"Yes, all night." I didn't tell him I'd actually broken in or that I'd been trapped in a broom closet for most of it. Neither did I say I *hadn't*. If he interviewed the Back to Earthers and anyone had gotten a decent look at my face … Well, I didn't want to be caught in a lie. I confined myself to the questions asked and didn't volunteer anything.

I doubted, though, that anyone at Back to Earth would be

providing me an alibi for last night. Given the body in my trunk, thankfully still breathing, I no longer thought it miraculous that I'd managed to escape. I thought it was design. Why catch and keep me when the cult could do away with two problems at once … me and Uncle Christos. I wondered if they'd expected Christos to live or if I was supposed to be on the hook for murder. The very thought made me ache for Christos and whatever he'd endured.

A fist pounded on the interrogation room door, making me jump. Good cop slipped up and smiled privately at what he must have perceived as evidence of my guilty conscience.

"Come in," his partner called.

A woman poked her head in, her sparse hair shellacked to her head and pulled back into an itty, bitty ponytail. She waved the detectives toward her, and they stepped into the hallway but didn't entirely shut the door. I was still feeling shaky and sick, but there was nothing wrong with my hearing.

"There's someone here with an alibi and bail for your suspect."

"What?" one of the cops exploded—good cop, from the sound of it. "She hasn't even been arraigned yet."

"Want me to tell him to come back later?" she asked, a bite to it. "Along with his potentially exculpatory information."

The cop blew out a breath, and I could almost imagine him rifling frustrated fingers through his hair … if he were the one with hair. "Fine, put him in interview room two. I'll get to him in a minute."

I thought quickly. It would help so much to know *who* had come to alibi me so that I had some idea of what he might say. Jesus? Apollo? Maybe Christie had even gotten through to Armani? What was I? Sister? Lover? Somebody's cheap date?

I pretended calm I didn't feel as the cops came back into the room.

"So, you were staking out the compound all night?" bad cop

said, eyeing me as though waiting in interview room two was the final nail for my coffin rather than a potential alibi witness.

"I already told you that."

"Alone?" he asked.

"I plead the fifth."

"That's for the stand."

"Fine, then I plead 'not without my lawyer.'"

"Have you got a lawyer?" he asked, looking around as though one might materialize.

"Have you got a phone for me to make my one call?"

He stalked to the door and yanked it open, startling the female officer on the other side—the same one from earlier, who was poised to knock … again.

The cop covered his own surprise by snarling, "What is it now?"

"Another man, another alibi, more bail money."

"Another—" He ripped a hand through his hair, I could see it this time. I was surprised he didn't yank it straight out by the roots he was pulling so hard.

His partner looked at me, no longer hiding his smile of amusement. "You're a popular girl."

I shrugged. "Well, you know, I put out."

I don't know what made me say it, but I thought good cop was going to swallow his tongue.

"Take her to booking," bad cop ordered the female officer. "Let her make her one phone call, though it seems like everyone she knows is *here*. We'll go talk to these *alibis*." He said it like it was a dirty word.

She looked me up and down assessingly, either to see if I was going to be any trouble or what was so special about me that I'd draw two witnesses out of the woodwork. She'd play a mean game of poker—I couldn't tell the verdict from her face.

We passed good cop and bad cop in the hallway, just opening the door to one of the interview rooms. The voice that issued forth from inside stopped me in my tracks. "It's about time," he said.

Hades.

Hades was my alibi? Poseidon's pearly whites, I was in trouble. If they allowed him to bail me out, I wondered whether anyone would ever hear from me again. Although, I'd done what he wanted; I'd found Persephone. I just hadn't actually told him as much. I'd barely had time to think about what to do about the situation, and now he potentially held my freedom in the palm of his hand.

I wondered who my other alibi was, but I was doomed to go unsatisfied on that point. I was through SFPD's version of cubicle city and into an elevator faster than Jesus could get his panties in a wad. Okay, maybe not *that* fast. Two floors later we were stepping out into the booking area, where I'd have mug shots and fingerprints taken and my criminal record would begin.

The booking officer behind the desk got a call as we approached and waved to the officer escorting me with his free hand as he picked up the receiver with the other. "Booking," he said into it.

I could tell by the way his gaze suddenly laser-focused on me that I was the subject of the call, and I prayed with all my heart that it wasn't someone ordering him to amend the charges against me to murder.

"Yes," he said cautiously into the phone.

The officer with me raised her brows to him in question, and he held a finger up to let her know he'd answer momentarily.

"Now?" he asked, as if unsure he'd heard correctly. "Before processing?"

"Now." It was barked. Even I could hear it from feet away.

"The Feds are taking custody," the booking officer said in disbelief as he hung up the phone. "They say she's part of an ongoing investigation. *And* that her uncle's awake and asking for her."

I went boneless with relief and had to force myself to stay upright. Christos was *awake*. He'd be okay. He had to be. I'd known it all along.

The female officer looked at me hard. "Who *are* you?" she asked.

"Just what it says on my ID."

"You're sure getting a lot of attention for a newbie private eye."

I smiled, grateful that I *could* smile again. "Lucky me."

She sighed and we backtracked up to cubicle city, where Agents Rosen and Holloway were waiting. Had Christie called everyone in my address book or had they found me on their own? Which begged all kinds of questions about bugs and tracking devices.

"Agents," I said, nodding to them respectfully, like a good little PI who should absolutely be released on her own recognizance.

"Officer, would you remove her cuffs?" Agent Rosen asked.

And give her a triple venti, extra hot latte and a sack full of scones, I thought, hopefully.

But unfortunately, the universe wasn't prepared to make restitution for all the recent crap. Still, the relief to my shoulders as my hands were freed from the cuffs was a pretty fine thing.

"You do know we found her uncle's unconscious body in the back of her car?" the cop said.

"He's asking for her," Holloway said. "That seems pretty compelling evidence of her innocence."

"Anyway, it's all been cleared through channels," said a man I just now noticed standing behind them, probably the same man who'd been barking orders on the phone. From the cut of his suit, he was pretty high up in the command food chain. "Mizz Karacis, you're free to go … with these agents."

"And if I decide I'd rather go back to my hotel and get some sleep?" Not that I would; I wanted to see Uncle Christos as much as they wanted to take me to him, but I had to see how far this freedom extended.

"That would be ill-advised. Besides, our techs are still going over your car for evidence; it's not ready to be released. I'm sure the agents will give you a lift back to your hotel once they're finished with you."

"Great," I said, trying to mean it. After all, they *had* gotten me free, at least temporarily. I didn't want to seem ungrateful. "Any chance we can stop off at a coffee shop on the way? I've been up all night."

"Due to your two alibis?" Agent Rosen asked slyly.

"No," I answered, glaring. "My stake out. Anyway, who—" I started to ask who my second alibi was, then stopped when I figured it was the sort of thing I should know. I wasn't about to peg any potential alibi as a liar.

The agents ignored my unasked question and escorted me out. Rosen fiddled with his cell phone as we emerged into the early morning sunlight hitting us full blast from just above the tree line. He drew cool black shades from his pocket and slid them into place with his free hand, then reached his phone out to me, already ringing.

"Your friend, Christie," he said. "She's been calling me all night, frantic. I thought you might want to talk to her before she has an aneurysm." There was grudging respect in his voice.

"Ohmagod, Agent Rosen, tell me you have her," Christie ordered as soon as she picked up the phone.

"Hey, girl," I said, so glad to hear her voice, which whooshed out now in the mother of all sighs.

"Tori, you're safe! You didn't check in. Jesus flew all the way up here. And then he said he distracted everybody at the compound so that you could get out of there. He saw you go. You were supposed to be right behind him!" she gushed accusatorily. "Then you disappeared. *For hours.*"

I tried to get a word in then, but she continued. "Jesus drove back and saw the police surrounding your car, and we feared the worst."

She was crying now. I could hear it in her voice. I felt terrible, even though I'd never meant to scare her that way.

"I'm good," I soothed. "You did good. *Great.* And they found Christos. He's okay." I saw the two agents exchange a look, and my heart sank. "Well, isn't he?" I demanded.

"Tori." The voice came from behind us, and my heart squeezed. I turned slowly, and the agents along with me.

Apollo stood there, just staring, looking me over from head to foot as though I might have wounds not readily apparent. My other alibi, I presumed.

"Did Christie call you too?" I asked, unable to think what else to say. I didn't want to be happy to see him, but the idea that he would have come when I was in trouble even after I said I was through with him made my wants a moot point. I *was* glad to see him.

"Who?" Christie asked in my ear. "Who's there?" I'd nearly forgotten the phone.

"Apollo," I answered.

"Tori," he said again.

"I didn't send him," Christie said. "Jesus, yes, and I called Armani. And the agents, but—"

"Christie, can I call you back?" I didn't wait for an answer. I'd make it up to her later. For *all* of this.

Of course, Apollo would have known I was in trouble, via our unwanted link. Still, the fact that he'd come ...

"Thank you," I said to him, "for coming. You didn't have to."

"We need to talk," he said, taking a step forward.

"Later," Agent Holloway cut in, moving between us and cutting off all eye contact. "Right now, she's coming with us."

"Where to?" he asked.

"The hospital," I answered, when Holloway didn't, "to see my uncle."

"I'll follow you."

Holloway grunted and turned back to me, steering me with a no-nonsense hand toward his car. I was almost thankful. I didn't want to talk to Apollo. It seemed like every time I did I fell further and less willingly into his debt. Someday soon I'd stop fighting and I'd be like a fly trapped in a web, waiting to be devoured. Worse, not even minding the thought.

CHAPTER THIRTEEN

"'Better, I say, to break sod as a farm hand
for some poor country man, on iron rations,
than lord it over all the exhausted dead.'"
—The Odyssey by Homer, Book 11, lines 579-81

When we got to Uncle Christos's room, my two agent escorts hung back. Far enough to give us the illusion of privacy but close enough to hear and to intervene if it turned out my alibis were full of crap and I was inclined to finish the job I'd allegedly started.

He was sleeping as I approached—mouth open, a little drool escaping from one corner, gentle snore like a buzz saw with a silencer. I took his left hand where it rested above the blankets. His eyes fluttered to half-mast and then shut again.

"Maria?" he asked.

It was my mother's name.

"Tori," I told him, concern kicking up my heart rate. "I'm here, Uncle Christos."

His eyes slowly peeled open again. "Can't be," he said. "Tori's just a skinny little thing. No bigger'n ... a bug."

The speech seemed to take a lot out of him, and his eyes closed again. That way he couldn't see the tears in mine.

"It's Tori, *theios*. I'm all grown up. Don't you remember?"

I spoke to him in Greek, hoping ... I don't know what, but he loved to hear it. He was always afraid that my brother and I would lose it. He'd made us practice with him all the time when we were kids.

The look on Christos's face was strained, like he was trying to remember and couldn't, and he seemed to have new lines creasing his forehead. In six months? Maybe I was misremembering his face, like he was misremembering my age. But the hale, vital man I'd known seemed to have gotten old and shrunken all of the sudden.

"It's okay, *theios*, sleep. We'll talk later." I kept the catch out of my voice, but a big fat tear rolled down my cheek. I brushed it away and stood watching his face until it relaxed and the buzz saw started up again. Then I turned to the agents.

"He doesn't remember," I told them.

"Yeah, we got that," Rosen said, relatively gently. "We hoped that your presence would spark ... something."

"What happened to him?"

If they exchanged a glance, I swore to myself I'd slap them, regardless of the charges for assaulting a federal officer, but Holloway said, "We don't know. The drug tests aren't back yet. There's no cranial damage on the X-ray, no pupil dilation or blurred vision to indicate a concussion. Just the loss of memory."

"Sleep deprivation? Brain washing? Hypnosis?"

"We're waiting on approval of more tests, but if it's any of the above, they won't do us any good. There was no evidence of deprivation or torture, if that helps. His bruising is more consistent with taking a run at something and being knocked on his butt than of direct violence. There's also some pooling of blood, as if he'd laid prone for some time, which would indicate at least the opportunity for sleep."

"Or that he was knocked unconscious."

"Or that. He's a little like Rip Van Winkle right now, like he fell asleep and half your life passed him by," Rosen said.

"Only he was there for it. All but the last six months."

But something he said, about Rip Van Winkle, gave me pause. Uncle Christos had slept the sleep of forgetfulness, and while it could have been caused by any of the things we'd discussed, one more disturbing possibility came to me—the waters of the River Lethe, which wound through Hades's realm. He'd have had no reason I could think of to use it on Christos, but Persephone ... she'd have had motive and means. She could easily have taken some when she won her freedom from the underworld.

I doubted any drug test or tox screen in the world was going to turn that up. I'd always thought the River Lethe was imaginary, a myth like Mount Olympus, gorgons, the Fates and all that jazz. I'd been wrong on everything else thus far, so why not this too?

Agents Rosen and Holloway turned at some kind of commotion in the hallway, the latter motioning me to stay back and presumably safe while the former slipped out to see what was going on, closing the door behind him.

A second later, he opened it again, and I couldn't even believe my eyes.

Nick stood there, looking about two cups of coffee down for the day, but nonetheless gorgeous with his dark hair ruffled, one wave, as always, half over his eyes, which were emphasized by the blue denim, button-up shirt he was wearing over jeans. I'd never seen him look quite so casual before except when he was wearing nothing at all.

"You're here!" I said, ever ready to display my brilliant grasp of the obvious.

"I took the red eye."

Then I was in his arms, my face buried in his shoulder as his arms went around me and held me fiercely. "Christie called," he said.

"She told me."

Nurse Nancy was goggling at us, and I remembered she'd seen that news footage of me with Apollo. She'd probably assumed he and I had been an item. If I had half the fun everyone suspected me of having ... well, I wouldn't have time to get into nearly as much trouble.

Rosen cleared his throat from the doorway. "Can we take this into the hall or to the visitor's lounge? Nurse Nancy says that we've exceeded the visitor room limit ... again. She was trying to explain that to Mr. Armani when he flashed his badge and went around her."

I looked up at Nick, who shrugged, totally unrepentant. I wanted to kiss him, but not with an audience. I supposed it could wait.

Agent Holloway led the way to a visitor's lounge, which was either naturally deserted or had been pre-cleared by the agents. It sported dirt-brown couches and chairs, seventies green plastic tables and two-year-old magazines, largely winners like *Field and Stream*. Nick and I took the couch, leaving the chairs for the agents. We promptly sank toward each other as the couch sagged in the center.

"So, you've been inside the complex?" Agent Rosen began.

"I never said that," I answered immediately, not about to admit to B&E.

"Earlier in the day," he prompted, "with a Mr. Apollo Demas." Agent Rosen held up his smart phone to show me a screen of words too small to actually read. "It's his statement. Plus, your car was logged by the side of the road around midmorning. A police officer approached to offer assistance and couldn't locate the driver of the vehicle. It came back clean when he ran the plates, except for a host of unpaid parking tickets."

Armani looked amused over that, but Rosen looked like a disappointed papa. Was he the one with kids? I couldn't recall.

I let out a breath. "Oh, okay, I was there. It's not a crime, is it?"

"We want you to get with our people and give them the layout of the place—structures, vehicles, population estimate."

I leaned forward, studying his face. "You found something? The lab results on the food?"

"Results were … inconclusive. There's definitely an additive, but it couldn't be identified. The chemical structure … it's not something we've seen before. It's definitely not on any black list."

"What about Alonzo's sister?"

"We have her samples en route to our lab, but results are not instantaneous, whatever you see on TV. Do you expect anything different?"

Damn, I didn't.

"We have no cause for a warrant. Nothing on which to go in."

"But you *suspect*," I said. "You wouldn't be here otherwise."

"We have several similar and very brutal crime scenes, one of which happened close to the site of a terrorist attack on domestic soil at the top of Mount Lee. *Six* deaths now, including the eviscerated man in the morgue and the tourists who were killed in the parking lot of your hotel. We have *one* common denominator—*you*."

Armani took my hand and squeezed it as I said, "But you told the officer at the station I wasn't a suspect," I protested.

"Honestly, that's up to you. Suspect or informant … your call. Whatever else is up, you know more than you're telling."

"If only I knew as much as everybody thinks I do, I'd have this solved by now. But—wait—what if I could get you that informant?" I thought of the questioning girl who'd come to check on the alarm bells with Casey Olivieri. *She* didn't seem to have drunk the cultish Kool-Aid. I wondered if she'd be as good at answering questions as asking them.

"You know someone?" he asked, leaning forward himself and studying me as if to determine whether I was putting him off or finally, truly, cooperating.

"I might. Look, I'll meet with your people. I'll give them all the info I have and you can put a sketch artist with me on the girl I think might be your weak link. If you can get her outside the compound, away from the others ... but first, I really need to use the facilities." Because that double espresso had finally run through me. I supposed that up until now I'd been scared literally shitless.

Holloway rose to go with me. I guess he'd drawn the short straw for the day. I squeezed Nick's hand as I rose and told him I'd be right back. Famous last words.

Holloway preceded me out into the hall so that he could check it out first, and it must have been clear, because he motioned me to follow him. The restrooms were in an alcove directly across the way, so we didn't have far to go. Within a few paces, Holloway was at the ladies' room door. He knocked loudly, and when no one responded, he turned the knob and pushed the door open hard. It was a small, cotton candy pink space with two stalls—one a large handicapped stall—and one small sink. There were no windows through which I could escape, even if I were so inclined. The doors to both stalls were closed, and Holloway motioned me to stay back while he stepped inside and shoved them both open to check that they were truly empty. I felt a tingle of warning, but nothing happened. Both doors swung in, completely unobstructed, and bounced back into place, closed apparently being their default.

Holloway rejoined me in the hallway and held the door open for me to enter. I thanked him and waited for the door to close behind me before heading to the first stall. I was mid-step when I heard the lock on that outer door click home. I whirled back toward it, and had only time to register ... nothing ... an empty room ... before Holloway threw himself against the door to bust his way back in, and I was suddenly pinned against the wall by an invisible pressure. Panicked, I kicked and struggled, but it was no use at all.

"She's there, isn't she?" a voice hissed out, a millimeter from my face. The pressure released enough for me to fall a few inches forward so that he could slam me back into the wall. "You ran out of the police station before I could talk to you, but you're not running out on me now. Just answer the question—you found her, didn't you?"

My eyes were bruised from being rattled in their sockets by the last impact of my head against the wall, but they weren't doing me any good just then anyway. I was frozen with indecision. There was no telling what Hades would do to Persephone once he found her or what he'd do to those he'd see as aiding her. I couldn't be responsible for that, even if she had maybe used the water of the forgetfulness on Uncle Christos. But—

He pulled me away from the wall and shoved me back against it again, brain-jarringly hard. It was not helping me think.

"Tell. Me," he ordered. "Where do they have her?"

I started to shake my head in denial, but when that hurt too much, I croaked, "No."

"Tori!" Holloway called. "Mizz Karacis, who is it? Who's in there with you?" I opened my mouth, though I didn't know what would come out. I never saw the blow that knocked me to the ground, my vision and head exploding as I hit, the world going all Dali-esque and then dim.

"Never mind," Hades was saying, ignoring the agent entirely. "I know she's there. I will raze the whole place to the ground. I will tear it apart stone by stone to find her."

I couldn't form an objection. My world winked out.

And then I was being shaken awake and crying out in pain. My eyes, when I opened them, weren't working right. Neither was my mind. I was afraid, and I couldn't remember why. There was something … Something … urgent.

"Stop!" I begged.

The shaking stopped, but it didn't help. The pain was such that I wanted to bash my own head against the tiles to open it up and relieve the pressure, but there was something I had to do ...

"The Back to Earth complex," I told the three agent Holloways before me. "Danger. You've got to get out there *NOW*. No time for a warrant. *Danger*."

I didn't know if I made any sense. It hurt even to talk, to think. I wanted to lie right down and pass out again to escape the pain.

A doctor pushed Holloway aside, and I flinched as he shined a light in my eyes. "She has a concussion," he announced, as if *that* wasn't obvious. "What happened here?" he asked.

Holloway ignored him. "I might be coming around to your way of thinking," he said to someone outside the bathroom. Rosen? "Whatever blew past me, it was ... unseen."

Like he couldn't bring himself to say "invisible."

"Ouch!" Whatever the doctor was doing *hurt*. Putting my head in a vise, it felt like.

"We've got to get to the Back to Earth compound. She says there's danger, and I heard a voice threaten to raze it to the ground. Call for backup," Holloway ordered.

"On it," Rosen said.

Nick poked his head in. Three of him. In triplicate. The mind boggled. I tried to rise. The doctor held me down. "You're not going anywhere."

"Have to," I told him, trying harder.

"No, you really don't," both he and Rosen said, almost in stereo.

"Nick, you've got wheels?" I asked.

Rosen and Holloway both gave him the evil eye, but he responded, "Yes."

"Good. Help me up."

The doctor tried to hold on to me while Nick tried to pull me up. I now knew what it felt like to be the rope in a tug of war. The agents took advantage of the tussle to leave us behind, getting a head start, no doubt hoping the action would be all over by the time we got things sorted out.

"I'm declining medical attention," I said, to make it official. If there was one thing the medical profession feared more than contagion, it was legal action. If I declined the doctor's help, he couldn't touch me, which he made immediately clear by leggoing Nick's Eggo.

I practically snapped to my feet, wobbling the whole way. The room spun around me and then stabilized. Like a 3D film without the glasses, everything had echo images, and they redoubled every time I refocused. I felt seasick.

"Let's go!" I said.

Nick kept hold of my arm, which was all that was holding me upright. Running *hurt*. My vision kept blacking out, swimming back into focus and then collapsing again. I felt more than saw the exit doors whoosh open ahead of us and hot air hit. Nick all but shoved me into the passenger's seat when we got to his rental car.

I closed my eyes and tried to breathe through the nausea, nearly losing it when something shook me hard. "Tori, stay with me. Don't go to sleep."

I opened my eyes, but the sun was right in them, stabbing jagged sun spears of pain up into my brain. I closed them again immediately. "Won't sleep, but can't see right now. Migraine."

"More like concussion," he answered. "I hope I'm doing the right thing."

"You are," I said. I tried to make it convincing. I didn't know what I thought. I could do in my condition, but Hades going after the compound was all my fault, and I had to help any way I could.

"Do you think they called ahead?" I asked, trying to remember the conversation that had gone on around me at the hospital.

"What?"

"To warn them. Do you think the Feds called the compound?"

"Do they have a phone?"

"The Feds?"

"The *Back to Earth* people."

"They must. Do you—" I hated to ask but, "—have Apollo on your phone?"

He didn't ask questions. "Yes," he said cautiously. "From the last time you were in trouble."

"Would you dial him for me?" Because right now I couldn't see clearly enough to tell which end of the phone was up. I wondered when my super healing was supposed to kick in. Had it been too long ago that I'd had the ambrosia? Had I taken too little?

I presumed from the small thing he'd pressed into my hand which was now ringing in my ear that his answer had been "yes."

"Tori?" Apollo answered instantly. "Where are you? What's going on?" Like he'd known it was me. Probably our damned mental connection.

"Hades?" he asked, after I told him. "*Skata*. That's bad news. How big a head start does he have?"

"How long since I was knocked out?" I asked Nick.

"Knocked out?" Apollo roared in my ear.

"Twenty minutes," Nick replied, "give or take."

"I'll meet you there," Apollo said, overhearing.

"Wait! That's not why I called. Do you have a number for Dionysus? He's got to get his people away to safety. If Hades comes with backup it's going to be a bloodbath."

"Dionysus is perfectly capable of using his followers for cannon fodder. You forget that we were in power during the time of sacrifices and tribute. Calling will only ensure an all-out war."

"Then what do we do?"

"I'll come up with something on the way."

"Great," I said unconvincingly. The phone rang in my hand as I hung up.

"How is she?" the voice asked. "*Where* is she? We went to meet you at the hospital, like you said, and you were gone. The staff will only tell us that she left against medical advice. I thought she was *fine*," Jesus said, putting his special emphasis on it.

"Jesus, it's me."

"*Dios gracias.* Wait a minute—you don't sound so good. Where are you? Are you … drunk?"

I guessed I could add slurring words to my blurred vision and crashing headache.

"Don't worry. Nick's got me. That's how I come to be answering his phone."

"Protective custody, that's what you need," Jesus sniffed.

I shot Nick a look. "Oh … right. Listen, we're a little busy right now." Trying to figure out how to stop an Olympian civil war. "Can we call you later?"

"Wait, boss lady—" I was already pulling the phone away from my ear when I thought I heard him say something about tying a cowbell around my neck. Yeah, like that would help.

"So, do we have a plan?" Armani asked as I hung up. "Apollo says he's working on it."

"*Great.*"

"Do *you* have a plan?"

"I'm working on it too."

"As long as we're all on the same page."

I ran over about a gazillion potential scenarios in my mind as we drove, but nothing prepared me for seeing the gates of the fenced-off complex crushed to the ground as though a Mack truck—or a three-headed dog the same size—had barreled right over them. Several feet of fence on the right-hand side had gone down with the gate. And there were bodies strewn across the yard. We could see them from just outside.

Armani stopped the car before we hit the fence, afraid he'd

drive over people along with the mesh if he continued. The Feds had apparently feared the same. Not one, but two dark, unmarked sedans also sat abandoned outside the gates. We jumped out, and I overran the fence on foot. I didn't see any bodies where I stepped, but just beyond lay a blonde woman whose hair had half escaped her ponytail to catch in the blood matting her face. I bent down to take her pulse and shook my head at Nick.

From the buildings to the left came a sound like gunfire, but my brain quickly processed with more clarity—something had cracked, all right, but it sounded more like wood, like something being put to use as a battering ram. There were screams and snarls.

I took off running in that direction, Nick hot on my heels. Any extra speed or prowess the ambrosia might have given me had been worn away by everything I'd already been through, most recently the concussion. My head felt like it would split every time a foot hit the ground. Any impact could crack me open like the San Andreas Fault. My vision was cutting in and out. I was running on instinct and adrenaline.

A body came flying out of the door of the guard shack or whatever I'd been trapped in last night and crashed to the ground in front of me with the fearful bonelessness of a rag doll. I vaulted it to get to the source of the trouble, suspecting the girl was already beyond help. But as if I had a third eye at the back of my head, I sensed Armani stop to offer aid. I hoped he didn't judge me and that there'd be a later when I could explain.

I was barely through the door when I was blown back by a gut-busting whack straight to the chest. It sent me flying. My healing ribs cracked. Pain exploded so that the impact of my butt with the ground barely registered. I was struggling to breathe, every inhale torture. A gurgle sounded with each exhale … not good. So not good.

I tried to blink my vision back into being, as if I was in any condition to avoid a threat even if I could see it coming. But the world had gone dark, like a stage when the show's over. I'd never been so afraid in my life.

Someone was calling my name. Or maybe it was "Toro!" and not "Tori"—someone wanting to play raging bull with whatever had smacked me around. I hadn't gotten a good look, but I suspected Cerberus's tail had delivered the whack that had sent me flying, which meant I hadn't even met the really dangerous end and already I was no match.

Someone grabbed for my jaw, and I gurgled something at him—probably blood. Then something was being shoved into my mouth, and I was choking. Or so I thought. There were definitely hands at my throat, but my breathing wasn't any worse than it had been … as if there was any room at all on the scale between "No breath" and "oblivion."

A strange tingle went through me, and my entire body arced up off the ground as the pain that hit doubled … quadrupled. I had a flash of vision. Two faces staring worriedly down at me. Two fallen angels. Eyes two impossible and entirely different shades of blue—midnight and Mediterranean. Then it was gone again, ripped away by pain. Every available nerve stolen away so that my body could scream with everything it had that Things Were Not All Right.

It went on forever … my forever … because I was sure at the end of it would come death. I even welcomed it. But when my round on the rack ended, I was left panting and spent. Distantly, I heard screams and forced my eyes open; those faces were still there. One looked anxious but relieved, the other relieved and furious all at once.

"What did you give her?" the furious face asked the other.

They had names. I knew they did. And they meant something to me, but right then it was as if my whole brain needed to reboot, like I had the files and the operating system, but couldn't remember how to make them work together.

"It's enough for you to know that she will be fine."

"It's that *stuff*, isn't it? The stuff I found in her fridge?"

"Do you think now is the time for this discussion?"

I gave up trying to think and decided just to act. I gritted my teeth, expecting pain, and found none as I sat up. There was a body beneath me, badly broken from what I could see, and in front of me—beyond the arguing men—was a doorway completely taken up with ... a gigantic dog's behind? Could it be?

I shook my head and it rattled my brains, but I was starting to remember—Apollo, Armani, Cerberus ...

The latter's back end was thrashing around like he was striking at something with his front, and I said, "Someone give me a gun."

That ended the argument. Both men stared down at me dumbfounded. "No gun?" I asked them.

Both shook their heads. "I don't even have my arrows," Apollo lamented. "Couldn't get them through airport security."

"There's always UPS," I said. But it was too late for that now. "Ideas?" I asked.

Both looked at me blankly.

"Right. Super."

I started to rise to my feet, but Armani jumped me ... and not in the good way.

"Where the hell do you think you're going? You nearly died."

I shoved his hands off and pointed to the downed girl beside me. "There was no 'nearly' for her."

I rose to my feet, tested their steadiness, so glad to have them under me again and my head and eyes in working order. Later I'd deal with the fact that Apollo had saved me—*again*—and that it was him I looked to, knowing without asking that we were on the same page. "Ready?"

He nodded.

I darted for that door, ready this time for the tail. I paused, watching the swing so that I could time it just right, and then I leapt, letting it catch me under the arms and hanging on for all I was worth. As it swung toward the body, I leapt, grabbing hanks of that thick, matted fur to use as handholds to pull myself up onto the beast's broad back. The hound shook like a dog after a bath, but I clung tightly and managed to hang on, even when the eau de pooch threatened to choke me all over again. But that was the least of my worries. I was most afraid one of the heads would snap back for me at any second, but now that I had the high "ground" I could see why they weren't.

Men and women lay scattered about the floor in front of Cerberus like discarded dolls, but a woman I'd never seen before still stood facing off with him. Her hair was wild and white, lighter in color even than her wheat-toned cult clothes. Her eyes were equally wild, but contrastingly dark and not the least sane-looking. One of Cerberus's heads was lashed to the floor by some kind of thick green rope, but the others still snapped at her as she faced him fearlessly. I yelled at the woman to run, but she ignored me, raising empty arms toward the beast and chanting furiously. She had to be crazy to choose prayer over retreat, I thought, but suddenly Cerberus shook again, more violently. Terrified, I hunkered down, holding on for dear life. It was then I realized that it wasn't *him* shaking, but the ground. Something erupted through the floorboards ... A vine. Thick and shiny, growing as it erupted like Jack's beanstalk.

Cerberus snapped at it, snarling and lunging suddenly, so that I almost lost my seat. I clamped down with my legs and held tight to keep from falling. The left head noticed me then and looked back, baring its fangs, but the middle head gave a yelp of startled pain and its partner whipped back around to bite at the vine that had wrapped itself around the central mouth. As it got close, a tendril from the vine snaked out and drove itself right up into one exposed nostril. The head reared back, howling pain, nearly deafening me.

I looked at the crazy woman with new respect. No mere mortal then. *Demeter?*

"Where's Persephone?" I asked. "Hades is here for her."

"He has her already," Demeter shouted so that she could be

heard over Cerberus's increasingly panicked noises. Her mad eyes met mine. "Karacis girl?" she asked, as if confirming something she already knew. "Your grandfather was a good man. You find Persephone and bring her back for me and I won't have to take your world apart to do it myself."

"My world?" I asked, voice strangled.

"All the current entrances and exits to Hades's realm are protected against us gods. I'd have to make my own. It would be ... messy."

One of Cerberus's heads got free and he lunged forward to snap at her again. I used their mutual distraction to slide down off Cerberus's back. Strong hands caught me as I landed, and I looked up into Armani's killer blue eyes, shaded by his dark brows and overhanging thatch of hair.

Neither man had been able to get past Cerberus's big ol' butt.

Gunfire sounded back in the compound, rapid, like in a frightened burst. "The agents!" Damn, I'd forgotten all about them. I should have known Hades would've come in full force, not just a man and his dog.

Apollo took the lead, racing in the direction from which we'd heard the shots, but Armani and I weren't far behind.

We burst on to a scene behind the buildings that looked like something out of a horror film. An entire pack of dogs, dark as nightmares, were chasing people through the vineyards. As I watched, one overtook a young man and pounced on his back, driving him to the ground and out of my sight. I couldn't bear to think what might happen next. Only Rosen seemed to be still standing, defending a woman and a group of frightened kids who were pinned down against one of the longhouses. He was backed up with them, firing away at the dogs taking turns drawing fire and darting in. The bullets didn't seem to have an effect.

Apollo put two fingers to his mouth and gave an ear-piercing whistle. Immediately, every hellhound froze, their ears pricked forward and heads turned his way. Then he did something that shocked the hell out of me—and them too. He began singing. *Singing.* To the dogs. In the middle of a massacre.

Well, he *was* the god of music, and they did say it soothed the savage beast, but … I'd never thought of putting it to the test. Certainly not in the middle of a battlefield. Of course, *my* singing would be more likely to incite than stop a riot.

But Apollo's voice … it was … there were no words. Painfully beautiful. Haunting. The song was something like a dirge mixed with the hope of Heaven … or the Elysian Fields. It made you want to cry and laugh and fall to your knees and rejoice all at once. I'd never heard Apollo sing before, and it was … transformative.

I didn't know what Armani saw in my face, but when he clamped his hands over my ears, I nearly took him down. Hard.

Instead, I chopped his hands away by throwing mine up between them and rounded on him.

"*What* is your problem?" I demanded.

His eyes bored straight into me. He was that intense. "You looked mesmerized, and we've still got a god to find and a girl to save, from what I've overheard."

My face flamed. "Right."

Only I had no idea where to start.

On the last lingering note of Apollo's song, the dogs all dropped to the ground, dead or dead asleep, then faded away before our eyes. Just … gone. I tried not to look on Apollo as … well, as a god.

"Where did they go?" I asked, not looking at him directly. I wasn't sure I could do it and keep my distance. I wanted … but I couldn't have.

"They are nightmares made flesh," he said. "And when *they* dream, it's not of this place. They've gone back where they came from. Hades has what he wants. I don't think they'll be back."

"They didn't leave when he did," I pointed out.

"No," Armani said grimly. "He wanted Dionysus's people to suffer for his loss."

"We can't let him win," I said. "We have to find Persephone. Demeter's threatened all kinds of chaos if she isn't found."

"No more than Hades, from what you've told me," Apollo answered.

Armani gave me a *look*. He'd only just heard everything in the car on the way, which meant he knew I'd confided in Apollo first. But it hadn't been like that.

"Hold it right there!" Rosen shouted at us.

Other agents were closing in now, herding people who'd run off into the fields or hidden in other buildings. I saw no sign of Dionysus, but someone had obviously called for an ambulance or three, because now that Apollo's song had ended, I could hear the sirens. So close. They'd be here any second, and from the number of bodies *not* rising from the ground to be rounded up by the Feds, they were going to be needed … or well beyond being needed by some.

Hades was going to have a hell of a head start by the time we extricated ourselves from all this. And he'd have the home court advantage. I didn't even have the directions to get onto the field.

"Do you think the … food additives will help them?" I asked Apollo, eyes still on the downed cultists.

"Some," he said. "It depends on how their bodies are holding up to it and what changes were—"

Rosen was right up on us now, and Apollo clammed up.

"What the *hell* is going on? Invisible assailants, ghoulish great Danes. I'm sure I even saw some ladies rip one to shreds with their bare hands. No one is going anywhere until I get some answers."

"You can't handle the truth," Armani said under his breath.

"Try me."

We all looked at each other, and Rosen stepped in the midst of us. "No!" he said. "No eye contact. No getting your stories straight. If this is some kind of doomsday cult, it's the damndest thing I've ever seen. And I've seen some strange things."

Paramedics flooded around us, and still Rosen held our gazes, one right after another, and wouldn't let us move.

We had only one hope that I could see of making him believe and convincing him to let us go while there was still time to catch up with Persephone's kidnapper. "Follow me," I said.

He gave me a hard look, as though sure I was up to something. Another agent came running up, whispered something in Rosen's ear. His face went angry/sad at the same time. Whatever he'd heard, I was pretty sure someone was going to pay. "Handle it," he snapped. "I'll be there as soon as I can. *Show me*," he said to us.

I swallowed hard, nodded and led the way—back to the guardhouse and Demeter and, hopefully, a three-headed dog still wrapped up in magically growing vines.

I led the way, but Rosen kept Apollo and Armani in his sights as well, and brought up the rear. All was eerily quiet in the guard shack as we approached, to the point where I had a sinking suspicion that we were going to find it empty, Cerberus vanished like the hellhounds. But just inside the open door was a great big furry butt, smelling of wet dog fur and sulfur. Such a lovely mix. The tail was still, and the great hound let out such a snore as we approached that it rattled the building around him.

I could just see the tops of his three enormous heads settled on his front paws. No surprise, I suppose, that at least one of them snored. Demeter, however, *had* vanished.

"What the *hell* is that?" Rosen asked, but not entirely like he didn't know.

More like he needed confirmation to truly believe.

"Well, you had it in one. *Hell.* What you saw outside were what you'd probably call hellhounds, but what we like to call the hounds of Hades. *This* is Cerberus. He's sort of the watchdog of the underworld."

Rosen looked to Apollo and Armani to see if I might be

pulling his leg. Neither cracked a smile. Apollo nodded. Armani looked bemused, like he was seeing what he himself looked like the first time *he'd* heard about all the insanity. "But ..." Rosen stepped forward, hand outstretched, to touch the beast's flank when the building rattled again, and he froze. "How on earth do I—"

"Animal Control?" I suggested. "And an elephant stampede's worth of tranquilizers."

"But—"

"Don't you have a *division* to deal with this sort of thing?" I knew there had to be something, because Zeus and Poseidon were still in custody, and I didn't think that was just good fortune. If they wanted to bust out, they had ways, and no namby-pamby prison was going to keep them in line. Oh sure, the gods had lost a lot of their power when they'd lost their worship long ago, but things like *Xena*, *Clash of the Titans*, Percy Jackson and even Yiayia's *Goddities* website kept them alive enough in peoples' minds and hearts to feed them a certain amount of strength. If only they'd use it for good. But the gods always had been petty.

"Don't you get it yet?" Rosen asked. "Why we've been investigating? Why we've been interested in your cases?" He looked around to see who might be close enough to listen in and, finding no one, continued. "*Power* we've seen—remote viewers, clairvoyants, telemetrics who can't move anything bigger than a bread box. Not much more than sideshow stuff. But *this*—three-headed dogs that can be sung to sleep. Hell, you say?"

So he wasn't just a spy guy, he was a spook. It explained so much. But it didn't bode well for actually blowing his mind. He wouldn't mentally explain away any of the weirdness. No, he'd want to *investigate*.

I'd said too much already. "Look, we have to go. Someone's life depends on it."

"I can't let you do that. You need to be debriefed. We need to be fully in the loop. If someone's life is at stake, you tell us, we'll handle it." Wasn't. Gonna. Happen. They had procedures and protocols … and no idea what they were dealing with.

"Rosen?" I said, making sure he met my eyes.

"What?"

"Freeze."

I put everything I had into it and saw his eyes go slightly panicked, but they didn't widen. Didn't *move*. And neither did the rest of him.

"Let's go," I said to Armani and Apollo.

I didn't run away. That would be too obvious. But I walked quickly. With purpose. Armani cursed and followed, Apollo silently taking up my left flank.

"I hope you know what you're doing," Armani murmured.

"And that I didn't just screw up your career," I added, something I should have thought about earlier. But what else could I do? Lead the government straight to the secret of gods among us? What would they do with that kind of information? Or to control that kind of power? They might consider it a national resource to be harnessed for the greater good. Armani aside, I never had really trusted people in power. Maybe it was all those stories of gods and demigods using people like playthings. I wanted to believe it could be different, but look at what I did with my one and only power. I used it to stop men in their tracks, and not just the bad ones. *I* decided when it was convenient for someone else to be subject to my will or free to act.

With paramedics now dashing back the way they'd come with those who could be saved and the Feds either interrogating witnesses or caught up in a turf war with the local law enforcement that had arrived, we made it back to the car. One officer tried to stop us as we pulled out, but Armani flashed his badge, and even though he had no jurisdiction or even standing here, it was enough for the officer to let us go.

"Where to?" Apollo asked as we were cruising down the long drive, going the speed limit or a little below to look like law-abiding citizens, certainly *not* fleeing the scene of a massacre.

"I was hoping you knew."

"Knew what?"

"Paths to the underworld, the closest entrance."

He took his eyes off the road to stare at me in the rearview mirror. In deference to his longer legs and my guilt over various Apollo-directed thoughts, I'd given Armani the shotgun seat.

"*Seriously?* First you think all Olympians have each other on speed dial, and now you think I'm on the VIP list for Club Hades? You have a better chance getting the intel from your crazy grandmother than with me."

"So you *do* know my grandmother."

I'd wondered at times, the way she always seemed to know everything about everybody. I knew she had a secret source, sure, but in the way of secrets, I didn't know *who* it was.

"Tori, we may not all know each other, at least not on sight, but we *all* know your grandmother. She's ..."

"Crazy?" I asked, using his word.

"Yeah, that," he said unapologetically. "You know, when you and I were seen together last year, she threatened to put my address and unlisted phone number on the web and sell it to those people who make maps of the stars' homes."

"Like they don't have it already?" I scoffed.

"You ever been on one of their self-guided tours? It's all stars' former homes or whatnot. They don't want to be liable for any psycho stalkers getting ideas."

"Well, there you go—they wouldn't use it anyway. It's an empty threat."

"The point is that she *had* the info to begin with. Your Yiayia is a scary woman."

He had a point there ... a very good one.

"You have her number saved?" I asked. At some point, I was going to *have* to replace my phone.

He sighed and handed me his, still all warm from his pocket.

"*Egona,*" Yiayia answered on the first ring. "I have been

calling you all night. Where have you been? And why are you calling from *His* phone?"

"How did you know it was me?" I asked suspiciously.

"*He* wouldn't call, but you … is there something going on? Is he there with you?" She lowered her voice as if she might be overheard.

"Yes and yes, but it's not what you think. I need to know—are there any paths into the underworld near Napa or San Francisco?"

Dead silence. "*Egona*, you are not going there. Tell me you are not going there."

I turned toward the window so that neither of the guys could see my face as I prepared to lie to my grandmother, just in case I had a tell. "Okay, I'm not going there."

"You know what happened to Orpheus when he tried to rescue Eurydice," she continued, clearly not believing me.

"Nothing happened to Orpheus," I answered. "Eurydice got sucked back into the underworld when he turned back to look at her."

Yiayia snorted. "That's the fairy tale version. Orpheus never made it home, not in one piece. He broke the deal he'd made with Hades. Some accounts say he committed suicide, but truly, his soul stayed behind in forfeit, and his body couldn't live long without it."

Oh, joy.

"Yiayia, I won't look back."

"So you say."

"Yiayia, if you don't tell me, I'll just find out for myself."

I could practically hear her thinking. "First, you tell *me* everything. There have been rumors of a three-headed dog …"

I debated. Rosen was already going to be furious with me when he snapped out of his paralysis, as he no doubt had by now. If I exposed his X-file to the world, would he use it as an excuse to lock me up and throw away the key, maybe citing something like a threat to national security?

But what if she could help?

"Yiayia, what would happen if the other gods found out, say, that one group was trying to create a new pantheon, like Latter-Day Olympians?"

I couldn't even hear her breathe on the other end of the line. "Who?" she demanded.

"What would happen?" I repeated.

"What could happen? Who could stop them? Zeus and Poseidon are in jail; Hades is all caught up with Persephone. Who is left?"

I looked to Apollo.

"It's all up to us, isn't it?" he asked. "Rescue Persephone, stop the cult?"

I nodded mutely.

"Good," he said. "You'll get to see my heroic side."

Nick shot him a look that, had it missed, would have melted the safety glass window beyond him. "I'll remind you … once. Boyfriend, right here. Badge and gun. Licensed to carry."

"But you're not carrying *now*, are you?"

"I don't need a gun to take you down," Nick growled. Apollo didn't dignify that with a response.

"Guys, as much as I appreciate the dick waving—and I do— we've got bigger things to think about here." They both grinned at that.

On the phone, Yiayia snorted, reminding me that she could overhear everything.

"Yiayia, save me," I said. "Tell me where around here I can find an entry to the underworld."

"W-e-l-l, I don't know specifically. It's never been a regular interest of mine, but the conspiracy boards have been abuzz lately about a few things."

"Conspiracy boards?"

"A woman needs a hobby. Besides, often there's some method to the madness. You'd be amazed how many leads …"

So if the conspiracy boards were a hobby, what was her Olympian obsession? A life's calling? Scary.

"Yiayia, *what* leads?"

She huffed. "Since I knew you were out there, I've been paying special attention to the San Francisco area. There've been a few rumors. For one, that Alcatraz is haunted."

"Old news," I cut in.

"Hush or I won't tell you more. A three-headed monster menacing the streets."

"Cerberus," Apollo said unnecessarily.

"And the Wave Organ picking up what sounds like a domestic dispute from the center of the earth. Very Jules Verne."

"What?" I asked, suddenly interested.

"Wave Organ?" asked Armani.

Apollo just nodded, like it all made perfect sense.

"I Googled it," she said, clearly proud of her accomplishment. "According to Alcaspaz2000, it's this amazing sculpture park on a jetty in the San Francisco bay, where the artist engineered tubes that lead into the underground caverns or straight into the bay and act like giant sea shells, where you can hear the sounds of the deep."

"Why don't I know about this place?" I asked.

"Because it's neither a mystery nor a man," she said matter-of-factly.

My face flamed. Both men smirked at me in the rearview mirror, and I vowed to buy Yiayia a muzzle for her next birthday. Not that she'd wear it.

"Wanna start a conspiracy theory?" I asked, trying to deflect, but also inspired. "Tell everyone to stay away from Back to Earth products and The Rustic Potato. They have dangerous additives. People have gotten ill … or addicted."

"Is this true?" she asked in horror.

"One hundred percent."

"I'll need specifics to make it convincing."

"I'll put someone in touch." And I would, if Alonzo and his

sister were up for another interview. "Thank you, Yiayia. I'll let you know how it all works out."

"Stay safe," she ordered. "And you two—" She raised her voice until it bounced around the car like an echo chamber. "You see that she comes home safe *or else*."

The look the men exchanged was still more glare than glance, but they said in stereo, "Yes, Yiayia."

She disconnected.

I tried to hide my amusement.

Armani wrecked the moment by asking suddenly, "Is it getting really dark outside or is it just me?"

The question had to be rhetorical, because there was no way he needed confirmation of what was perfectly clear. Or rather, perfectly *un*clear. The sky *had* darkened, thick steel-wool clouds moving in to blot out the sun. I'd been so focused on talking to Yiayia I'd never even noticed. A flashbulb of light went off out the left side window, just caught in my peripheral vision. I turned too late to catch the freaky fork of lightning, but only a few heartbeats later thunder rocked the car.

"Demeter mourning her daughter's abduction," Apollo said, at the same time Nick kicked in. "Ten Mississippi. It's about two miles away."

"I thought lightning was Zeus's bailiwick."

"She can make sure the conditions are right for it," Apollo said grimly.

"She said she'd give us time," I protested.

"Did she say how much?"

We were all silent at that, which made the shock of a sheet of water hitting our windshield that much more deafening. There were no warning droplets. It was more like someone had simply thrown several buckets full of water straight at our car. The heavens had opened like a sluice gate.

We fishtailed down the street. Apollo cursed and struggled for control of the car as the fishtail threatened to morph into a full on spin out. The back of the car seemed to want to overtake the front.

"You want us to get your daughter back, you have to *stop* trying to kill us," I yelled at the heavens.

Both men winced at the volume in the small car, but miraculously—or maybe just coincidentally—the rain slacked off from deluge to downpour.

"Thank you," I said, just in case Demeter was actually listening.

"It's like déjà vu all over again," Nick said. He was thinking, like I was, about the night we'd gone up against Poseidon and Zeus. We'd survived that. Demeter's hissy fit probably wasn't going to destroy us, but I didn't want to take the risk.

"Underground caves, possibly with under*water* entrances are going to be pretty treacherous if this continues," Apollo said.

"Maybe it's localized," I answered hopefully.

"We can hope."

"We're going to need supplies," Nick cut in. "Unless you can make like Aquaman and call fish to our aid or whatever. We're going to need special equipment, a map of the caverns as accurate as possible. We can't just rush in."

"Give me my phone," Apollo said, reaching a hand back for it.

"You're *driving*," I pointed out. And given the slick streets, I didn't really want him dividing his attention.

"Fine. Call Hermes. He delivers everything to everybody all over the world. He'll be able to put us in touch with someone who can get us what we need." Hermes being helpful? I'd never even considered the possibility.

"You sure he'll help?"

"A potential war brewing between Hades and Demeter, possibly pulling in Dionysus, you, me, your boyfriend …" Petty emphasis on the *boy*, although Nick was hardly that, though if we were comparing our lives to the centuries Apollo'd lived, I guessed I was a mere child as well. "He'd probably pay for front row seats. Chaos is kind of his thing," he reminded me.

"But he runs a worldwide business. That's got to take organization."

"Even Hitler made the trains run on time," Apollo said, "and he was about the most destructive force I've ever seen."

"Mercury wasn't …" I couldn't even finish the thought.

"In character at the time? No, but it wouldn't surprise me if he'd been somewhere behind the scenes. Manning the supply lines at the very least."

"Great galloping gorgons."

Apollo smirked. "I like that one, you should keep it."

"Thanks."

Nick cleared his throat to break up the moment. "Hate to intrude, but *rescue mission*. Special equipment, phone call to make, caves to spelunk."

I blushed and looked down at the phone, because Nick was right. Apollo and I had been having a moment. There'd been too many of those lately, and that was dangerous. I felt like a shit over it, but I'd been right before. After this was over, no more contact. It was the only way. I didn't trust my willpower.

Apollo called his people, who called other people, and inside a half hour we were in a dive shop being outfitted in wetsuits and warnings. According to the pros, we were either: A: crazy—the weather made visibility nearly nil and the churning waves would be doing their best to smack us up against the rocks, or B: suicidal—neither Nick nor I were scuba trained, so they refused to rent us *that* equipment … something about licenses being revoked. We'd be counting on whatever breath we could take on the way down and our senses of direction to find the way back up for more. It was easy to become confused with no visibility to light the way back to the surface.

Apollo couldn't come with. As he explained in the car, Hades had his kingdom warded against other gods. Humans not so much. If a soul wandered in unannounced, well, it was just too bad for them. One more subject to add to his rolls. But a *god*, that was a clear threat and distinctly unwelcome. Whether an Olympian wanted to rescue a lost love—their loves were always falling prey to this misfortune or that wrongful death—or stage a hostile takeover, any infiltration was seen as an act of aggression and treated with extreme prejudice.

Apollo's presence would only make ours completely conspicuous … and actionable. I didn't realize until he said it how much I'd come to count on his backup. Now was a good time to start tapering off my Apollo addiction. He promised to keep an eye on things topside so that we wouldn't emerge into an ambush. It was something anyway.

We were quiet on the ride to the Wave Organ jetty. Even with the GPS on Apollo's phone confidently spitting out directions in a voice that seemed specially chosen to give geek boys wet dreams, I wondered whether we were on the right track. I didn't see a thing as we approached but a discreet sign and a parking area long before we hit the end of the jetty. From here it looked like any other—a spit of land jutting out into the San Francisco bay, the skyline of the city off in the distance on another, much larger, spit of land. I guess I'd expected to see, well, something like a pipe organ, now that I thought about it, rising from the earth like a churchly instrument and sounding like whale or dolphin song.

Apollo pulled off into the parking area where only three other cars sat. "This is it?" Nick asked, as if we had the answers.

"I guess so. They probably have people park here to keep the car sounds from interfering with the ambience," I said. I sounded half-convincing even to myself.

We got out. Armani and I hefted our dive packs onto our shoulders, even though Apollo tried to take mine from me, and started trudging down the jetty. Despite the lack of cars in the lot, the path was well trod. Not paved, exactly, but sand, shell and stone had been compressed almost to the point of concrete.

I kept waiting for some monumental construction to come

into view, but we were almost to the end of the jetty when instead I saw cut stone stairs leading downward. We took them, and I caught my breath as we descended into ruins … or anyway, a sculpture park made to look like ruins. Artfully tumbled stones, terraced walls with wildflowers and weeds growing up between them. It looked like a cross between an old armory and a Greek temple. Doric columns here and there, half crumbled or carved into the stone walls should have contrasted with the rest of the feel, but strangely they seemed in harmony with the site. But more than that, they gave me the strong sense that we were in the right place. There was no point at all to those columns in this place unless they'd been inspired, consciously or unconsciously.

The breeze whipped my dark hair across my face, saturating it as well so that the strands bound together into a lash. I spat the hair out as it flew into my mouth before gathering it up and twisting it into a knot at the base of my neck that I knew wouldn't hold. It never did. But it would give me a temporary reprieve so that I could listen.

The whole place was the organ. Among the ruins, pipes stuck out like gun muzzles or canon barrels, and I realized that was what had given me the impression of an armory. I tried to tune out the wind and listen for the sound of the sea, which was all around us. The pipes acted as speakers, amplifying the music of the deep, some sounding like, yes, whale or dolphin song, others as though the sea breathed into underground cave entrances like a flutist into his instrument. Only the sound was deeper than a flute. More melodic than a tuba. It was a sound all its own. I was entranced. Whoever had built the wave organ was a genius. There'd been a sign back toward the stairs that had probably said, and I vowed to pay more attention on the way out, assuming I was in any condition to do so.

"Everybody pick a pipe," Nick directed, "and start listening."

I gave him a saucy salute, even though I'd been about to suggest the same thing.

My first two tubes were a wash—like holding giant seashells up to my ears. Beautiful but completely unhelpful. I was about to move on to the third when Apollo announced, "I've got something."

Nick was closest, and he got there first. The look of concentration on his face as he listened was nearly comical, only I didn't laugh. I hadn't been in water, beyond the daily shower, since I'd nearly been drowned by the twin of the Creature from the Black Lagoon just weeks ago. Oh sure, I visited the beach, but I stayed well away from the surf. When I needed to cool down, I went with a rum punch.

Creature—Glaucus—was no longer a threat, but he had friends. He was far from the only water divinity, none of whom were happy with me after my part in taking down Poseidon. If they came gunning for me … well, water wasn't exactly my element. I preferred the much more breathable air.

"Let me listen," I ordered, pushing Nick gently out of the way. He went, but not far, standing beside me with a dazed expression on his face. He'd been exposed to enough weirdness now that he *knew*. He believed, but every once in a while, the evidence still seemed to strike him dumb.

There were definite voices, raised, heated. But what they were saying wasn't immediately clear. There was too much interference.

"Can you make it out?" I asked the men.

"It's all Greek to me," Nick quipped.

"Really?" I asked. "You really went there?"

He just shrugged. In all honesty, it'd been bound to come out some time. I stuck my tongue out at him.

"You know, I have better uses for that," he said, leering.

"It's an argument," Apollo cut in. "A lot of name-calling. Nothing helpful like 'it's too bad we've left the north gate unguarded.'"

No, of course not, because that would be too easy.

"Any way of tracking where this tube goes?" I asked, but not with any real hope.

All three of us tracked with our eyes where the pipe disappeared into the ground.

"Not without schematics," Apollo answered.

"Then I guess we're going in."

There was a family of four roaming the ruins, two kids under ten having a field day climbing the rocks, and a lone fisherman casting his line, probably futilely, into the turbulent waters. I didn't see any sign of whoever might belong to the third car. Of those I did see, none looked terribly interested in us until we started stripping down to our bathing suits, purchased at the dive shop on Apollo's titanium card, in prep for getting into the wetsuits that would protect us from the cold. At that point, the father of the family kept an eye on us, part suspicion and part interest, I guessed, from the way his wife playfully swatted him when she saw him staring our way. She caught my eye and shrugged, like "men, can't take them anywhere." I smiled back. It helped distract me from what we were about to do.

Mostly, though, a nearly naked Nick was distraction enough. Because the man was *fine*. His shoulders were every bit as broad as Apollo's. *Damn*, I immediately killed the comparison. His chest was peppered with dark hair that only seemed to emphasize his abs. His really rock hard abs, as I had reason to know. His legs were about as finely formed as those of a marble statue. I couldn't help but watch as he tucked himself inside his suit and had to squelch the urge to offer my assistance. I don't think his suit would fit any better for my contribution.

Apollo watched it all in silence, then looked away, purposefully looking *anywhere* else, scanning the horizon.

"The storm is headed this way," he reported ominously. "You'd better go now, while things are relatively calm."

"Ready?" Nick asked.

"No, you?"

"Hell no."

"Great, let's do this."

I fastened the latch on my utility belt, trying to tell myself I felt like Batman with my dive knife, spear gun and other suddenly inadequate-seeming gear we'd picked up at the shop.

We carried our flippers and walked barefoot over to the closest entrance to the water from the tube we were interested in. The stones beneath our feet were cool enough to numb them ... or maybe that was fear giving me cold feet. When we were right up on the water, Nick and I sat to put on the flippers, and the father came up to talk to us.

"You sure you want to do that?" he asked. "In *this* weather?"

The splash as Nick hit the water made me jump, but I slid my mask into place to follow him in before I could come to my senses, leaving Apollo to answer for us.

The water hit me like a Heimlich, nearly shocking the breath I'd taken right out of me. Unlike footy pajamas, wetsuits didn't cover *everything*, and the areas of exposure were enough to rip away at my body heat. I knew wetsuits were about protecting core temperature, and that I'd get used to the cold, but in the meantime ... *day-um*!

Nick turned to smile at me before breaching the surface for a new breath. I did the same, catching the tail end of his "Whoo hoo!"

I didn't have the breath to answer it, so I just tried and failed to smile back before pointing back down. Nick winked and dove back under. I took off after him.

The masks made things as clear as possible. As long as we stayed close, we could see each other, though silt floated between us, and very little light penetrated. It was easy enough, anyway, to tell which way was back to shore, because the waves wanted to smack us right into it. We swam down deeper, arms close to our sides to streamline ourselves and kicking hard, but I couldn't sustain it. I was afraid to smack head first into something I couldn't see, and had to reach out, slowing myself. We bumped around and resurfaced, explored crevices that went so far and no farther, found the outlets to some of the pipes, covered over with mesh to keep anything from swimming in and getting trapped inside. I'd just felt a strange current I wanted to follow, something that seemed to suck at me and only reluctantly give back when the water ebbed away in the traditional flow pattern when my air gave up. As I breached the surface, Nick was just diving again. I took a deep breath and chased him, tapping his foot and miming for him to follow me with the hand signs we'd been taught at the dive shop. He nodded and changed directions, following me.

Instinctively, I found the current again and followed it as far as I could with my hands. It was big enough, I thought, to follow whole hog … or whole PI anyway. The risk was that I might go too far and not be able to make it back to the surface in time. I'd faced the fear intentionally, waiting for my precognition to go off with sirens wailing, but nothing happened, which I took to be a good sign.

I signaled. I was going in. Nick grabbed my mask and shook his head, the universal sign for *oh* hell *no*. But this was what we were here for. I nodded and shook him off. Probably I could have used a fresh breath, but the mystery was calling to me, and I had to follow.

I kicked furiously, leading with my hands to keep myself out of trouble, but I didn't hit anything. It was dark now. I reached for a dive light at my belt and turned it on, aiming it before me, but all I could see was silt and, beyond, darkness.

Still, the push of that current, like a hand to my back, kept me going. Armani swam up beside me, and I had a moment to fear for him. He'd dived before I had and would run out of air that much sooner. Already, my lungs felt squeezed, as if the lack of air was creating a vacuum. I desperately wanted to take a breath to fill it but couldn't. Instead, I kept swimming dead ahead. There were no alarms but my own panic. We'd be okay. I had to believe that.

Spots started to swim in front of my eyes, blotting out the

silt, darker than the darkness, and then I felt something change. To the right, the water was … colder. I should have been too numb to notice the difference, but … I turned toward it, hoping Nick followed, trying to signal him with the light I could myself barely see. It was getting hard to hold in what breath I still had, harder still to move, but I forced myself. It was easier to kick my legs than move my arms, which floated uselessly now at my sides. And then even they stopped. I began to float upward. Up, up … or maybe down? I didn't know. My eyes closed, and I thought that it was peaceful here. Like the wave organ up above. A watery grave.

There was still no panic. Peace, acceptance, but no panic.

Then I broke the surface of the water, and the breath I'd held gave out. My mouth gasped open, and no water flooded in. It took me a sluggish second to grasp that fact, certain it was a dying dream, but beside me was another gasp, and then a choking, coughing fit. Nick!

I blinked away the spots before my eyes, but they weren't so easily moved. They continued here, but around them I could begin to see things in the faint glow of my dive light. We were in an underground cave. Honestly, it looked like something out of Scooby Doo, where they'd find glowing webbed footprints or a guy in a sea monster suit. The roof of the cave wasn't high above our heads, but high enough to let us breathe and look around a bit.

I pointed Nick in the direction the water seemed to want to flow, and he nodded. Neither of us wasted the breath that suddenly seemed very precious. We swam on top of the water instead of under it until we came to a kind of shelf where the cave seemed to balloon up and out and where we could pull ourselves out of the water. My muscles were shaking almost too much to accomplish the job, but I managed with a strong kick to gracelessly flop myself onto the shelf like a beached whale. Nick's exit wasn't much better, and we both lay there for a minute just breathing, oxygenating our muscles so they'd support us when we decided to rise again.

He looked at me and rolled to brush a long strand of hair out of my face. I'd been trying to work up the energy to do it myself. "I take you to *all* the best places," he said.

I laughed and coughed.

"When you said *underworld*, I thought you were talking about the movie," I quipped when I could talk again.

"Fiction, bah," he answered. "I prefer the source material." Then we heard it … *them*. Voices. Bouncing around like pinballs. "—don't want to be here when she does," a voice was saying.

Hades.

I strained to figure out directionality.

"That way," Nick said, sitting up and pointing. Break time was over.

"You sure?" I asked.

"Eagle Scout," he announced proudly. "I'm sure."

My muscles shook and threatened failure, but I managed to sit slowly and creak to my feet. I kicked off the fins and grabbed for the small spear gun at my belt.

"Let's go."

Nick didn't like the idea of me leading, but he'd seen the gorgon glare in action, and he knew what it could do.

I crept forward, pointing the dive light at the cave floor, afraid to send it out ahead of us and alert anyone to our presence.

But I didn't think they were too worried. Hades wasn't just making plans to bug out and fall back to his well-defended stronghold, he was giving orders to collapse the tunnels behind them.

The same tunnels we were in.

Nick and I shared a glance, and I shut off the light. We were close enough to the source of the voices that it could give us away.

Blind, we had only our hearing. We moved ahead. I couldn't see Nick, and he was quiet enough, but not so quiet, as close as we were, that I couldn't hear him moving beside me. The air seemed to shift ahead of us, take a dogleg, and I reached out to confirm the impression with my hands. Sure enough.

"Left," I whispered to Nick. It was eerie, but I could almost feel his nod.

Left it was, and only a few steps before I heard a low rumbling growl. Then another. And a third.

Cerberus, back where he belonged? Hellhounds? We should have come armed with Scooby Snacks, not spears. My warning system flared up. Actually, it had been trying to get my attention since we'd gone dark. But at first it had been polite, like a tapping on my shoulder. Now it was a cattle prod to the heart, sending volts of electricity through me, trying to goose me into flight. *Away* it seemed to say. *Ahead there be dragons.* Or at least their canine equivalents.

I ignored it.

"You can't!" Persephone pleaded ahead of us, off to the left. "Thanatos, you can't do it! Listen to me, I'm your *mother*."

"Yes, but he's my Lord."

There was the sound of a slap, of flesh hitting flesh hard enough to leave a mark, and a woman cried out.

"Silence," Hades bellowed. "You've done enough on your own. Now you encourage mutiny?"

I'd heard all I needed to hear. Hades and Persephone were not alone. At the very least, Thanatos was with them. And canine companions. We were beyond outnumbered, but we'd known that was likely going in.

The growls rose in volume, became ominous, and caught Hades's attention. "You hear something boys?" he asked. "Go— hunt!" Over the sudden sharp baying of the hounds we heard him order Thanatos, "Set the charges."

CHAPTER FOURTEEN

"Bravery is being too stupid to know fear. Courage is standing firm in the very face of it."
—Christos Karacis

The precog kick to my chest urged me to run, but I stood my ground, aiming my spear gun for the point where I thought the dogs would appear. I let my hearing guide my aim on my first shot and released the bolt. A yelp upon impact nearly deafened me, bouncing around the caves and battering my ears from all sides. Beside me, Nick yelled, "Close your eyes!"

It was immediately followed by a sizzle as he lit up a flare, which ... *flared* into life, lighting up the room beyond my lids, which I'd gotten shut just in time. The dogs howled in distress and seemed to stop their rush. If sound could be trusted, one even slid into another, sending them sprawling across the floor. But I couldn't keep my eyes shut for long. I was going to have to let them adjust before the dogs' did or I'd be a sitting duck.

I blinked away the tears that formed at the pain of the sudden brightness after all the dark and looked toward the hounds. Away from the flare. One was already shaking its head, trying to clear its vision to focus in on us. The other two were getting to their feet, lips pulled back from their teeth to show wicked-sharp canines bared against us.

I reached for another bolt, but didn't have time to load it before the closest hound leapt for me.

"Freeze!" I ordered, terrified, staring straight into its hellfire eyes, but it was already in midair, and while its snarl did seem to freeze on its face, its momentum carried it on. I dove to the side to escape the landing but it struck me a glancing blow that sent me crashing to the ground and the spear gun clattering out of my hands. The beast landed hard, but I could hear the other two going wild to take advantage of its felled prey … me.

Nick gave a huge battle cry, and I spun on the ground, already getting my feet under me. Trying to find the lost gun would cost me time I didn't have. I reached for my fairly impressive dive knife. Nick was brandishing the flare, trying to drive the dogs back, but they snapped at it, barely intimidated. One caught it in his jaws, and shook it like an animal, trying to break its spine. The light went out, and I heard the broken flare hit the floor off to the right.

I feared the darkness would give all the advantage to the hellhounds. My mental alarm bells were ringing, and for a millisecond, I thought my ears were playing tricks on me, as a whistle sounded back from where the hounds had come, and I thought I heard them drop, one woofing in protest. And then light flared again, and standing there in the entrance deeper into the cave, with the dogs heeling at his feet like hunting hounds at rest, was a tall young man with ice in his eyes and hellfire like a small sun cupped in his hands. Thanatos, I thought at first, without his trademark cape and cowl, but then I realized that it wasn't quite right. No, Thanatos must have gone to set the charges. At a guess, we were facing his brother Hypnos, rumored to be his near spitting image. His hair stuck straight up like a flame that started dark at the face and was golden-red tipped at the ends. He looked like I'd imagined Hades before meeting him—all punked out in lots of leather and chain with a ... was that a safety pin? ... sticking through his nose. I didn't want to get close enough for a good look. I could practically hear Jesus in my head, though—"Oh honey, nothing you can buy at a pharmacy counter should ever count as jewelry." The thought made me smile inappropriately in a way that I hoped conveyed confidence rather than the fine edge of ensuing hysteria. Because whoever we faced was certainly spawn of Hades/Pluto/Dis ... the very god who put the "dis" in "discord" and "dissociative disorder."

Hypnos or whoever didn't wait to exchange witty repartee, but immediately launched that hellfire at us. Nick and I dodged in opposite directions, and the cave exploded into sparks between us. I smelled something burning, and realized it was my hair, singed at the ends. I rolled onto my shoulders and kipped back up to my feet as another hellfire orb was growing between his hands. I knew why he'd called the dogs to heel. He wanted the pleasure of killing us himself.

I weighed my chances of getting close enough to use the knife in my hand versus hitting him with the actual blade should I hurl it ninja-style, and realized neither had great odds of success.

Meanwhile, while we fought, I assumed Hades was dragging Persephone farther and farther away from us. We had to finish this. Rephrase: we had to *win* this, and fast.

"Nick," I yelled, "whatever you do, watch him. Don't worry about me. Look for your moment."

Hypnos laughed, as though our attempts to survive were just adorable, and launched the second hellfire grenade straight for me. It was what I'd counted on. Instead of dodging this time, I got my body behind it, just like I'd been taught playing ball with my circus friends. I caught it at chest level, dropping my knife as

I did and crying out at pain so intense I nearly blacked out on the spot. I launched it back before my flesh could burn down to the bone.

He was so stunned, he threw his hands up to block his face, and Nick saw his moment, firing his own spear gun straight for Hypnos's center of gravity. One of the hellhounds snapped at the bolt as it flew, snatching it out of the air and throwing it to the ground. I hadn't counted on that. And my fingers were too raw, the flesh at the ends actually burned away, for me to dash for any weapon of my own to help him.

Hypnos laughed again and whistled to release the hounds. Apparently, murder was all good fun until the victims started fighting back. Three beasts flew at us—one coming for me and the other two going for Nick. Panicked, I whirled out of the way of the one coming at me, but he was agile, turning on a dime and dripping menace as he gathered himself for another run.

"Freeze!" I ordered him, and he did, but Hypnos was suddenly right beside me, pinning my arms to my sides with a bear hug, his breath hot and poisonous in my ear.

I thrashed, trying to go to Nick, who was fighting off two dogs at once. He'd managed to get a bolt into one, but that had only made it cautious, waiting for its moment as another attacked. There was blood at the gut of Nick's wetsuit, and I suspected we wouldn't be getting our deposit back. Ah, our brains and their defense mechanisms. As if *that* was the problem with a bloody Nick facing down two hellhounds.

"Do you give?" Hypnos asked Nick, whose eyes flashed to me, giving the wounded dog the distraction he was looking for to go for Nick himself.

"No!" I cried, struggling to get to him.

I smashed down on Hypnos's instep, hard, and threw my head back into his face, catching his nose just right—I could tell by the crunch of caving bone. He let go, and a growl rose behind me—the hellhound I'd frozen coming free of the compulsion. Quickly, I grabbed Hypnos and whirled him in front of me like a shield just as the dog launched himself. I bolted out of the way as Hypnos howled and was knocked to the ground. His head cracked on the cave floor, but I was too focused on Nick to make sure he was okay.

I tried to grab the nearest hound, but the pain of it dropped me to my knees. I'd forgotten my hands were useless, but the hound rounded on me, giving Nick at least that much reprieve. I was still gasping in pain, fighting back the wave of nausea and unconsciousness that wanted to swamp me. I didn't get the chance to defend myself before I was suddenly pinned with razor claws digging into my shoulders. I was less than a breath away from the death strike.

"Freeze!" I cried desperately, hoping it would work even though I couldn't see into his eyes, even though it hadn't done me much good so far. Nothing happened. No teeth ripped into me or claws shredded my stomach. The next thing I knew, the weight was knocked aside and Nick's voice came out of the darkness. "Tori, are you all right?"

I whimpered. It wasn't what I'd meant to come out, but Nick had caught at my hands to help me up, and it was suddenly the only sound I could make.

"Oh, sorry!" He pulled back. "I saw you catch that hellfire ..."

"Is everyone down?" I asked. The pain was starting to recede, bless the ambrosia that was already healing me up.

"For now."

"We've got to get after Persephone."

My vision was clearing as the healing progressed, and I rolled onto my side to get to my feet still without using my hands. It wasn't pretty, but I succeeded.

I wobbled as I stood there looking at the four downed hellhounds and one god of oblivion. There was blood spreading out around his head, but he was breathing, and if I was tough to kill ... well, I was nothing compared to a god. He'd be coming after us. No doubt. I summoned up my inner strength, consoli-

CRAZY IN THE BLOOD

dated it into my core, and told Armani to plug his ears and start after Hades. It was only then I unleashed the power, ordering Hypnos with every fiber of my being to stay frozen.

I felt the power wash out of me and sweep the room, almost like a flash flood. My legs wanted to give out as weakness rushed in to fill the void left behind, but I ignored it and went off in search of another god of the underworld and his kidnapped bride, turning my back on Hell's hand-minion.

They hadn't gotten far with Persephone thrown over Hades's shoulder like a sack of potatoes. They didn't hear us as we approached, not with their argument and Persephone's repeated pleas that he put her down. For a second, I entertained the wish that I was the kind of girl who could shoot a man in the back. It would make things so much simpler. But I wasn't and never would be.

"Hades!" I called. Beside me, Nick leveled his spear gun so that we were both aimed at Hades. "Let her go."

He turned, slowly, shock on his face that we'd gotten so far. But he covered it quickly. "You *dare*?" he asked, though I thought the answer was pretty obvious. "She is mine."

"Here's the thing; I think the lady feels differently. Let. Her. Go."

He glared and let Persephone slide to the floor, holding her like a shield in front of him. "Never," he answered.

Crap. I looked at Nick, who shook his head that he didn't have a shot.

Persephone flew into action, kicking back at Hades's knee, and whirling as he began to buckle to thrust three fingers into the soft spot at the base of his neck where there were no bones to get in the way.

Hades fell back, making choking noises and clutching at his throat. Persephone threw herself forward toward us, out of his reach, and Nick shot Hades in his center of mass—gut, not chest—for good measure. He went down in an explosion of blood spatter and gore.

I shot a shocked glance at Nick and caught Persephone in my arms as she ran toward me sobbing.

"What?" Nick asked. "He's a god; he'll heal, right?"

"Right. Let's get out of here before that happens."

"Or the charges go off," Persephone said, voice breaking. "Thanatos is going to blow the place to hell." She wasn't in any condition to appreciate the irony.

Would Thanatos set the place to blow with his lord and father still in the tunnels, never mind that a god would heal? Would he even realize Hades and Persephone hadn't gotten out? That thought right on the heels of "we've just shot the god of the underworld … we have to live forever or we're totally screwed" sent my panic level straight to apocalypse (on a scale from zero to oh-my-gods).

We *ran*. Persephone continued to cling to my arm, but I had to shake her off to really throw on the speed. Hypnos was coming to groggily as we hit the cave, and I veered to deliver a hard kick to his head. He *oomphed* and went down. One of the hellhounds snarled, but it couldn't bring itself to give chase just yet. That wasn't going to last.

I started pulling an extra wetsuit out of my pack, but Persephone shook her head and tossed it to the side as I handed it to her.

"No time. I'll be fine."

We reached the ledge where Nick and I had pulled ourselves out of the water, where we'd left our fins, but Persephone's fear was feeding mine until it raged like a forest fire. I pushed my mask down over my eyes and dove, trusting that the others would be right behind me, and struck out hard from the surface.

I could just see the faint change in the light up ahead that indicated the mouth of the cave when my precognition exploded … a hair's breadth before the tunnel itself did the same. Superheated water blasted my back, pushing all the air out of me and sending me spinning through the water. With no more oxygen for buoyancy, I started to sink. Frantically, I kicked and struck at the water, trying to control my fall, aiming toward what I thought was the surface, but one of my feet was caught. I pushed off, thinking I'd hit bottom and my foot had gotten sucked between two rocks or into the muck, but whatever had me held fast. In the churning water, I couldn't get a decent look, but something seemed to be moving down there … and then the thing that held me started to crawl up my legs, hand over hand. My heart was pounding too quickly, and my oxygen level dropped equally fast. Spots started to appear before my eyes, but I summoned up whatever reserves I had to thrash around. I was caught too tightly to kick, but I could squiggle and squirm, eel-like, and make myself as difficult to hold on to as possible. Only there was no give.

I twisted back on myself like a netted fish, looking for escape, but found only the most frightening creature I'd ever seen floating before my facemask. She was odder even than Glaucus, who'd at least looked like something out of film. But this woman had a lizardlike mouth—wide and beaklike, but with sharp pointed teeth—and delicate fins, it appeared, where her ears should be. Her eyes were cold and reptilian, oversized, as though she spent a lot of time in the dark depths. Her green matted hair flowed all the way to her torso, which divided into two serpent tails, not scaly like something out of a Cher mermaid movie, but sinuous, like moray eels with a fine fin running down the back of each. I didn't know what she was. A water divinity certainly. My doom equally likely.

With her tails wrapping my legs, I gave up fighting for the surface and fumbled instead for the spear gun at my waist, but she swatted it easily away, and we began to sink into the depths. My lungs, muscles and mind were all screaming out imminent death as I tried to catch her gaze. It wasn't hard. She clearly wanted to watch my death throes. I couldn't order her to freeze, not in so many words, but I willed it with all of my being.

Nothing.

We continued to sink, and those spots that had haunted my

descent were back, stealing away my vision. *Not okay*, I thought. So not okay.

I struggled to take back some portion of my brain for planning rather than panic, but it was hard to think when my lungs were collapsing. I had to have some resource or her some vulnerability that I could exploit. My useless hands accidentally brushed the fine fins all along her tails wrapped around my legs. The spines burned me like coral, carving up my flesh and releasing fresh blood into the water. But it gave me an idea. Fins were thin and membranous between the spines. If I could do enough damage … I forced my shredded hands into claws to rip and rend those sail-like fins. The serpent woman let out a cry that was eerie and otherworldly. If my hearing weren't fading along with my vision, I'd guess it would have deafened me.

There was a splash to my right. Something else coming in fast, maybe attracted by my blood. I'd never survive a second attack. I didn't let it distract me, but got one leg free in serpent-woman's distraction and struggled to free the other.

Only then did I turn to the new danger and see Nick yanking on that skanky green hair. Her other tail loosened, and I kicked free of it, barely able to propel myself to the surface, which didn't seem to be getting any closer. I despaired of ever reaching it, my vision and movements getting fainter and fainter, and suddenly there it was. My autonomic system took over, gasping in the breath I'd been starving for. Nick appeared beside me and took me under his arm, pulling me against his chest to swim me to shore. There was no way I would have made it on my own.

The sight of the entire family that had been playing so peacefully now watching my rescue made me feel especially vulnerable as Apollo and Persephone helped Nick get me onto the jetty. I ignored them, ignored everything and closed my eyes. It had been a helluva day.

CHAPTER FIFTEEN

"Young gods have no impulse control; old gods no patience. But power…always they have the power. And smiting, I hear, is a great deal of fun."

—Pappous telling tales of old

Now what?" Armani asked.

Everyone looked at me, but I hadn't gotten so far as a plan that would avert Hell on earth. And I realized at that moment, when I was thinking about everyone I cared about getting caught in the middle of a godly grudge match, that I'd forgotten something.

"Crap!" I said, earning a disapproving look from the happy family. "Hades knows about the hotel. It's the first place he'll look for us. Christie and Jesus are there, defenseless."

"Not for long," Nick said. "Apollo, you get word to Demeter to meet us at the hotel. We'll grab our people, hand over Persephone to her mother and be done with it."

Persephone started sobbing. "It's not going to be that easy. Hades will punish you for helping me. This is all my fault."

"No, it's *his*," Nick said, putting an arm around her. "We can take care of ourselves."

A flash of jealousy warred with my sympathy for her, but I was distracted by Apollo's muttering.

"I've told it to the West Wind," he said at my look. "Demeter will get the message. Let's go."

I didn't need to be told twice, but I did need to be helped to standing. Since Nick had his arms full with Persephone, it fell to Apollo. I swatted him when I realized he was reaching down to carry me, but realized it was sheer bravado when he pulled me to my feet and my legs nearly went out from under me. I'd call them jelly, only they didn't seem even that firm. Apollo seemed to feel it and didn't let me go, supporting me as my legs tried with every step to let me down.

We reached the car, and this time Apollo growled as Nick approached the shotgun seat. Nick gave him a dark look, but backed away to leave it for me. I went boneless as Apollo poured me into the car, and waited until he got into the driver's side and was pulling out to ask, "You got any ambrosia?"

I was beyond caring that Nick might overhear. This was survival. If any more craziness came our way right now, I'd be defenseless.

Apollo shook his head, tight-lipped and driving like a fiend. I had some ambrosia back at the hotel, and very shortly Nick was going to know it. It took effort, but I forced my hand up to flip down the vanity mirror and angle it so that I could see his face.

"Ambrosia?" he mouthed.

I nodded but refused to look away in shame, defensive that I even felt the urge.

"We'll talk." His lips barely moved.

I didn't answer. I could already imagine how the conversation would go. Nick would see me as a junkie. He'd want to get me clean and … I knew that should be what I wanted as well. But now … with everything going on … I wasn't so sure that kicking the habit was the way to go. I couldn't have beaten Hades or Hypnos or even survived them without the extra punch it gave me. I couldn't have rescued Persephone. But were those reasons or excuses? *Was* I an addict, rationalizing my continued dependence?

Now I did look away, afraid my own uncertainty would show and fuel Nick's arguments when the time came for us to have it out. First, we would save the world. Then we could worry about me … if I even needed saving.

Before us, the storm clouds seemed to melt away, and the sun came shining through, but it didn't do anything for my mood. All I could see in my mind's eye was Jesus and Christie being ripped apart like the couple in the hotel parking lot.

"Faster," I told Apollo.

He shot me a look. "Prophecy?" he asked.

I closed my eyes, thought about it and shook my head. "No, just worry."

"Then I'd like to get us there in one piece."

I nodded, but the lack of danger warnings did not unclench my gut. I didn't know whether there was some kind of range on my precognition. If so, the hotel might be outside of it. Not knowing was making me crazy … er.

"Phone," I said urgently.

Nick handed his up from the back seat, and I quickly dialed Christie. Her laugh caught me by surprise. She had to choke it off to say, "Hello?"

"Christie, are you okay?" It seemed like a silly question in the face of her laughter, but my gut would not unclench.

"I'm fine. A friend of yours stopped by." Panic fluttered my heart. "He says his name is Thom Foolery."

Hermes? Here?

Apollo and I shared a look.

"He said something about grabbing 'front row seats.' That mean anything to you?"

"*Shitshitshit,*" I said under my breath.

"Christie, make sure you and Jesus are packed and ready to go. And ... if anything happens, you can't trust Thom to protect you."

She laughed again, and I had a feeling she wasn't listening to me at all. "Christie, this is serious, okay? You can't trust him."

But the voice that answered me wasn't hers. "*Agape mou,* what an unkind thing to say. I've never been anything but helpful to you, and the chance to see you in a wetsuit ... I couldn't pass that up."

"I am *not* your love. We'll be there in ten," I told him. "No hanky panky."

"Neither hanky *nor* panky? You ask a lot of a man."

And he promised nothing, I noticed, but he was already gone before I could say as much.

Now my early warning system was starting to blare.

"What I wouldn't give right now for Chitty Chitty Bang Bang," I said under my breath.

"What?" Apollo asked.

"A flying car," I snapped, even though none of this was his fault. "I don't suppose you still have your sun chariot stashed away somewhere?"

"That belonged to Helios," he answered, "and Phaeton smashed it all to bits. No more chariot."

"Too bad."

But we were almost there. I recognized the turn. The parking lot, when we pulled into the inn, was eerily quiet. The crime scene tape from days ago fluttered in the breeze where people, probably impatient for the parking spaces blocked off behind it, had blown through. My Spidey senses were tingling.

"Quickly," I told the others.

We were barely out of the car when the shadows all around

us took on form, at first just vague shapes rearing up out of nowhere, then becoming more sharply edged.

Persephone cried out and shrank back, but I didn't spare her a glance. My gaze was riveted on the closest of the horrors, a man so gaunt there was barely enough flesh to cover his bones. Every rib stood out above his caved-in stomach. His lips had peeled back from his over-large teeth. I could make out the individual arm bones. The *radius* and the *ulna*, my brain supplied in a sanity saving non sequitur. The apparition licked its lips when it saw me, and the moisture it left behind convinced me that this thing had substance. It was no mere shade.

Others closed in, looking like extras in an old zombie film. One had its chest torn open just where the heart should be. Another had been flayed, his skin hanging from him in strips, some held on by mere threads of tissue. All of him was red and bloody, except for white greasy gobs of fat poking out here and there … or maybe it was bone. Yet another was bloated, washed out, fish belly white, eyes bulging, hair a ghastly sludge slick molded to her head. *Drowning victim?* I wondered. *Murder? Suicide?*

Had Hades made good on his threat and opened up the gates of his realm, starting with Tartarus and all those poor souls the gods saw fit to torment for all eternity?

All the dead eyes were on us. Hungry … ravenous … not the least bit sane. "Apollo?" I said, not really sure what I thought he could do.

When I didn't hear him respond, I looked over to see him shaking his head. "Can't sing them to sleep. They're not given any such peace. And they've no souls left to soothe."

"Any suggestions?"

"Don't let them get you."

"Great."

Behind those horrors were more like them. Just as hungry, just as grotesque, coming on as inevitably as death and taxes. An undead army. We were surrounded.

"Persephone!" someone yelled from beyond the horde.

"Mom!" Persephone cried. "Mom, help!"

"Oh, my baby."

Baby? She was how many years old? Someone seriously had to learn to cut the cord. If we weren't careful, the Tartarus terrors would do it permanently.

"Take cover!" Demeter ordered.

Apollo and Armani were on the far side of the car from Persephone and me. They instantly ducked back against it. I had to grab Persephone as she would have ignored Demeter and rushed to her side. I pushed her up against the car and shielded her with my own body. The wind began to whip up, blowing my hair into my face and chilling me to the bone. I fought my way free of the blinding hair to see a funnel cloud beginning to form. Distracted as I was by it, I completely missed the closest terror lunging for me until it was too late. Sharp, ragged nails raked my arm, and I cried out. Instinctively, I lashed out and hit ... something. My brain didn't even want to process the wet, meaty sound of impact. Eyes that had been hollowed out and refilled with crazy bored into mine as the remnant of a man wearing his insides out grabbed me and ripped me away from Persephone. She screamed ... or maybe it was me. The horror swung me around, bashing me against the hood of the car. My chest took the impact, which was a nice break for my head, but it crushed all the air straight out of me.

Wind was whipping all around, so fast I couldn't catch it for breath. That cone of churning chaos came for us, and I had just time to grab on to the car for dear life before my attacker was ripped away from me with a howl of denial. The wind lessened almost immediately, as the tornado seemed to skirt around me then, collecting the debris of a thousand tourists—fallen wrappers, receipts, maps, fast food leavings. They swirled on the air, fuel for the funnel. More snarls split the air as other ghouls were swept up in it, and Demeter yelled, "Run for shelter."

I spat out hair that had whipped into my mouth and blinked

grit out of my eyes. Demeter had cleared a path between us and the hotel.

"Come on," I urged the others, like they needed it.

We ran full out for the hotel room. The door opened before we even reached it, the impish face of Hermes appearing in its place. I knew it was him, even if this wasn't a form I'd seen before. The glint in his eyes was unmistakable.

We all flew past him into the room, and he slammed the door behind us. "Mom!" Persephone cried, when she noticed Demeter wasn't with us. "She's in control," Apollo assured her. "Just finishing up."

Christie pushed Hermes aside and threw herself into my arms. "You're okay!"

I hugged her back, so glad the same could be said for her. I searched out Jesus, who stood on the other side of one of the beds in our now overcrowded room, arms crossed.

"Boss lady, you need a keeper."

I would have laughed, but my inner alarm system was still tugging at me like a boy who'd spotted the ice cream truck disappearing around the bend. All urgency.

When the knock sounded at the door, I jumped, even though I knew it was Demeter.

Persephone leapt to open the door, but confusion chased the joy off her face, and I pushed her aside to see what was wrong. Dionysus stood in the entryway, backed up by three female acolytes in the wheat wardrobe from my nightmares. They crowded into the room, Demeter trailing behind them, leaving barely enough room for the door to close behind them.

"Take Persephone and go," Dionysus said to Demeter. But he was staring at me, practically radiating menace.

Apparently, she sensed it too. Demeter swept him a startled glance. "What are you going to do? They saved my daughter from Hades—"

"After leading him *right to her*," he cut in sharply. "Go. If you get in my way on this, I'll destroy you too."

Beside him, the bacchae hissed, bristling like guard dogs eager to jump the leash. They watched us with a fanatic hunger that was both disturbing and almost completely inhuman. I was startled to realize that one was Casey Olivieri. She no longer looked like a nature cultist so much as a wild woman with her hair a rat's nest from the earlier fight at the compound and blood caking the front of her clothes as if … as if she'd been a sloppy eater. My stomach lurched at the thought.

"No," Persephone said, stepping in front of me. "I didn't escape one horror to give anyone over to another. This has all gone far enough."

A deadly smile spread across Demeter's face as she moved to stand shoulder to shoulder with her daughter. "You heard her. This is over. The Feds have invaded the compound. *Hades* has invaded the compound. It is no longer safe. Your 'paradise' is no more."

Dionysus snarled but didn't answer with words. Instead, he gave a sharp gesture that unleashed the bacchae on us. They dove for the closest targets—Apollo, Armani, *me*. Dionysus himself turned on his former allies.

"Get back," I heard Hermes call to Christie and Jesus before he snapped his fingers and was instantly out of the fray. The smell of popcorn suddenly filled the room, and I swore that if he'd just materialized himself a snack, I'd kill him … if I lived that long.

Claws flashed at my eyes, and I threw my hands up just in time to deflect one of the bacchae. The nails diverted to rake across my scalp. Teeth snapped at me, and I reared back. My flinch gave her the chance to raise a knee … fast, striking in a spot no less painful for women than men, even with our plumbing on the inside. My eyes instantly watered, and my knees buckled, but I locked them and refused to fall. I'd beaten Olympians. I was *not* letting some crazy cultist take me down. I swiped the tears from my eyes so that I could see straight, and met her crazy with my own.

"Freeze!" I thundered. I felt it flow out of me with all the force of my determination. The bacchae before me stiffened. To my right I felt another figure falter, and looked to see that it was Demeter, staggering from a blow Dionysus had dealt her. In the close quarters of our room, she couldn't summon the perfect storm. Persephone caught her as she reeled, and Dionysus raised an arm to strike again while they were vulnerable. I dashed the frozen bacchae aside and caught Dionysus's hand as the blow started to fall. The power behind it pulled me off balance, but Dionysus grabbed me with his free hand and pulled me against him. He looked straight into my eyes, and I wished with every fiber of my being that my gorgon glare worked on the elder gods. And then the alarm bells chased that thought away along with any other I might have had. It was so hard to concentrate … and then the blare of the alarms became muffled, as if someone had slammed a door on them. One line of a song, just one, played through instead. *The girl with kaleidoscope eyes.* It didn't make any sense, and I didn't have time to ponder as someone tried to tear me away from Dionysus, but I was held fast.

… *kaleidoscope eyes* …

The eyes staring into mine spun and telescoped, as if all the secrets worth knowing lurked there, hidden in the shadows, and if I just concentrated they would reveal themselves. I couldn't break contact. Any second now … any second, I would know.…

A huge rumble shook the room, and the earth moved under our feet.

No! my mind cried. The shift lost me a secret I'd been stalking, a mystery about to be revealed. Gone forever. Then those knees that had been threatening to buckle gave out on me. My feet were torn in different directions, as the floor burst wide open.

The big one, my mind jabbered, the panic of every La La Landian. The steel bands that held me in place, Dionysus's hands, released as he flailed to keep from going down with me.

Stars exploded across my vision when one of my knees struck the floor. The pain cleared away the last shred of wonder and awe. The for-real fall had kept me from falling under Dionysus's spell, but if this *was* the big one, I could hardly be thankful.

I looked around frantically at the world jumping around us. Nick's gaze met mine, and he reached out for me, heedless of the bacchae riding him to the ground, but the earth jumped again, and our fingers missed by inches. My legs split farther as the fissure beneath me grew, until I felt like a wishbone, and when the air escaped, hot as Hades, I feared that one way or the other, it was the end. Either we'd gotten so unlucky as to choose a hotel on a previously uncharted fault line or all hell was about to break loose.

I pulled my legs back together and twisted around to face whoever was coming, just in time to see Thanatos rising from the depths of … whatever lay beneath. He was dressed like the traditional grim reaper—black cowled cape and sickle that danced with the reflected flames from down below.

My inner alarm jingled until I yelled, "Enough!" out loud, drawing Thanatos's extremely pissed off gaze right to me.

I kicked out for his knee a fraction of a second before I noted the fall of his sickle and that I'd have been better to roll out of the way, but he had gravity going for him, and the sickle beat my foot to impact. My shoulder exploded in pain. Someone leapt for Thanatos's back, or so I assumed based on his sudden *oomph* and lurch forward, and the sickle jerked with him, slicing straight down through my collarbone.

The pain overwhelmed my alarms, which fell silent as the world went black. Everything receded—the flames, the fear, the pain … all a distant star, meaningless to me in the void of space.

I silently cried out as the star raced toward me, denying it and what it represented. If life was pain and death was the absence of it, then maybe I was ready for the end. But as the light hurtled toward me and resolved into three separate stars, I had a funny feeling …

"*Again?*" Lachesis said dramatically. "*But it's so unsatisfying. Where's the climax? The character arc? The denouement?*"

"*This is life,*" Clotho said.

"*No, it's death,*" Atropos argued, "*and I agree, wholly unsatisfying.*" She raised the scissors to a multicolored string. It wasn't smooth like silk. No, my strand had burls and kinks, crazy combinations of color along its length, coming to a very dark end.

"*Wait!*" Lachesis cried, putting a long-fingered hand to Atropos's wrist to stop her as the shears started to close around my cord. "*Look.*"

As the three sisters peered at my strand, the end seemed to lengthen and the color to return—the red of blood or roses or hellfire, and I felt the sisters' light pulling away again.

"*Damn,*" said Atropos.

"*So unsatisfying,*" grumped Lachesis.

They swirled away from me and winked out just like that. Suddenly, pain convulsed me, arcing me up off the floor, stealing my breath and nearly my sanity. Apollo loomed over me, hand pulled back as if he were about to slap sense back into me. *Again?* I wondered, but the pain of my cheek was such a small ache in the grand scheme of things that I couldn't be really certain I'd felt it at all.

Thanatos was turned away from us, having moved on to another target, but I must have gasped at my sudden return to consciousness, and he whirled back around on me, sickle dripping with my blood … or maybe others' at this point. I didn't know how long I'd been gone, and I couldn't see around him to check on anyone. His sickle was already crashing down, and I used the renewed fire of my weave to buck hard, rolling Apollo off of me, out of the path of the blow meant for me. I caught the blade between my forearms like some kind of gorgon ninja. The tip pierced my chest, but not far. Blade trapped, I rolled with it, twisting it out of Thanatos's grip. He came down with it, landing hard on top of me, purposely or not, leading with an elbow as hard and bony as a hilt. I felt something crack and realized for a wonder it wasn't my rib but the haft of the sickle, unequal to handling our combined weight working against it. I quickly adjusted my grip on it to thrust a broken end back at him like a stake, but it vanished right out of my hands like it had never been. Nice trick, that, only I was now defenseless, prey to a god with a grudge whose hands were tangled in my hair, ready to bash my head into what was left of the floor.

Thanatos rocked with a blow as someone—Apollo?—attacked him from the side and it knocked us closer to the fissure in the floor.

"Stop right there!" a voice rained down on us with sudden authority ... and nearly its own reverb. Certainly, the walls rattled, just a bit.

Thanatos rolled off of me to stare up in shock at Persephone, who stood above him holding the now-mended sickle, pointed straight for him. I looked quickly around to see the few battles still feebly being waged cease at the power of her voice.

"*I* am your mistress," she thundered. "I am your queen—by the marriage Hades refuses to dissolve. You will heed *me*."

Apparently, there was something to that, because Thanatos stared as if he had no other choice ... until he bowed his head and lowered his gaze in silent acceptance.

"You tell Hades that as long as we are bound, his power is *mine*. I am claiming my share. I am through with the fear, with the obedience and with *him*."

The door to our overcrowded room blew open, and Hades stood in its place, face a mask of anger and pain. It was hard to look at and harder to know which emotion was coming out on top.

"Tell him yourself," he said.

We all watched Persephone to see if she would waver, but she only shifted the aim on the sickle and looked him right in the eyes.

"It's over," she said. Firm. No explanation. No apologies. No room for argument.

"But I still love you," Hades said, voice ragged with torment. But I remembered the sound of his slap in the tunnels and the sight of her reddened face, and I was unmoved. I hoped she'd stay the same.

"You've never understood the word," she spat back. "Love takes into account what the other wants. I don't know what you ever felt for me, but it was *never* love. And now, it's over."

No one moved. I wasn't sure anyone even breathed.

Until Hades, like Thanatos before him, finally hung his head. "As you wish," he answered.

CHAPTER SIXTEEN

"It's not about the climax, it's about the clean-up afterward."

—Yiayia, in an OMG, she did not just say that moment

I called Agent Rosen, though I hardly needed to do it. Little things like localized earthquakes, tornados and battles to the death and back again tended to attract attention. The local police announced themselves with a no-nonsense knock on the door that Hades had slammed back into place when he left and the order that we open up. The agents were barely a step behind them.

"Quick," I hissed to anyone who would listen. "Demeter and Persephone—" I paused, because I had no idea what names they were going by among us mortals.

"Demi and Sinestra," Demeter supplied.

"Sinestra? Still? Okay, whatever. You two were trying to escape the cult. The others—"

But the door burst open before I could get any further.

Thanatos had disappeared from whence he'd come. There one second and gone the next. Hermes had done the same, which surprised me. If he liked trouble, he could have gotten a firsthand look at another round, but apparently he'd had his fun. Sticking around to answer questions probably didn't seem a fitting encore. At least he'd gotten Jesus and Christie out of the way. They'd ridden things out locked in the small hotel bathroom. At least I could be thankful to him for that much.

They arrested us all until they could sort things out. This time, Rosen and Holloway didn't rescue me from custody, but stood, I suspected, behind mirrored glass watching the interrogations. We were all, of course, separated. I had no idea what tales the others were spinning or how I was going to explain any of it to my assistant and BFF, who were certainly going to want explanations for what they'd seen.

It was long and grueling. I was left alone for vast periods of time with nothing but the burnt brown sludge they called coffee. I even fell asleep for a time, too exhausted to remember whether that was supposed to be a sign of guilt or innocence. I was very much afraid it was the former, but the needs of the body totally outweighed any concern.

Finally, *finally*, Agent Rosen entered. He didn't look like he'd slept at all, probably not since before the raid on the Back to Earth compound. He gave me a tired smile as he sat down across from me.

"After the murders at the hotel earlier in the week, the inn decided to reactivate the parking lot cameras they'd shut down to cut costs. You'll never believe what they showed. Oh wait, you were there. I don't suppose any of those—things? people?—who attacked you will be available to answer for their crimes?"

I shook my head, completely at a loss. It had been caught *on camera*? What about Demeter's tornado? How on earth did the authorities explain all this to themselves? How were they planning to keep it quiet? And why was I just hearing about it now? Had the Feds gotten to the footage before the regular police?

"Of course, Dionysus Bach and his followers are claiming they were invited to your room, where you jumped them."

"Is anybody buying that?"

"Not with two former cultists willing to provide evidence against them, including regarding your claim of drugs. Although, it might be a little difficult given that one doesn't seem to have much of a history before, say, right this minute. Still, we've offered them Witness Protection."

"They're taking you up on it?" I asked.

"Looks like. Marshals should be here within the hour."

It was the best thing for Demeter and Persephone, in case Hades changed his mind about letting Persephone go or Dionysus got out and went looking for revenge. Unfortunately, the rest of us would be a lot easier to find.

Speaking of … "What does this mean for the rest of us?"

"You're free to go. Police will be by themselves in a minute to tell you so. You'll have to keep yourselves available to testify."

I stared at him, and he stared back. I was better at it, but then, I'd slept. "So that's it?"

"That's it. Except maybe for you. I have no idea what kind of charges there'll be to your credit card over the state of that room."

I laughed, surprising us both. "That is the *least* of my worries."

Rosen eyed me steadily. "Well, if the rest of those worries ever catch up to you, give me a call. But no more of that whammying crap or whatever you did to me. Next time I'll have you arrested for assaulting a federal officer."

"I'm not sure I can make any promises."

"You could have lied."

"As you just pointed out, you're a federal officer. I think there are laws against that."

"And you being so law abiding …"

"Exactly."

"Just call us next time you get in over your head, okay? You're not alone." No, I wasn't. In addition to big brother, always watching, I had Nick and Apollo, Christie and Jesus. My merry misfit crew. I owed them … well, everything … but a huge meal at the very least. Breakfast or lunch or whatever the hell it was time for at this point. I couldn't even remember the last time I'd eaten, and if I didn't find something to soak up the battery acid the station called coffee soon, it might just eat its way through my stomach.

One by one, we were all released and gathered in the lobby. Jesus was the last, because apparently he'd mouthed off to one of the detectives about his shabby treatment and the complete heinousness of the man's tie and was subsequently held a bit longer in the fervent hope they could find something to charge him with.

My heart hurt at the sight of him with butterfly bandages marching from his right eye up to his hairline and the claw marks at his neck from one of Dionysus's crew.

"Don't worry," he said at my horror. "It makes me look dangerous, no? There will be many waiting to comfort me. And the tale—by the time I tell it, it will be beyond recognition."

"Of that I have no doubt."

I looked around at my people—Christie with no worse than a fat lip, Apollo and Nick, who'd thrown themselves into the fray, a little worse for wear, but nonetheless too sexy for the room.

My heart was full and my stomach empty.

"Come on, all. Breakfast or … whatever. I'm buying."

As long as the hotel charges hadn't yet hit my credit cards and I could still afford it.

But first, we had to swing by the hospital. I had to see Uncle Christos and let him know it was all over. I hoped he'd be in a condition to appreciate it.

The others waited for me in the lounge as I ventured to his

room alone. If he was ... not himself ... he probably wouldn't appreciate the audience when he got back to rights. And he *would*. The Karacis family was tough. Nuts were like that ... hard to crack. *Eccentrics*, I heard in Yiayia's voice. Whatever.

But when I got there, he wasn't alone. Someone had beaten me to him. I pushed his door open quietly, in case he was sleeping, and found a woman at his bedside, her back to the door. She didn't turn at my entrance. I didn't think she was even aware of it.

Detective Beverly Simon had eyes only for Uncle Christos. And he had eyes only for her. They held hands like teenagers, and as I watched she bent to kiss him.

That was enough for me. I ducked out quickly and quietly. Christos was in good hands. He and I could catch up later. For now, it was clear enough that all was well.

Breakfast beckoned.

ABOUT THE AUTHOR

Lucienne Diver does not actually come from circus folk, though you'd never know it to meet her family. She is, however, in no particular order, a wife, mother, literary agent, book addict, sun-worshipper, mythology enthusiast, travel-junkie and crazy person. In addition to the *Latter-Day Olympians* series, she writes the *Vamped* young adult novels (*Vamped, Revamped, Fangtastic, Fangtabulous* and *Fangdemonium*) as well as YA suspense. Her short stories have appeared in the *Strip-Mauled* and *Fangs for the Mammaries* anthologies edited by Esther Friesner (Baen Books) and *Kicking It* edited by Faith Hunter and Kalayna Price (Roc). Her essay "Abuse" is included in the anthology *Dear Bully: Seventy Authors Tell Their Stories* (HarperTeen).

More information can be found on her website at luciennediver.com. You can also follow her on Twitter @luciennediver.

www.luciennediver.com

IF YOU LIKED ...

IF YOU LIKED CRAZY IN THE BLOOD, YOU MIGHT
ALSO ENJOY:

Dan Shambles, Zombie P.I., Tastes Like Chicken

by Kevin J. Anderson

Griffin's Feather

by J.T. Evans

OTHER WORDFIRE PRESS TITLES BY LUCIENNE DIVER

Bad Blood

Rise of the Blood

Battle for the Blood

Blood Hunt

Our list of other WordFire Press authors and titles is always growing. To find out more and to see our selection of titles, visit us at:

wordfirepress.com